WILDE LOVE

He leaned down, even closer. "I'm going to kiss you now."

"Good. I don't know what's been taking you so damn long."

"I wanted you to be clear about who I am."

"You're the man who tells me and shows me the truth. Everything else is outside of you and me."

His eyes went wide. "You do get it."

"I'm trying, because I think you're worth it."

His lips met hers with an urgency and need that stunned her at first, then warmed to something so intimate and consuming it nearly buckled her knees. She didn't need to worry about falling off the world: he wrapped his arms around her, pulled her up to her toes, and kissed her like his life depended on her feeling everything he poured into the start of them.

WILDE LOVE

A DARK HORSE DIVE BAR NOVEL

JENNIFER RYAN

AVON

An Imprint of HarperCollinsPublishers

WILDE LOVE. Copyright © 2023 by Jennifer Ryan. All rights reserved. Printed in the United States of America. No part of this book may be used or reproduced in any manner whatsoever without written permission except in the case of brief quotations embodied in critical articles and reviews. For information, address HarperCollins Publishers, 195 Broadway, New York, NY 10007.

First Avon Books mass market printing: September 2023

Print Edition ISBN: 978-0-06-331971-4
Digital Edition ISBN: 978-0-06-331972-1

Cover design by Amy Halperin
Cover image © Stephen Carroll/Arcangel; © Shutterstock

Avon, Avon & logo, and Avon Books & logo are registered trademarks of HarperCollins Publishers in the United States of America and other countries.

HarperCollins is a registered trademark of HarperCollins Publishers in the United States of America and other countries.

FIRST EDITION

23 24 25 26 27 BVGM 10 9 8 7 6 5 4 3 2 1

To those who have faith in others and trust in love.
You brave souls.
To those who guard their hearts, I hope you find
someone who makes it worth it to open up.

Author's Note

Dear Readers,

I am so excited to bring you Lyric and Mason's story. It's one that's been living in my head and heart for a long time, ever since Mason appeared in *Love of a Cowboy*, and because these two were so meant to be.

When I came up with the concept for the Dark Horse Dive Bar, I knew Lyric was a songwriter and what better way for her to express herself than through the songs she sends to Mason? It's even sweeter that he talks to her in her love language, too.

Because music is such a big part of their story—and I'm not allowed to use lyrics from actual songs in the book because of copyright—I'm adding the playlist here so you can listen to the song or look up the lyrics and know exactly what they're expressing. Most of the songs are sent from Lyric to Mason, but I've also included the songs playing in the bar and a song Lyric sends to an unwelcome guest. It's my soundtrack to the book.

Dark Horse Dive Bar Playlist:

"Come Over" – Kenny Chesney
"Alone" – Heart

"Soul" – Lee Brice
"Angel" – Aerosmith
"Uninvited" – Alanis Morissette
"Strangers" – Maddie and Tae
"You Make It Easy" – Jason Aldean
"Safe" – Katie Armiger
"Pick Me Up" – Gabby Barrett
"I Will Always Love You" – Whitney Houston
"The Best" – Tina Turner

Enjoy the book and the songs if you choose to play them while you read.

XO Jennifer

P.S. I am not a songwriter. Kudos to those who can put words and music together. I admire you and your talent. I am not one of you. But I did my best with Lyric's song, "What's Your Name," to Mason. He'd love it because Lyric wrote it, even if it has no rhythm.

WILDE
LOVE

Chapter One

Apair of warm hands covered her eyes. Lyric's heart jackhammered as the person drew even closer behind her. Her mind wanted to believe it was *him*, the man whose hands swept over her body in her dreams, leaving her in a feverish need. But he wouldn't do something playful like this.

"Guess who?" The unfamiliar voice ratcheted up her fear.

Definitely not *him*. She really wished it was her badass-biker enigma.

The disappointment made her shoulders sag.

Viper. She hated the ridiculous name, but that's all he'd given her. A man of few words and hot looks, they'd had this thing going on between them for months that couldn't be defined or explained, except to say they both avoided giving in to the pull between them. She'd gotten used to him being there at the bar, a mostly silent presence who offered protection when some drunk got mouthy or handsy with her.

But it had been twenty-three days since she'd seen him.

The loss of him in her life left her feeling colder than the mid-January Wyoming temps.

Whoever was playing this stupid game wasn't one

of her siblings. Jax knew she hated being scared. He'd learned her retaliation wasn't worth the joke.

So would the stranger who had snuck up on her now.

This whole drama amped her impatience because she didn't have time for this. Especially from someone she couldn't name by the sound of their voice. And with that realization, fear washed over her annoyance, and she went still. With nowhere to go she had only one recourse and shoved her elbow into the guy's gut. He released her, and she spun around, ready to face off with whoever snuck up on her in the barn.

"Ouch. Damn, Lyric. It's just me."

She stared in incomprehension at someone she barely remembered. He'd obviously followed her home all the way from Nashville, where she'd recently traveled. Alarms went off in her head. "What are you doing here?"

And how did he know it was her morning to work on the family ranch? She took turns with her sisters while her brother Jax worked the cattle and their parents handled the cabin rentals. The rest of the time, they worked the Dark Horse Dive Bar.

Their grandmother had run it for years, giving the small town a gathering place not only to get drunk and rowdy but also have a good meal, an event space, and community. Grandma had left the bar to her and her siblings when she passed three years ago.

"I knew you'd be surprised." He glanced over the stall gate at her horse, Bruin. "Damn, he's big."

"Your name is Rick Rowe, right?" They'd met in Nashville at the Whiskey Bent Saloon where she'd gotten a dream New Year's Eve gig playing with her best friend and cowriter Faith Jordan. Faith lived in

Nashville and had landed them the coveted spot to be one of the early openers that night.

He smiled, his eyes bright with joy. "I knew you'd remember me. We clicked. I couldn't wait to see you again, so we could write together, like you said."

She remembered him always crowding into her personal space and trying to dominate the conversation. He forced her to focus on him, preventing her from talking to the others around them. They were people Faith had wanted her to meet and mingle with in hopes that they'd make connections with others in the country-music business and sell their songs.

Lyric didn't have dreams of being up on stage. She wanted to hear someone else singing her songs on the radio and to a coliseum crowd. Lots of artists, not just her.

She fulfilled her singer fantasy just fine by playing at the bar and posting videos on her YouTube channel. She curated her personal channel and the one she ran for the Dark Horse Dive Bar. Both did well, but her personal one had gotten her a huge following. If she kept at it, she'd hit a million followers in a few months.

She made some decent revenue off the channel with select advertisers. She wasn't in it to be a millionaire, but she had to pay the bills. And her little nest egg had burgeoned into an I-could-buy-a-house-retire-early-and-live-well territory.

And recently she and Faith had sold a couple of their songs to up-and-coming artists.

She liked her life, her work, her place just fine for now.

"What are you doing here? In Wyoming? How did you find me?"

"I follow your YouTube channels. Obviously the bar you work at is closed this morning, but I asked around about you. Everyone is so friendly in this town. They all know you. One of them was kind enough to tell me you're usually at the bar early to start cooking, but on Tuesdays and Thursdays you spend your mornings here. All I had to do was look up the address for the Wilde Wind Ranch." He looked so pleased with himself.

She'd been so careful online not to make it this easy for people to find her. She never used the name of her town. She didn't even use her last name. But it was impossible to stay completely anonymous, and everyone knew she worked at the Dark Horse Dive Bar. Still, she never thought anyone in town would naively send someone out to see her at the ranch. Luckily, it seemed they hadn't given Rick her home address, not that it would be that hard to find her at the apartment above the bar.

Damn.

This was not good.

She seriously needed to reevaluate her security.

She'd had some trouble in the past with overzealous fans leaving messages for her online that crossed the line from supportive and appreciative of her songs and singing to becoming way too personal and possessive. One guy had even made some threats about what he'd like to do to her, thinking she'd be open to his sleazy suggestions.

No. Not even a little bit.

Rick showing up without an invitation or any indication from her that she wanted to see him didn't just cross a line, it scared her a little.

"So you saw me play last week and you thought you'd just fly from Nashville to Wyoming and show up here—and what?" She really was confused and caught off guard by all this. It wasn't even eight in the morning and he'd come looking for her.

"You said we could write together sometime." He'd asked if she'd write with him. At first, she'd told him she wasn't planning on staying in town long. She'd flown in on the twenty-eighth, after she celebrated Christmas with her family, then flown home on January third because she was needed at the bar.

The second time he asked, she'd said maybe next time she was in town, if she had the time. Faith often set up writing sessions with other writers and singers working on projects. Lyric usually flew in for a few days every other month or so.

That still didn't appease Rick. He asked a third time. Annoyed, she'd simply said, "Sure, we'll do that soon." She never intended to follow through with it.

So she put her foot down. "I'm not available right now. I have a job, responsibilities, a schedule. If you want to set up a writing session, you should have contacted me online instead of coming all the way here."

Rick stared down at her. "I need you, Lyric. You're my only hope of turning the bits and pieces of ideas I have into something worth singing. I know, with your help, I'll hit it big. We'll do it together. We'll be the next big Nashville power couple."

That was taking things too far.

She took a step back from him and the intensity he gave off that it was meant to happen. "Rick, I appreciate that you think—"

"I know we'll be great together." He took a step closer.

She didn't like being cut off.

He reached for her, and she stepped back again.

He frowned. "Give me a chance to prove it to you."

"It's not about that," she snapped. "You can't just show up here and expect me to drop everything and write you a song."

"I don't." He eased off, though it seemed to take effort. "I just wanted to come by and see you, to let you know I'm here. You're busy right now. I get that."

She relaxed. A little.

He pulled out his phone. "Give me your number."

She really didn't want to do that. "You give me yours, and I'll call you when I have some free time." *Never.*

His head tilted to the side. "Or you could come by my cabin later."

Her heart tripped over itself as a shot of adrenaline raced through her. "What?"

"When I looked up the address of this place, I saw that you rent out cabins."

In the dead of winter, January especially, they rarely had guests. Mostly people came to hunt, fish, and hike in the spring, summer, and fall. Jax ran the business with a couple of guys who helped him with the trail rides and taking people out on daylong fishing trips. Their mom hosted campfire cookouts. The rentals supplemented the ranch's income when times were lean, cattle prices dropped, and feed and water prices skyrocketed.

"It's perfect." Rick practically beamed with excitement. "You'll be here. I'll be here. We'll be together."

That last part sounded a bit too intimate and made her very uncomfortable.

She wanted to tell Rick she didn't live on the ranch full-time. Yes, she still had her room, but she mostly stayed in town because she was the first one in to work to prep and cook all the food.

"The website said I couldn't get into the cabin until two today. Any chance you can speed that up?"

Give in on one favor, he'd ask for a dozen more. "Uh, no. I'm not in charge of that." First, she needed to talk to her parents about him. "My mom takes care of the cabins. I know she'll want to make sure it's clean and stocked for your stay. And I need to get to work. I've got a lot of horses to groom and exercise before I head to work at the bar."

"Okay. Well, you know where to find me. Plus, you'll have my number." He notched his chin toward her.

She didn't plan to call him, but to get this over with, she pulled her phone out of her back pocket and unlocked it. Before she knew his intent, he snatched it from her hand. "Hey! Give it back."

He bent his head to her phone and typed. "I'll put in my information."

She fumed. Her heart raced. She wanted to snatch the phone back and order him out of here, but something told her that wouldn't go over well. Rick tripped her radar in a way that felt dangerous.

Viper never did, even with his formidable presence. Tall, broad, always dressed in black from head to toe. He never smiled. She'd never heard him laugh. With one hard look, he could send other men in the opposite direction. One hot look could melt a woman into a puddle of lust. But he never looked at any woman, except for her, like that. And he never did anything about it either.

He seemed indifferent to everyone. But Viper had played an integral part in returning the kidnapped baby Cyn and Lyric's cousin Hunt had been desperately searching for after Cyn's sister was murdered. Viper called Lyric out of the blue to set up a meeting between Cyn and the motorcycle-club president who'd ended up with the baby. Viper made sure Lana got home to her family.

He had a big heart buried under his tough exterior. She knew it. She felt it.

But Rick . . . There was something off about him.

Maybe it was just that he was pushy. He wanted what he wanted, and he didn't seem to care about her feelings on the matter or if she even wanted to work with him.

He'd deemed it so, so he assumed it was going to happen.

Arrogant.

That's what put her off.

She tried to remain calm and let him finish. She didn't want him to see her aggravation.

Normally, she liked most people. She never got bad vibes from anyone. Sure, drunk people in a bar could be obnoxious, rude, unruly even. But this was something different.

This was in-your-face.

He'd flown hundreds of miles to see her after one chance meeting.

That wasn't right. It was creepy.

His phone dinged. "There. Now you have my number." He turned his phone. "I sent myself a text, so I have yours."

Fuck! She did not want him calling or texting her. She'd have to block him.

And as soon as he left, she'd do something else about him, too. "Now, if you'll excuse me, I have work to do."

"When can we meet to write?"

Never. She didn't think that would go over well.

"Soon." Her brain couldn't even think about what else she had on her schedule this week to come up with a day or time.

Maybe she'd give him a chance and work on one of his songs and hope that ended this.

She knew it wouldn't.

"I've got my guitar. We could do it in my cabin later, or I could come to your place where you film all your YouTube stuff. I've been following you forever. I'm LyRick." She guessed what he meant before he could spell it out. "Get it? Our names together. It's perfect."

She went still, a new, creepier understanding coming over her.

He grinned, victory in his eyes. "See? I knew you'd be happy it was me."

She'd already mentally put him on her caution list because of how much he posted on her channel. This proved she'd been right to be wary. "I appreciate all the comments you leave."

"You always answer. You've even done a couple of my song requests."

Shit. She'd interacted with him for months without knowing he'd bonded with her to the point where he believed they were friends. Of late, she'd pulled back because his posts had become increasingly familiar, his questions more personal, straying from talking about music and writing songs to asking about her personal life. She always tried to stay on the topic of music, but he wanted to know if she was seeing anyone and what she liked to do in her spare time.

Every time, she either responded with something about the song she posted or didn't answer at all.

And now he was here.

On her family's ranch.

In her life.

Shit. Shit. Shit.

He gave her a look she suspected he thought was flirtatious. "I loved that white frilly blouse you wore in your last video."

Comments like that hinted at something intimate. After she'd posted the video, she'd wondered if she should reshoot it because the blouse had dipped way low, showing off an uncomfortable-for-her amount of cleavage. But her sister Melody had come in asking for help with something in the bar, said she loved the look and the ballad, and told her she should embrace what their mama gave them and post it.

Now she regretted both listening to her outgoing little sister and posting the video.

"Rick, I want to be very clear. I appreciate that you're a fan of the online stuff I do and that you think I'm a songwriter you'd like to work with. But if we collaborate, that's all it is. Work. I'm not interested in anything beyond that."

"You want to keep things professional."

Hope flared that he understood and would abide by her wishes. "Yes. Exactly."

"There's a time and place for everything." With that, he turned and walked away, leaving her feeling like he hadn't heard her at all.

Alone, she let loose. "Fuck!" She hardly ever swore out loud, but Rick had flustered her, and she didn't like the feeling one bit. Or this situation.

Bruin raised his big russet head and stared at her wide-eyed, his ears back.

She tried to soothe him. "Sorry for yelling, baby."

Her dad's truck pulled into the drive by the barn.

Feeling frustrated and exposed, she ran out to him and threw her arms around him.

He hugged her back. "What's wrong? Is this about that guy at the bar?"

Her whole family wondered about Viper and whatever it was they had going that had seemed to disappear along with him.

Where was he?

What had happened?

Why would he just disappear like that?

Was he coming back?

Was he okay?

Was she? Because she couldn't stop thinking about him. And maybe that made her a little obsessed.

She leaned back and stared into her dad's concerned eyes. "Not him. He'd never do something like this." She knew that to her soul. Viper, for all his gruff, quiet ways would never impose himself on her. He'd be direct and ask for what he wanted, not steamroll right over her.

Her dad raised a brow. "What happened?"

"You know how you're always telling me to be careful online?"

He frowned. "Is someone harassing you again?"

She'd blocked a couple people, who'd just come back under different names. She'd blocked them again, sometimes multiple times before they gave up.

"I don't want to sound the alarm when nothing bad has happened"—*yet*—"but I think I have a situation that maybe I can't handle on my own."

"Lyric." Her dad said her name like she'd exasperated him, even though he was the kind of man who had infinite patience for his four kids. "Spill it in a concise manner that I can follow."

"A guy I don't really know, who follows me online, showed up at the New Year's gig I did in Nashville. At the time I met him there in person, I didn't know he was the same guy I've been purposely ignoring the past few weeks online."

"Okay. So did he post something about seeing you at the performance?"

"No. He showed up here this morning."

Her dad eyed her. "Here. At the ranch."

She nodded.

"Did you invite him?"

"Absolutely not. I barely remembered his name."

"He followed you here from Nashville." Her dad looked stunned, then pissed. "That is not okay, Lyric. Did you tell him to leave?"

"He rented one of the cabins. He's moving in this afternoon."

"What? No." He fisted his hands. "How did he even get your address?"

"Some helpful person in town told him that if I wasn't at the bar and it's Tuesday morning, I'm at the ranch. He looked it up online, booked a room, then drove out here."

Her dad's eyes went wide. "What the hell?"

"It's a small town. Everyone knows everyone's business. Still." She gave him a look he read all too well.

"They gave that information to a stranger, who could be anyone and want anything from you."

She scrunched up one side of her mouth. "He wants to write a song."

"That's what he said?" Confusion joined the anger in his eyes.

She nodded. "But the vibe I got . . . He's . . . I don't know how to explain it. He's here for me." That sounded conceited, but she didn't care. It felt like the truth Rick was burying under pretense.

Her dad cupped her face and looked adoringly at her. "I'm calling Hunt."

Her cousin was a cop. Maybe he could help.

"I think that's a good idea."

Her dad looked even more distressed that she agreed so readily when she usually insisted on handling things herself.

He pulled her into a hug. "I don't like this."

She pressed her cheek to his chest, taking in his comfort and protection. "I don't either. But right now, I think we need to tread carefully." She stepped back, and he released her. "I don't want to make Rick mad. That could go wrong in a lot of ways. But I also don't want to give him any hope that something could happen between us either."

"I bet Hunt's going to say the same thing. Maybe he can run a background check on this guy, and that will tell us who we're dealing with. Let's go tell your mother, so she knows what's going on, especially if this guy is going to be here for a little while."

They bypassed the truck in favor of walking up the short road to the house in silence. She could only imagine what her dad was thinking about all this.

Someone had parked a white Subaru in the driveway.

Her dad glanced at her, then rushed up the steps to the porch and burst into the house.

Lyric was right next to him.

Her mom looked up from her spot in the kitchen behind the big island and across the huge living room. As always, her mother had music playing in the background. This morning it was classic Tim McGraw. "Wade? Lyric? Everything all right?"

Rick turned on the barstool and glanced at them. "Lyric, honey, your mom makes the best cinnamon rolls." He licked his fingers.

That *honey* was another too-familiar endearment she didn't want coming from his lips.

Her dad glanced down at her, then turned to her mom. "What's going on here, Robin?"

Mom raised a brow, catching Dad's not so easygoing tone. "I was just welcoming Lyric's friend to the ranch." She looked at Lyric. "Why didn't you tell me he was coming to stay?"

Lyric chose her words carefully, knowing her mom would pick up on the caution in her voice. "He surprised me. We just met last week in Nashville."

Her mom's eyes changed to that of knowing this wasn't someone Lyric knew well and welcomed here.

"But we've been friends for a while now," Rick supplied, then turned back to her mom. "Online. You know. Where everyone meets these days. Lyric and I can't wait to collaborate and make some really awesome music. Maybe I'll play at the bar, and she'll put me up on her YouTube channel."

Mom eyed her. "Well, that sounds amazing. But Lyric, are you going to have time between working at the bar, here, and your other activities?"

She did a lot of catering and cooked for those in need who stopped by the Dark Horse Dive Bar kitchen looking for a hot meal or even a bag of groceries to tide them over.

Jax walked into the kitchen from the mudroom holding his hand, blood dripping down his finger. "Hey. It smells really good in here."

Mom immediately went to him. "What happened?"

"Sliced it on, of all things, a bag of grain. It's

nothing. Just an annoying paper cut that won't stop bleeding."

Mom rushed into the half bath below the stairs and came back with a Band-Aid from the medicine cabinet.

Jax finished cleaning the cut and stared at the stranger in their house. "Who are you?"

"Rick Rowe. Lyric's friend. I'm staying in one of the cabins for a while."

"I'm Jax. Lyric's brother." Jax raised a brow at her.

"I'll tell you later. Right now, I've got horses to ride."

"Can I come?" Rick asked.

Fuck, no. "Have you ever been on a horse?" *Please say* no.

"No."

She tried not to show her relief. "Then, no," she said, not wanting to spend time with him or teach him how to ride. She had a schedule, and she was already behind. "I don't have time for a lesson. You'll slow me down." Okay, maybe that was too blunt and dismissive.

Rick didn't drop it. "Come on, it can't be that hard."

Her dad intervened. "Jax, you're all patched up. Mind taking our guest to his cabin, make sure he's got everything he needs?" The tone didn't make it a question of any kind.

Jax picked up on the off feeling in the room and hopped to it. "You bring yours." He picked up one of the cinnamon rolls. "I'll bring mine."

Mom handed Jax a key. "Cabin ten." The one farthest from the house. "It's got the best heater. You'll need it." Mom eyed the coat Rick wore that would barely block the biting wind.

"Let's go." Jax headed for the front door.

Rick came to Lyric and smiled. "Your family is so nice. You're lucky." She didn't want to read into that statement that maybe his family wasn't good to him. "See you soon."

Lyric held her mom's gaze as Jax and Rick left. The second the front door closed, Mom asked, "What the hell is going on? He said he was your friend, but you're acting like you don't know him."

"I don't. Not really." Lyric explained the best she could, telling her mom all she'd told her dad.

Her dad pulled out his phone. "I'm calling Hunt. We need to check this guy out." He made the call, putting it on Speaker.

"Hey, Uncle Wade, how's the family?" Hunt sounded relaxed and happy. He should be, after his recent honeymoon with his beautiful wife, Cyn.

"We have a problem."

Hunt didn't even pause. "How can I help?"

Chapter Two

Viper lay on the massage table gritting his teeth as the physical terrorist worked on the knots in his shoulder breaking up the scar tissue from an old gunshot wound.

"Relax. Breathe."

Easy for her to say. She wasn't the one with an elbow digging into soft tissue. She wasn't the one who had to endure not just the gunshot but the rehab, too.

And that got him thinking about the past couple of years and the state of his life. He hated everything about what he was doing, except for the reason he was doing it.

Two months ago he'd returned a kidnapped baby to her family. That felt pretty damn good. Lana was safe with her aunt Cyn, who'd recently married Lyric's cousin, Hunt. He'd shown Lyric he could do the right thing, even if he looked and acted sometimes like he was on the wrong side of the law.

Last month, he'd ended up in a gunfight with one of the guys in the biker club he was currently neck-deep in, who was hell-bent on taking out someone else connected to Lyric's family. He'd ended up having to shoot the guy himself, then give the club president a bullshit story about how the FBI had taken out their buddy. Lyric's cousin, Max, and his fiancée were safe now too because of him.

Not that Lyric knew that.

All he wanted to do was find out who in the club was the head of the snake who set up all the shady shit going on, including the contract killing. It seemed like the club president—who went by the name of Lobo—didn't know anything about it. Either that or he had the best poker face Viper had ever seen. Which was possible, but his instincts told him otherwise. The guy Viper had killed, Bleaker, had played things close to the vest and had never revealed who set up the jobs, leaving Viper still trying to weed out other members so he could find the mastermind and stop him.

Living a double life was exhausting, especially when you didn't know who to trust or who'd stab you in the back.

"Ow." He groaned, and the PT let up on a particularly tender spot.

"Sorry about that. You're so tense. You need to relax."

Yeah, try doing that when you're surrounded by a bunch of thugs. No one fucked with him, but he was tired of the game he'd been playing for years now.

Maybe it was time to change things up and do something different.

The only bright spot in his life was something he wanted but couldn't have. Not right now. Not when he put everyone around him in danger all the time. He was happy to risk himself for the reward of taking down the bad guys, but not someone else.

Not her.

But wanting her had become an almost tangible

gnawing inside him. The more he tried to stay away from Lyric, the more he wanted to see her. Just being in her presence eased him. Watching her cook or sing or dance or laugh with her friends and family . . . Yeah, he wanted to be part of her world.

But he was stuck in his.

"You're good to go. See you in a few days. We'll work on that range of motion. Drink lots of water. Ibuprofen for the swelling and pain. You should be feeling better in the morning." His PT left with a smile on her face and him feeling worse than when he'd walked in. But she was right, by tomorrow his shoulder would feel better. And if he took better care of himself, it might last.

Viper sat up on the table, hung his head to stretch the muscles in his neck and back, then glanced at the man sneaking into the private room and closing the door behind him. "Hey."

"How's the shoulder?" Nick didn't ask simply because he was Viper's boss, here to get an update without anyone seeing them together, but because they were brothers.

"Fine."

Nick frowned at him. "That's what you always say, but here we are."

The shoulder was an old wound that plagued him.

His phone rang. He hopped off the table and grabbed it from where he'd left it on his thermal. He checked caller ID. "Huh. Interesting."

"What?" Nick asked on the second ring.

"I need to take this."

Nick waved him to go ahead.

Viper picked up, not one bit ready to hear her voice and loving it all at the same time. "Hey."

"How did you get my number that time you called me about my kidnapped baby cousin?"

Viper held back a grin. She'd obviously saved *his* number.

But Lyric sounded off. This wasn't her usual cheerful self others got to experience while she remained suspicious of him. But she didn't sound cautious today, more like inquisitive and scared.

He didn't like that at all.

So he answered her. "You call your sister from the kitchen to the bar all the time." He found it odd since they were in the same building, less than twenty feet away from each other. But then again, Lyric couldn't just leave whatever she was cooking back there unattended, so she would call Aria behind the bar for whatever it was she wanted. "I see your number light up her phone all the time." He had a knack for remembering details like that. "I put the number in my phone. Why?"

"That's what I want to know. Why?"

"In case I needed to call you. Which I did that one time."

"Did I ever thank you for reuniting Cyn with her niece?"

"Not the way I wanted you to," he said under his breath, hoping Nick kept his mouth shut, because the last thing he needed right now was his big brother giving him shit about distractions Viper surely didn't need. But Lyric wasn't someone he could ignore. Now. Ever.

"What did you say?"

He got back on track. "You thanked me. And that's how I got your number. So?" The pause unsettled him when nothing ever really did anymore. "Lyric, what's wrong?"

"It's just that easy for anyone to find me, to get my information."

"I only called you once." It wasn't like he made a habit of it. Though, he probably shouldn't mention how often his finger hovered over her contact information. But he never pressed the button to send the call through, no matter how badly he wanted to hear her voice and have her all to himself once in a while. He stared at the picture of her on his phone whenever he was alone. Because even he had limits to his loneliness. So he indulged them by watching her YouTube videos. He loved watching her sing and hearing her songs. She was so talented.

But she didn't need to know that either.

"I'm not talking about you."

That got his attention. Just like this random call did.

He had noticed a couple of her followers left some rather personal comments, hoping she'd respond to them with as much interest as they showed in her. She never did. But lately one in particular had seemed a little too enthusiastic.

"Who got your information? Did someone contact you?"

Nick raised a brow, catching on that this personal call was also something serious.

She didn't respond.

"Lyric, you can talk to me. Tell me what's going on."

"Maybe it's nothing."

"*Nothing* doesn't make you call me." They didn't have that kind of relationship, though he wished he could change that.

"I'm probably overreacting."

He knew her well enough to know she wasn't dramatic.

"It's just . . . You wouldn't do something like this. And he did. He looks like a nice guy. You don't, particularly. I mean, you seem one way, but I don't think that's really who you are."

If she only knew.

And he couldn't help but feel those words sink deep inside him. She saw past the image he portrayed and saw something else. He hadn't seen the man he used to be for a long time. He had to bury that guy deep to do what he did.

And maybe he needed to resurrect him because Viper didn't have a hell of a lot going for him.

Well, except for a girl named Lyric, who saw more than he ever showed her.

"Who is this so-called nice guy, and what did he do to you?" He bit out the words, trying to control the rage building inside him. Because if someone hurt her, they would not escape his wrath.

"I'm sorry. This isn't your problem. It's mine."

"You called me. Now, tell me what's going on."

"I just couldn't believe it was so easy for him to follow me home all the way from Nashville and then find me at the ranch like he knew me."

"What the fuck?" Every protective instinct in him flared to life.

"Exactly."

All kinds of alarms went off in his brain, and his heart jackhammered in his chest. "Who the hell flew all the way here and showed up at your family's house?" She didn't live there. She lived above the bar. He knew that because he made it a point to know where she was when she wasn't working.

Who sounds like the stalker now, asshole?

"His name is Rick. I'm not *really* sure who he is, except a fan. I know, that sounds pretentious, but I don't know how else to describe him." She sighed. "Do you know this is the longest conversation we've ever had?"

He was wholly aware of that. He wished they were talking about something else entirely. Anything else than her being in danger. "Can we focus on this guy?"

She sighed. "My cousin Hunt is looking into him."

"How so?" He wanted Hunt up this guy's ass and kicking him out of the state. Now.

"Background check."

That was a start, but not enough in Viper's mind.

"Maybe he's harmless and I'm just paranoid. Maybe I'm creeped out over something that is nothing. Maybe I should be flattered he wants to work with me so badly he rushed here looking for me."

He thought she knew exactly what was what with this guy. "Is that how things are normally done?" He didn't think so.

"No. It's usually a scheduled thing. I do most of it online, since I'm here and my writing partner is in Nashville."

Yeah, he'd heard her talking to her sister Melody about her New Year's trip and another she had planned for March. It sounded like something she did every couple of months.

He'd love to know more about her songwriting but stuck to her overzealous new arrival. "If you got a bad vibe from him, trust your gut." His had saved him more times than he could count.

And hers had told her that Viper wasn't what he seemed, and she was dead-on there. But he couldn't tell her that because then he'd have to explain. Not going to happen. It would put her, and him, in more danger.

Nick pointed his finger and circled it in the air, indicating for Viper to finish up so they could talk business.

He ignored the gesture and his brother.

If Lyric wanted to talk, he'd talk to her. It was little moments like this that fed his faith in humanity and reminded him not everyone was terrible. He just wished she'd called about something not potentially horrible.

Hell, at this point, he'd swap recipes with her just to have a chance to talk to her longer. Of course, he'd have to call his mom for help with that one, because he barely got by in the kitchen.

"I'm sorry." She sounded so lost, nothing like the vibrant, happy woman he'd come to know. "You're probably busy. I'm bothering you with this. Whatever *this* is."

He couldn't let that stand. "You can call me anytime you want. It's not a bother. At all."

Nick glared at him.

He should really shut up. But he couldn't seem to stop talking now that he had her attention.

"I know this was totally random. Thank you. Now I have to go exercise a bunch of horses." She paused again. "Do you ride?"

"Yeah. But not in a long time." Too long. He missed the ranch in Montana, his family, everything about having a normal life.

"Hmm. Okay." She sounded like she didn't know what to say anymore.

"What's the dinner special tonight?" He often ate at the bar. She was the best cook. And if his mother ever heard him say that, she'd kill him, but it was true.

"Are you back in town?" She'd noticed his absence.

That gave him hope, even if he couldn't do anything with it. "I got back last night."

"Were you hoping for something?"

Her. But he remembered they were talking about food. "Pot roast with those garlic mashed potatoes." His stomach grumbled because all he'd had this morning was coffee.

Nick picked up Viper's shirt and threw it in his face. He glared back at his brother.

"I could make you that."

He didn't expect that answer because pot roast wasn't really on the menu at the Dark Horse Dive Bar. He just really wanted it on this cold January day.

"See you tonight." She hung up.

He didn't mind. He was too stunned by her response and that she'd called him at all.

"Care to share?" Nick asked.

"Call Hunt Wilde. I want to know who he's doing a background check on for his cousin Lyric. I want to know everything and more on whoever this guy is."

"Why? She's not your concern. Let Hunt handle it. You have other business to finish."

He pulled his shirt on over his head and bit back the pain in his shoulder. "I can do both." Back to his usual irritated self, he dared his brother with a look to contradict him.

Nick frowned. "This isn't smart."

"I have stayed away from her for months."

"You got involved with her cousin and the baby. You shot the guy who went after her other cousin and his girlfriend."

He didn't need the reminder of the shooting. "Then, keeping one more Wilde safe isn't exactly beyond the scope of my job here."

Nick's stare didn't waver. "She's different. Isn't she?"

"She's not a part of the other stuff, if that's what you're asking."

"You know exactly what I'm asking. Why her? Why now? You know better than to lose focus."

He held his arms out, then let them drop. "I have been nothing but focused on the job for years. What has it gotten me?"

"You know the payoff has always been worth the risk. That's the job."

"And what about my life?" he snapped, then realized he'd revealed too much.

Nick took a seat and stared up at him. "I've felt this coming for the last several months. Talk to me. Tell me where your head is at, so I can help."

"I don't need help. I need something that's mine. That's real." The need for it clawed at him.

"It can't be real with her. She doesn't even know who you really are. And you can't tell her."

He leaned back against the massage table. "I know that. I didn't call *her*. She called *me*." And it meant a lot that she'd felt safe enough to open up with him.

"Because you intervened. For a good reason," Nick tacked on. "Can you finish this, or do you want out?"

Out wasn't an option. Not anymore. "I'm in it until it's done. We're close. I can feel it."

"Then, enjoy your dinner tonight. Tomorrow things go back to the way they need to be. For now." Nick held his gaze, making sure Viper understood and complied with the order. Nick was his boss. But the brother side of him toned down the look enough to convey that Viper could go after what he really wanted once he finished the job.

But that also meant reevaluating his future.

And where Lyric fit into it.

If she even did.

Nick pulled him back on track. "You need to focus on the motorcycle club, its members, and who's really in charge there. People's lives are at stake."

He knew that all too well, because his life was also on the line. One wrong word, one wrong move, and he could be killed. "I'm ready for whatever happens."

"I hope so." Nick stood and faced him again. "When this is done, we'll talk about what comes next." Nick held his gaze.

It took Viper a long moment before he asked what had been on his mind for months now. "What if nothing comes next?"

Nick gripped Viper's shoulder. "As always, I have your back the way you always have mine." Nick smacked him on the back, then left before him, so no one would see them together.

Not that anyone was watching him here. He'd made sure of that before he arrived. But he'd been trained and learned on the job to never be too careful.

Which made him hope and pray that Lyric took whatever was happening seriously and remained cautious.

He had a bad feeling about a guy who'd hop on a plane and show up unannounced without so much as an invitation.

He thought about how she actually talked to him today, like she wanted to get to know him.

Rick probably saw what Viper saw in her: a woman with an open heart too sweet to turn him away. So he'd taken a chance. One Viper had to stop himself from taking every time he saw her, every time he thought about her—which was becoming all too often—and distracted him from his job.

And there, he needed to stay focused and on alert.

Time to get back to it. The sooner he finished this, the sooner he could do what he wanted for a change.

Chapter Three

Lyric couldn't believe she'd called Viper and dumped her problem on him. Granted, he hadn't brushed her off. Not that she thought he would. And once she started talking to him, she couldn't seem to shut up. She'd finally hung up because if she didn't, she'd give in to the urge to simply keep him talking about anything and everything just so she could hear that deep, sexy voice.

They'd spoken more words to each other this morning than they had the whole time she'd known him. Everyone around her told her to keep her distance. But . . . he seemed nice. Interested.

She wanted to know more about him, not what people thought about him. Because, like her, they didn't really know him at all.

And people shouldn't judge others until they really knew their story.

An hour ago, Hunt had given her the good news that Rick Rowe wasn't a wanted serial killer and had no prior convictions or speeding tickets. But for all that, he wasn't squeaky-clean. There was one report of trespassing on private property and a separate charge of breaking and entering that was dismissed by the district attorney due to lack of evidence. She found it interesting that items had been stolen from the woman's home but weren't found in Rick's possession, nor was there evidence he took them. But the woman had been adamant he did.

Hunt said plainly he saw this as a red flag. One she should heed until Rick proved to be a good guy, despite what he'd been accused of in the past.

She couldn't get the woman's claim out of her head.

Why steal things like a plant, a sweater, and a pair of socks? The list of items seemed so random, from those things to a pen and a tube of toothpaste. Also, a half-eaten jar of salsa. So weird.

She checked the time on her phone: 9:01 p.m. No messages. And it was time to close the kitchen. Tuesday nights weren't very busy. The Dark Horse Dive Bar was much more than just a bar. It served the community as a place where all could gather to eat, hang out, dance, meet friends and make new ones—even in a small town, where you knew practically everyone—if you were twenty-one and up.

"What's with the long face?" Her younger sister Melody had asked her something similar twice already tonight. Aria was up to three or four.

Was she that transparent? "I'm fine." Except for the fact that Viper—she would make a point to get his real name out of him the next time she saw him—had stood her up.

She had gone out of her way to make him the dinner he wanted, and he hadn't even shown up to eat it.

"Do I smell pot roast? That wasn't on the menu."

"I made it. If you want it, have it."

Melody studied her. "Is this about that guy who hung out here all night trying to get your attention? Are you trying to impress him? Because your pot roast would certainly do that."

Rick had sat on the barstool closest to the kitchen window where the waitresses put up their food-order tickets and took the meals out to customers. He stared at her mostly, then he started trying to carry on a conversation with her through the window. It was a lot of yelling because the place was so loud during the rush. He tried to come back to talk to her while she worked, but she'd put an end to that, telling him customers weren't allowed in her kitchen. She and her staff worked in concert with each other. It was chaotic and potentially dangerous with all the hot burners, pots, pans, and people moving around. They had a rhythm, a shorthand, and knew how to stay out of each other's way.

Rick did not and would only annoy her and the others by distracting them all.

"I'm not interested in him."

Melody gave her a half frown. "Are you stress-cooking again?"

She did that sometimes. "No. I just wanted to make it." She'd had it for dinner. Alone. Since *he* hadn't shown up. "See if Aria and Jax want some, too, before I put it away." Maybe she'd make pot-roast sandwiches tomorrow for the crew. A perk of the job.

Her staff did not go hungry. Ever.

Melody didn't move, just stood there eyeing her. They were all so close; if anyone seemed off, one of the siblings, if not all, would know it with a look. "Are you sure you're all right? Is it that biker guy who always comes in?"

"Why would you ask about him?"

Melody's eyes filled with knowing. "You two have your thing."

"What thing? There's no thing." Maybe there was a thing. A thing she wanted but wasn't sure if it would be a good thing.

If she kissed him, she'd know.

Kissing told a lot about a person and how they felt about you.

"You're awfully defensive. Whatever." Melody dismissed it with a wave of her hand. "Keep it to yourself. Just be careful."

"There is nothing going on." Even if she wished that wasn't true. They'd had a moment today. Well, not exactly a romantic moment, but some kind of something. A normal conversation, at least. Then again, not exactly.

She was kidding herself if she thought a guy like him and someone like . . . Wait a second. That was so not the right kind of thing to think. She didn't judge people like that and she wasn't about to put other people's perceptions of him in her head and think they were real when he'd been nothing but . . . nice? Yes, nice. In his way. And maybe he only showed that side of himself to her. Or so it seemed.

But then he hadn't shown up.

Maybe he had a good reason.

She gave him the benefit of the doubt, pulled out her phone, and texted him.

LYRIC: You didn't show for dinner. Are you okay?

She read the message over three times and decided it wasn't too forward or desperate, just concerned, and sent it.

And waited for a response.

Chapter Four

*F*uck *my life!*

Viper read the text message from sweet Lyric. He stared out the windshield of the truck he was in with one of the guys from the Wild Wolves Motorcycle Club and wished he didn't have murder on his mind. He felt terribly guilty for standing her up. Not that it was a date or anything. Still, it would have been a chance to talk to her again, have a real conversation. Over a meal she'd made for him. Instead he was sitting in a deserted parking lot waiting for a guy who wanted to put a hit out on his wife because he didn't want a divorce.

After a few bittersweet weeks home for the holidays—most of the Wild Wolves club members dispersed for the holidays anyway, so he hadn't missed anything—he was back on the case. He hoped to figure out who in the biker club was setting these things up. And here he was back in the thick of things and hopefully one step closer to knowing who was making these deadly deals.

He didn't like the setup, sitting in a parking lot in full view of the road, no cover.

If this shit went sideways . . . He didn't want to think about it.

He definitely couldn't take the time to text Lyric back and apologize.

"Are you clear on the plan?" Spike, aka Darrell Kelly, asked, his knee bouncing like a jackhammer and hitting the steering wheel.

"Dude shows up, we confirm what he wants done and when, count the money, and take off."

"And you're sure you're cool with this?" Spike's nerves rubbed Viper the wrong way; he didn't like that the guy was so wound up.

If Spike was so inexperienced and ruffled by this, things could go wrong fast.

"Are you okay?"

Spike bit at his thumbnail. "It's good money."

"Yeah, but you have to kill someone to get it." Viper had a lot of bad shit on his conscience and a lot of good reasons why he'd done what he'd done. It didn't make it any easier to carry the burden of it all. He justified his actions in a lot of different ways to cope. But the body count was stacking up, and he had the scars, visible and not, to prove he'd lived a dangerous life.

Spike suddenly turned to him. "I thought you were up for this."

Viper shrugged. "I'm here."

"This has to go right." Spike's leg sped up. "I don't want to end up like Bleaker."

Not the same. "Don't get into a shoot-out with the feds, then." Viper thought that one was a no-brainer.

"The boss was not happy about losing him. Bleaker brought in a lot of money for doing protection and things like this."

He tried to get Spike to open up even more. "Bleaker spent a lot of time out of state."

Spike nodded, his whole body vibrating with the

bounce of his knee. "There's money to be had all over if you've got the network to insulate you from exposure."

"I know Lobo isn't running this. He protects the Wild Wolves at all costs. If he finds out someone is putting the MC at risk . . ."

Spike glanced at him. "What makes you think he doesn't know?"

"Because this is never talked about in the MC."

"The pres has plausible deniability by remaining on the fringe."

Still, Viper wasn't so sure Lobo knew about this. Someone might have told Spike the club president knew and to keep it quiet because talking about it could expose them all.

"Where the hell is this guy?" Viper wanted out of here. Now. The longer he waited, the more he felt like this could go sideways. Civilians thinking they could step into this world often got caught up in something they had no business being involved in, in the first place.

Headlights swept across the parking lot, highlighting the bait and tackle shop, along with a mom-and-pop sandwich shop. Both were closed this time of night.

What he wouldn't give for something hot to eat and drink. It had to be nearly freezing, and the temperature was dropping.

The other car stopped, facing them about fifteen feet away. The headlights went out.

"I'll follow your lead." Viper opened his door and stepped out.

Spike met him at the front of the truck, both of them shivering in their leather jackets. They stared at the other vehicle's windshield, barely able to make out the two occupants.

Viper swore under his breath. "I thought you said it was one guy."

Spike's eyes narrowed. "It's supposed to be the husband."

"If that's a fucking cop with him . . ." Viper let that hang.

If the cops were involved now, this whole thing could go down the drain.

"Fuck." Spike got even more jumpy.

The two in the SUV climbed out and walked toward them. One of the guys did look like a manager of some office job or something, in his long coat over slacks, and a matching knit cap and scarf to keep him warm. His shoes were not suited for the cold, rugged outdoors.

The other guy was a bit more rugged in jeans, work boots, a heavy flannel, down vest, knit cap, and gloves.

"That's far enough," Viper said, making the two stop five feet away from them.

"Are you Spike?" the office guy asked.

Spike spoke up. "You Rich?"

"Yeah."

"Who's your friend?" Viper asked.

"Who the fuck are you?" the friend asked.

"Your worst nightmare," he answered because in many ways he could be and was in this situation.

Rich held a hand up toward his friend. "Let me handle this."

The friend rolled his eyes but shut up.

Rich looked to Spike. "I didn't want to come alone with all this money."

Viper wondered, why not? He was here to pay to

have his wife killed. If he got robbed, that was the least of his worries.

Spike took charge. "First things first. We're going to pat you down, check for weapons and wires. Arms out."

Viper hoped they were unarmed and not cops. That's the last thing he needed right now.

Rich complied with Spike's order readily.

The friend eyed him.

Viper glared. "You got a problem?"

The friend reluctantly held his arms out.

Viper patted him down a little rougher than necessary, just to make sure the guy understood Viper could take him and not to try something stupid.

Spike stepped back from Rich and folded his arms over his chest. "Now let's talk specifics."

Rich glanced at his friend, then back at Spike. "I want you to do what you said you'd do."

"Which is?" Spike asked, being very helpful to Viper because he'd like to know very much what exactly Rich wanted done to his wife.

"You have to make it look like an accident."

"What did you have in mind?" Spike asked. "You want her to trip down the stairs? Crash her car? Slip in the shower and conk her head?"

"Any of those things are fine, so long as it's quiet and she's dead. I don't want to know how."

"It will be more believable if he's actually surprised by her death," the friend said.

So the two had hatched a plan. Great. Viper wanted to crack their heads together, but what good would it do? Neither of them seemed to have a brain.

Rich nodded in agreement with his friend. "Yes. And it has to be done tomorrow night. I have a business dinner in Willow Fork." Which meant he'd be out of town with witnesses. "It needs to be done between six thirty and eight. That's when I'll be in the restaurant, not on the road."

Spike nodded. "And where will the missus be? What do you expect her to be doing during this time?"

"She'll be at home. Watching TV or reading a book. She never goes out."

Maybe if her husband invited her to these business dinners or took her out once in a while they'd have a better relationship, Viper thought.

Maybe if he'd showed up for dinner at the bar, he'd have a foot in Lyric's life, instead of being the dick who asked her for something and then didn't even call to tell her he couldn't make it.

He got back to what he was supposed to be doing instead of thinking about her.

"Why do you want her dead?" Viper asked, wondering what drove this man to hire someone to kill his wife.

Rich stared at him. "It has to be this way." He sounded so sure.

Viper believed him but wanted to know how it came to this. "Why don't you just divorce her?"

"She's worth more dead than alive," the friend said. "Divorce is expensive. Why should she get half of everything? She's not worth it."

Rich glared at his friend. "She's your sister."

"She's your wife," the friend shot back. "This helps both of us. You get to keep your new piece of ass, and I get out of debt."

So the two were in this together.

He felt sorry for the missus with the cheating husband and asshole brother.

Viper waved his hand out to them. "Get their money. Let's go."

"We're not paying until it's done."

Viper and Spike shared a look, then turned for the truck.

Two steps in, Rich called out. "How about half up front, the rest when it's done."

Spike turned back. "How about you go fuck yourself? You want the job done, you pay up front, we do it, and you never see us again. That's how this works. And there's no take-backs. Once you commit, it's going to be done. So if you're not sure you can stomach this—"

"I want it done." Rich ran back to his car and opened the door.

Viper's adrenaline surged when the dude went to his car. He could be pulling out anything. He slipped his hand to his back and wrapped his fingers around the gun grip.

The friend held up his hand. "It's just the money."

Rich took out a paper bag, rushed back, and gave it to Spike, who pulled out the bills still wrapped in the bank bands.

Viper bet the guy had gone to the bank in the last few days and pulled out the cash. Idiot. He really was banking on the fact that his wife's death would look like an accident and no one would investigate further.

Spike counted the two stacks, then tucked them into his jacket. "Nice doing business with you." Spike headed back toward the truck.

Rich called out, "Don't you want the address?"

Spike opened the truck door and grinned at Rich. "Don't you think I checked you out before this meeting? I know where you work, where you live, where your girlfriend lives, how often you've stopped by her house to fuck this week, and how your wife spends her days."

Rich paled, then glanced wide-eyed at his brother-in-law.

"Drive safely," Spike said, climbing into the truck.

Viper followed him.

Their two murderous guests ran to their car, climbed in, and sped out of the lot first.

Spike turned to him and laughed.

Viper pretended to laugh with him, to keep up appearances.

"Can you believe those two?"

Viper put a little doubt out there for Spike to think about. "I wonder . . . which one of them actually hatched this plan?"

"I think the husband got caught cheating on the wife by the brother."

"Maybe. I just hope the two of them have kept this between them." Viper could spin this to his advantage.

"Rich seems smart enough to keep quiet. He's got too much to lose. The other guy . . . he seems like someone who runs his mouth."

Viper nodded, not needing to say anything more and happy as hell this was over. Now he could try to smooth things out with Lyric.

Chapter Five

Lyric sat by the fire in her little apartment above the bar, strumming her guitar and staring at her phone, which she was using to record her singing the song she wanted to post on her YouTube channel tonight. Anything to distract her from thinking about Viper standing her up and not returning her text.

So stupid. She'd read things all wrong. Still, she couldn't help hoping.

She tapped Record on her phone. "Hello, music lovers. I'm so happy to see you all tonight. It's been one of those days where everything seems out of sorts and I find myself alone. With you. And my thoughts and a lot of feelings. This song seemed perfect for tonight. So here goes. Kenny Chesney's 'Come Over.'"

She lost herself in the sound of the guitar, the lyrics, the feeling behind the song about being home alone, wanting someone who maybe isn't good for you but you crave them anyway, and all you want is for them to come over and be with you. Just for tonight. Just for this moment. Just to make everything else go away, and it's just the two of you wrapped up in each other.

She finished the song with the title's plea over and over again, wishing the man who probably wasn't right for her would come over anyway.

When the last sounds of the guitar strings silenced and all that was left was her breath and the popping and crackling of the logs behind her, she laid her head on the guitar and gave a wistful smile to the camera. "Good night, music lovers." She held the pose for another moment then tapped the Stop button.

It never failed. Music made her feel better.

She sipped her wine, then took her phone, edited out her starting and stopping the recording, then posted it to her YouTube channel not really caring who saw it tonight.

That one had been solely from her to him.

Someone knocked on her door.

She sat upright and stared at the shadow behind the curtain-covered window. The distorted image didn't give her a hint of who'd come looking for her. Probably one of her sisters, who were still down in the bar closing out the night. At nearly midnight on a Tuesday, they'd already had last call: the two o'clock closing was only for Thursday to Saturday.

She bet Melody wanted to check on her again.

She hoped they didn't want her to help clean up. She'd already done the kitchen.

She opened the door ready to tell her sister to mop the bar floor herself but stopped short with her mouth open in shock.

"Hey." Viper stood on the little deck outside her second-story apartment taking up every square inch of it and looking uncertain of his welcome.

The freezing cold seeped into her skin and made her shiver as the warm air in her place rushed out the door.

"You're losing all your heat. Can I come in? I only need a minute." Despite his not showing up earlier, she was ready to let him stay as long as he wanted.

How did he make her want him so much?

She tried to play it cool and stepped back so he could enter. She closed the door on the freezing night. It took her brain a second to truly comprehend he was suddenly taking up a lot of the small space—just like he took up her thoughts. "What are you doing here?"

He stuffed his hands in his jeans pockets, his leather jacket making him look even bigger and broader than he already appeared. "I'm sorry."

She couldn't believe he'd come here to apologize. "You could have texted that."

He shook his head and shivered. "I wanted to do it in person. I . . ." He pulled his hands out of his pockets and brought them to his mouth and blew air into them.

She grabbed his sleeve and tugged him over to the fireplace. "Sit. Warm up."

He stared at the two sleek, navy blue recliners, unlike their overstuffed counterparts, then at her. "Are you sure?"

She sat and held her hand out toward the empty chair.

He sat, looking much bigger in the cozy chair than Jax did when he sat in it. "This is actually really comfortable." Viper settled in and rubbed his hands together, letting the heat from the fire warm his side and hands as it filled the room again.

She put her elbow on the arm of the chair, her chin in her hand, and stared at him. "So. You're sorry for standing me up."

His gaze shot to hers. "Was it a date?" Shock, surprise, and regret filled his bourbon-brown eyes.

Her cheeks heated, and it had nothing to do with

the fire. "I . . . uh . . . thought you planned to have dinner at the bar." She kept it vague, unsure what he really wanted with her, because up until now, there'd been an imaginary boundary between them. Tonight, he'd crossed it by coming to see her at her place and not in the bar.

He leaned forward, everything about him intense. "Lyric, I'm sorry. Really, I am. You have no idea how much I regret not making it tonight." His stomach rumbled.

A grin tugged at her lips. "I take it you didn't eat somewhere else?"

"No. I got caught up doing something with one of the guys from the MC."

Yeah, the motorcycle club, where a bunch of equally rough and tough guys hung out. One of the reasons everyone kept warning her away from him. But she couldn't seem to help the pull he had on her. "You guys all seem really tight."

He seemed to think about what he wanted to say. "I couldn't get out of it. I'm sorry."

"You said that already. Like three times now. And it's fine. I was just . . ." She couldn't tell him she was disappointed.

"What?" It felt like he wanted her to say something specific.

She eyed him. "Are you busy right now?"

"No. Why?"

"You're hungry. I've got a ton of leftover pot roast."

He shook his head. "You don't have to do that."

"I offered. So?"

A hint of a grin tilted his lips before it disappeared with his words. "I'd love some. And the company."

Me, too. "Then, you can have both."

"Can I have a glass of that wine, too?" He notched his chin toward the bottle and her glass on the little table between them.

"I'll get you a glass, then run down to the kitchen to make you a plate."

She stood but didn't even take a step when he gently took her by the wrist. "I don't want to put you out."

"You're not. I'll only be a few minutes. Relax. Drink some wine. Warm up."

"You're not worried about leaving me in your place?"

She looked him in the eye. "No." Not even a little bit.

He seemed nervous for some reason but said, "Okay. Thanks."

"You're welcome." She went to her little kitchen area and pulled out another wineglass from the cupboard and took it to him. "Back in a sec."

"Take your time."

She stuffed her stocking feet into her boots, pulled her coat off the rack by the door and tugged it on, zipped it up, and off she went down to the bar, leaving Viper alone in her apartment.

She went in through the back and pulled the leftovers from the fridge. She was making the plate when Aria walked in. "I thought I saw someone back here. Midnight snack?"

"Yeah," she lied to her sister because she didn't have time to explain why Viper had come to see her and why she'd invited him to stay a while. She spooned a huge helping of garlic mashed potatoes onto the plate and spread them out. Then she scooped two big helpings of the pot roast with all the veggies on top of that.

Aria's eyes popped. "Wow. You are hungry."

"I worked hard tonight. We had a good crowd."

"Yeah, including that guy who couldn't take his eyes off you." Aria eyed her and grinned. "Anything going on there?"

"No. He's a singer-songwriter who wants to collaborate with me."

Aria's eyes softened. "Oh, that's nice."

"Yeah. Not really."

Aria opened her mouth to ask more, but Lyric didn't want to talk about it. Especially when Viper was waiting for her. "Listen, I was working on something upstairs, and I want to get back to it."

"Sure. No problem. See you tomorrow." Aria was used to Lyric being in songwriting mode and not wanting to lose an idea or get distracted from it before she got it worked out on her computer or with the guitar.

Lyric picked up the plate and rushed back to her place. She found Viper right where she'd left him, though he'd taken off his jacket and hung it next to the door. He sat in the same chair, a full glass of wine in his hand, his face turned to the flames as he stared at them looking lost in thought.

"You okay?" she asked, wondering about how quiet and intense he looked.

He turned and held up his phone. "You posted a song tonight."

She went still. "You follow me?"

"You sing in the bar sometimes. Well, all the time in the kitchen. And then sometimes with the bands that come to play." He went quiet for a moment but didn't stop looking right at her. Then he surprised her again and said, "I like listening to you sing."

"Thank you."

He leaned forward with his elbows on his knees,

the wineglass in one hand. "Was that song meant for me? Or is that just me, having a stupid idea?"

She held his gaze, feeling this moment, knowing it meant something. Hoping it was the start of something. "It's not stupid at all."

He raked his fingers through his hair. "Me being here is crazy."

She shook her head. "I've had *crazy* today. This . . . this is nice."

He fell back in the seat and stared into his wineglass. "I thought maybe it was just me."

"It's not just you." She needed something to do, so she popped the plate in her microwave with a cover over it and nuked it for a couple of minutes.

Viper didn't say anything.

She watched him watching the flames dance.

"I like your place," he said without looking at her. "It's so you."

She laughed under her breath. "How so?"

He looked around, his gaze following the huge birch-tree branch behind her bed and sweeping across the ceiling with the strands of white lights casting a soft glow over the room. He stared at her bed for a moment, then at the pictures on the walls, the kitchen where she stood, and the little dining table with a bouquet of white and pink spider mums in the center. "It's warm, inviting, bright, and colorful."

She grinned. "Is that how you see me?" If so, she liked it.

He glanced over at her. "It's how everyone sees you. There's not a person in the bar who doesn't think you're their friend immediately upon meeting you."

"Maybe that's why Rick seems to think he can just walk right into my life uninvited."

"You let me in the door," he pointed out.

"At least I know you. Him . . . I spent more time trying to politely excuse myself from his presence so I could be with my friend Faith than I did trying to get to know him."

"You don't *really* know me." It sounded like a warning.

"You're right. I don't. But you're . . . familiar." She pulled the plate from the microwave, grabbed a fork from the drawer, and brought them to him. He took the plate. She took everything off the small table she'd been using to record her video along with her notebook and pen, and tossed it all on the pale blue down comforter on her bed, then moved the table in front of him.

"You didn't have to do that. It looked like you were working on something."

"A song. It really wasn't flowing tonight. I was too distracted. I'll work on it later."

Viper took a big bite of the pot roast and rolled his eyes with pleasure. "I can't believe I almost missed out on this."

She picked up her wineglass and enjoyed watching him eat the meal she'd made especially for him. "I'm glad you stopped by."

His gaze shot to hers. "Really?"

"Yeah." She thought of what her cousin Max had said to her at Hunt's wedding last month. "You're not what everyone thinks you are."

He didn't look at her this time.

"You've always been good to me. You stepped in when Dan got caught cheating on Aria and tried to get me on his side."

Viper looked at her then, anger simmering in his eyes. "He shouldn't have grabbed you like that."

"You tossed him out of the bar. He hasn't been back since."

"Good riddance." He dug back into the food.

"And there's been other times when some guy's liquored up and feeling frisky."

The familiar glare made her grin. "You don't like that kind of attention."

She wasn't into random guys putting their hands on her. "It's what you do that shows me I matter to you in some way."

He didn't say anything.

She leaned in close. "Tell me I'm wrong."

He met her gaze. "I'm here. Despite the fact I know this could go terribly wrong, even if you don't see that."

She pushed a little more because she needed to know it wasn't just her feeling this way. "Are you here because you want to be with me?"

"Yes. But that doesn't mean it's a good idea. There are things you don't know. Things I can't tell you right now."

That intrigued her. "But you could later?" She didn't know exactly what she was asking because she didn't know what he was hiding. But if this was a matter of trust, she'd earn his.

"Yes. But I can't tell you when that will be, because . . . I can't." His agitation showed her how much he wished he could confide in her.

She pointed at his plate with her glass. "Eat your dinner."

He picked up his fork and took another big bite, like he needed to hurry up and eat it before she booted him out the door.

She put him at ease, even as she settled back into

her seat. "I'd really like to spend more time with you."

The next forkful of food hovered in the air as he stared wide-eyed at her. "Seriously?"

She took a leap. "The song I posted tonight was definitely for you. I was very disappointed you didn't show earlier. I wanted us to share a meal and talk and get to know each other better."

He set the fork down again. "If I could have been here, I would have. I really need you to believe that."

"I do. So finish your food, and let's get to know each other better."

He took a sip of his wine and stared at her. "There's something you need to know about me. I will never lie to you. But I also can't tell you everything about my life either."

"Are you into something illegal?"

"No."

"Is whatever you are into dangerous?"

"Very."

She didn't know what to say to that. "I'm not going to be able to guess what that really means, am I?"

"I really wish you wouldn't, because I can't tell you."

She held his steady gaze. "Then, at least tell me this. What's your name?"

His gaze intensified. "Everyone here calls me Viper."

Here. Interesting.

She shook her head. "I want your real name."

He sighed, his eyes full of secrets and regret. "And this is where you either trust me or you don't, because I can't tell you that."

"Are you a wanted criminal?"

He almost grinned. "No."

"I'm not calling you Viper."

"Call me whatever you want, and I'll answer to it."

Mine. The resounding claim rang through her heart and mind. "You want to be with me so much that you'd just let me call you anything because I don't want to use that nickname."

"Yes. It's just a name, Lyric. What I'm missing in my life is someone who sees me, not all the other stuff going on around me. I don't know how to make that make sense to you when I can't tell you everything right now." The earnest words and utter intensity and hope in them sent a wave of sympathy through her.

"You need me to have faith."

"I'm asking for a hell of a lot more than that, and I know it, and I'm sorry for it, because it would also be best if we kept this, whatever this is that's happening, between us."

"You don't want people to know we're seeing each other." She didn't like hiding things from the people she cared about.

"It would be better for you if they didn't."

"Why?"

He simply held her gaze and didn't say a word. He didn't want to make up some story and lie to her.

She scrunched up her lips and shook her head. "I didn't expect it would go this way."

"I didn't expect you to invite me in or say that you wanted to get to know me better. Not now, anyway."

She heard what he didn't say. "But you saw a day when we did have a conversation like this?"

"I hoped."

"I don't want to wait for whatever it is you're waiting for. It already feels like we've been missing out on whatever this could be."

He leaned forward and hung his head. "I don't

know if I deserve this. Your faith in me that I'm not exactly what everyone tells you I am."

She waited for his anxious gaze to meet hers. "I'd like to decide who you are for myself."

His massive shoulders went lax. "I should have known you'd say that. You see people with an open heart."

"Everyone is the same, but different. We all love and laugh and hurt and make mistakes. We are all capable of good and bad. We learn. We grow. We get stuck in bad habits."

"I want to be something good in your life, even if we can't have the kind of thing you might have with someone else right now."

"Well, we're off to a good start. You're definitely the most open man I've ever talked to. And at the same time, the most guarded."

"I'll try not to be that way around you."

Someone knocked on her door.

Lyric frowned. "Busy night around here."

He stared at the door over his shoulder and whispered, "Are you expecting someone?"

"No. It's probably one of my sisters."

He turned to her, his whole body tense and on alert. "They can't see me here. It's too dangerous for you to be connected to me."

She went along. "The only place big enough for you to hide is the bathroom."

He moved quickly, ducking behind the door but not closing it.

She went to the front door and opened it, expecting Aria or Melody but getting the second surprise of the night.

"I got your message." Rick smiled at her and took

a step forward, but she stood her ground, blocking his entrance, the cold chill up her spine not all from the biting temps outside.

"What are you doing here?"

He put his hands on the doorframe and leaned in, a cocky grin on his face. "You posted that song, and I knew you wanted me to come over."

Stunned, she didn't know what to say.

He looked past her. "Were you just having dinner?" His gaze dropped to hers. "Why two glasses of wine? Is someone here?"

She thought fast. "My sister came up before she closed the bar. It's late. You shouldn't be here. How did you even know where I lived?"

"I asked the waitress where you went after you closed the kitchen. She told me you have a place up here. Then I saw the video and realized this is where you post them all from." He shivered in his inadequate coat. "It's really fucking cold out here."

Her T-shirt and flannel pajama pants weren't keeping her warm at all. "I didn't post the song as an invitation. It's late. I've had a long day. And I don't think it's appropriate for you to just show up like this. Again."

"You didn't answer my call."

No. She'd ignored all three calls. "I keep my phone on Silent when I record."

"Makes sense."

"If you'll excuse me, I'm going to bed."

He didn't budge and gave her a pleading look. "Can we please get together tomorrow to write?"

"I need to check my schedule. I'll text you."

"You will? You promise?" He eyed her. "Because it seems like you're not happy to see me." The words held a tinge of anger masked as hurt.

She remembered what Hunt had told her about antagonizing someone who had an obsessive personality. "I wasn't expecting you."

"Right." He seemed to soften a bit. "Yeah. That's okay. We'll have plenty of time to spend together soon."

She raised a brow. "What do you mean?"

"The bar is closed on Sunday and Monday. We can spend those two days together."

"I have other plans. And when I write with someone, I usually keep it to a couple of hours."

"Then, it's a date." He shivered again. "You sure I can't come in and warm up? We could hang for a while."

"No." She inched the door closed even more.

"Okay, then. See you tomorrow."

She closed the door and locked it, not giving him a chance to try to worm his way into her apartment again.

She walked toward her bed and found Viper standing just outside the bathroom door, out of sight of the front door and covered window.

"What the fuck?"

She folded her arms over her chest. "You sure I can't tell him the badass-biker dude is my boyfriend?"

He stalked toward her very slowly and stopped an inch from touching her, looming over her as she stared up at him. "Is that what you'd tell him?"

She dropped her arms. "Hell yes. In a heartbeat."

He leaned down, even closer. "I'm going to kiss you now."

"Good. I don't know what's been taking you so damn long."

"I wanted you to be clear about who I am."

"You're the man who tells me and shows me the truth. Everything else is outside of you and me."

His eyes went wide. "You do get it."

"I'm trying, because I think you're worth it."

His lips met hers with an urgency and need that stunned her at first, then warmed to something so intimate and consuming it nearly buckled her knees. She didn't need to worry about falling off the world: he wrapped his arms around her, pulled her up to her toes, and kissed her like his life depended on her feeling everything he poured into the start of them.

The kiss ended with one long touch of his lips to hers, like he didn't want this to ever end. But then he pressed his forehead to hers and took a long steadying breath.

She kept her arms around his neck and watched him finally open his eyes, and the relief and need were there, along with something more. Something deeper. Something she'd never seen before.

"I've wanted to do that almost since the moment I laid eyes on you."

"That would have been weird," she teased. "This was . . . amazing."

His fingers slid through her long wavy hair.

She realized he'd pulled the tie out of her messy bun. "When did that happen?"

"Sorry. But I've wanted to get my hands on all this forever."

"Oh. Well." She grinned at the greedy look in his eyes. "Have at it."

He pulled two fistfuls over her shoulder, let the strands slide through his fingers and land on her chest. "Stunning."

She spread her hands over his rock hard pecs. "So was that kiss."

He brushed his thumb down the side of her face. "Why did that guy think the song was a message to him?"

She pressed her lips tight. "You know it was for you. Right?"

"Yes. So he's the reason you called me this morning about how I got your cell number?"

She fell back flat onto her feet, her hands sliding down his rock-hard abs. "What's your take on him?"

He took a chunk of her hair again and let it slide through his hand. "He's delusional. You say one thing, he insists another."

"You caught that, too. He's moved into one of the cabins on the ranch. He spent the whole night at the bar watching me until I closed the kitchen. He didn't look at any other women, his focus solely on me." She eyed him. "Kind of like you do when you come in."

He narrowed his gaze. "Am I that obvious?"

"Not really. Sometimes. Mostly, maybe, I wanted it to be true."

He slid his hands over her shoulders and to the back of her neck, his fingers buried in her hair. "It is true. You're the only woman I see and want."

"Then, we're on the same page now, even if we'll try to keep it just between us."

He touched his finger to her chin to make her look at him. "Just for now. Not forever." It sounded like a vow.

She loved hearing that he was thinking long-term, not just in the moment as long as it lasted.

The intensity returned. "I don't like that guy. You need to stay away from him."

"As you can see, it doesn't seem to matter what I do, he just shows up. And thinks I wanted him here."

His brow furrowed. "That's not right."

"But is he just awkward, or what?" She really wanted his opinion, because to her it felt all kinds of wrong.

"Don't make excuses for him. Don't ignore your gut feeling or the fact he dismisses everything you say."

"He wants a song. Maybe if I sit down with him and write one, he'll take it and go home."

He gathered her hair at the back of her head. "You know it won't be enough."

She stepped away from him, her hair sliding through his fingers again. She stared into the fire.

He came up behind her and brushed his hand down her hair in a gesture meant to comfort. "I don't want to scare you. I want to keep you safe."

She leaned back into him. "I know. I'll handle it."

He put his hands on her shoulders. They were strong and warm and steadying. "With someone like him, it's not enough to stand your ground. You need to cut him off."

"I'll try. Like I said, maybe all he wants is a song."

"He didn't come here tonight for a song. He came because of the one you sang, asking for the person you wanted to come over."

She glanced up over her shoulder at him. "It worked. You came."

"I came because I owed you an apology, not because I expected something from you."

She turned to face him. "And that's why you're still here and he's not. And that's the way it's going to stay."

He gave her a determined look but dropped it. "It's late. We both need some sleep."

She didn't want him to go but didn't ask him to stay either. She liked what they'd started and anticipated things to move quickly now, but not that fast. "Will I see you later today?"

He grinned. "I would love that, but I've got something going that I can't miss."

"When will it be over?" She was starting to sound desperate.

"Late. Like tonight."

"I'm usually up late."

He brushed his hand down her arm. "I don't want to be the guy you're always waiting around for."

She appreciated that. "Then, I'll assume you're not coming, unless you text me that you'll be here."

He studied her face. "You're okay with that?"

She nodded and used his words. "For now."

He kissed her softly. "I don't deserve you or your patience."

"You have them both." She wanted to put him at ease, afraid he'd change his mind and pull back from her.

He cupped the side of her head, her chin in his big, warm palm, his thumb brushing softly against her cheek. "You never said what you want to call me."

"M."

Surprise lit his eyes for a second, then a question filled them.

She gave him the answer. "Because you're mine."

Wonder softened his eyes as he stared at her. "You have no idea what you do to me."

She went up on tiptoe and kissed him. Soft, sweet, a tempting without any pretense or wildness, just a tender message. "I'm so glad you stopped by tonight."

"Not half as much as I am." He kissed her. Long and deep, it spun out until she wondered if he planned to stay or go, because he didn't seem inclined to stop or move. He just held her close and kissed her like he could do it all night.

She liked that about him. He sank into the moment and stayed there. He didn't rush. He didn't need to keep it moving in one direction or another. So she went with it. Actually, she stayed with him in the kiss, the feeling, the here and now without worrying or anticipating what came next.

She'd never enjoyed kissing someone as much as she liked kissing him.

And when they finally came up for air, he had his fingers in her hair and a look of pure desire in his eyes. "I don't want to leave you, but I should go before we take this too fast and miss all the good stuff."

"So far, it's all been good stuff. The talk. The kiss. You being here as just yourself. I even like that you're a little worried about me."

"Will you do something for me?"

She raised a brow. "The pot roast wasn't enough?"

He touched his forehead to hers. "Best meal I've ever had. Don't tell my mother."

She giggled. "If I meet her, I'll keep your secret."

His gaze turned serious. "I know you would. And I want you to meet her."

"Well, that's something, isn't it?" Her stomach fluttered with excitement that this was really happening. He liked her. He wanted to be with her.

"Make me a promise."

"What?" She felt a little dazed by this man and how, when he opened up, he didn't hold back.

"If you feel like this thing with Rick is turning into something that even remotely makes you scared, you'll call me or tell me right away. Not when he's finally crossed a line, but before any of that happens, and you feel like it's not just awkward but possibly dangerous."

"Okay."

"Have you told your whole family about him yet?"

"Just my mom, dad, and Hunt know."

"Tell your brother and sisters. They're at the bar the most with you. They'll have your back when I'm not there."

"I'll be okay," she assured him.

He hugged her close. "I've seen people turn on others with no provocation."

She slid her hands up his back and held him tight. "I promise I will let you know if this escalates in any way or I simply can't take it anymore and want him gone." She heard how that sounded. "Not gone-gone. Just away from me."

He stepped back and mock-glared at her. "Do you think I'm going to shoot him or something?"

She raised a brow and tested him. "If I asked you to, would you?"

"No." The disgruntled and offended look he gave her told her he meant it.

"I wouldn't ever want that, anyway."

He brushed his hand down her hair again. "You're too sweet and kind to do anything like that."

"You should ask Jax what I'm capable of."

There was that almost grin again. "I bet you can hold your own. I just don't want you to have to do it." He kissed her quickly. "We're both stalling my leaving."

"It's worked so far. I've gotten a few more kisses, and you seem to like petting me."

He brushed his fingers through her hair and actually smiled. "Your hair is so soft."

"So is yours." She went up on tiptoe, pressed her nose to his, looked him in the eyes, and ran her fingers through his longish light brown hair, the ends of which were brushing the collar of his thermal. "Say goodbye to me."

"Never." He kissed her again, soft and sweet, so tender it made her eyes tear up. "See you soon." He touched her chin with the pad of his thumb, then released her all at once, like if he didn't he'd just keep holding whatever was still in his hands. He grabbed his jacket and pulled it on, then headed for the door.

"See you soon, M."

He turned before he stepped out the door, the cold air hitting the back of him. "Can I tell you a secret? Something you promise not to tell anyone or ask me more about it."

"I promise not to tell or ask anything more about it. For now."

"*M* is the first letter of my real name."

A smile so big it hurt her cheeks came over her. "Thank you for sharing that with me." It felt like a gift, this small bit of trust.

That familiar serious look came back. "I want to share everything with you."

"I hope someday soon you will. Until then, I'll take all these happy surprises we share, like you showing up tonight and me calling you M."

"I like being yours. It's been a long time since I felt like I belonged anywhere."

"You know where to find me."

"I will definitely be back for more of you." He turned to go, then shifted back to face her again. "Thank you for dinner. I really enjoyed it. This has been one of the best nights I've had in years. And the others that have come close were spent down in your bar watching you."

Her heart melted, and her throat clogged. "I don't know what to say to that, except that I loved our time together tonight, and I can't wait to see you again."

"This bad idea is probably the best one I've ever had. And maybe it's selfish to be with you when my life isn't really my own right now, but I can't help myself. I want you in my life too damn much to wait any longer."

She touched her hand to her heart.

"See you soon, Angel." He left her standing there staring at the door wishing she'd called him back and asked him to stay the night. Because now that they'd taken this huge step forward, she didn't want to spend a second without him.

The feeling was thrilling.

Angel?

She liked it.

She couldn't wait to see him again.

She just hoped Rick didn't spoil it next time.

Chapter Six

By eight o'clock the next morning, Lyric had three meat smokers going. She didn't mind M's late-night drop-in. She hoped for another tonight, though she knew that was a long shot, since he'd told her he had plans.

She checked the temps. Everything looked good. A couple more hours to go and she'd have the meat for their most popular item on the menu, pulled pork sliders. She still needed to do the tandoori chicken skewers, but those didn't take very long, and she'd put them on the grill when they opened tonight.

The aroma on the back patio outside the bar's kitchen was amazing. It was so cold, but she loved being outside. She sat with her guitar on one of the benches under an outdoor heater. There were several tables set up out here for family dining in the spring, summer, and fall because kids weren't allowed inside the bar. In the winter, she and the staff hunkered down under the heaters for their breaks and a chance to get out of the loud space.

She loved music, but it could be a lot with the noise from the crowd, the thump of the music, and the clanking of glasses and dishes.

Sometimes, she just needed some peace and quiet.

Like today.

Her dad came out of the kitchen, grinning. "That chili you've got simmering in there smells delicious." Her dad loved a good chili dog. So did many of their customers.

In the winter, she liked everyone to have something warm and hearty. "I'm thinking about making sloppy joe sliders tomorrow." She had a set menu of items the bar offered regularly, but she liked to add a special or two each night to mix things up. The one thing everyone loved was the burger and fries for five bucks. It had been that price since her grandma owned the bar. They'd keep it that price forever. They made a hell of a lot of money on the booze to cover fluctuating costs on the food. They worked together on keeping to the budget. Aria ran the bar business and took care of the books; Melody and Jax ran the bartenders and waitresses; and Lyric ran her six-person kitchen crew.

"Do you have any catering going on this week?" Her dad sat next to her on the bench under the heat.

"No. It's quiet."

"What's going on with Rick?"

"He was at the bar last night. Then he showed up at my door after midnight because of the song I posted."

"What was the song?"

She didn't really want to say. "'Come Over' by Kenny Chesney."

Wade stared wide-eyed at her. "He presumed it was an invitation?"

"He did. But it was actually meant for someone else."

Her dad raised a brow, then a knowing look came over him. "I see. The other guy who is interested in you."

Just the thought of M and the time they'd shared

together last night brought a grin and a bunch of warm feelings. "He's not what everyone thinks."

"How do you know?"

"Because we had a really good talk last night. A talk like I've never had with a man. He was honest about not being able to tell me everything about his life but promised that he'd never lie to me."

Her dad took a seat beside her. "Why can't he talk about his life?" The question wasn't accusing but interested.

"To protect me and himself. I don't exactly know why, except that maybe the things he knows about the motorcycle club aren't entirely safe for others to know. He swore he isn't into anything illegal, and I believed him."

"Don't you think he'd say that just so you'd think he's a good guy and want to be with him?" Again, her dad kept things inquisitive.

"He wasn't trying to convince me he's a good guy. In fact he told me now is not a good time for us to be together. He cares about me. He wants to be with me, but he also thinks it's best no one knows we're seeing each other because he doesn't want to put me at risk."

Concern filled her dad's eyes. "Lyric, doesn't that tell you something about his life?"

Yes. But . . . "I can't explain it. I believe he's trying to get away from whatever is going on in his life, so he can be with me. But it's also not just about me. I think he really wants something different for himself, and I'm just a part of what he wants."

Wade sighed and stared off into the distance. "I don't like that these two men are inserting themselves into your life, and neither is doing it in a way that makes you feel safe."

She put her hand on his arm. "That's just it. I know M would never hurt me. If I'd asked him to leave immediately last night, he'd have walked out the door."

"*M?*"

"He goes by Viper, but I didn't want to call him that."

"Why not call him by his real name?"

"He wouldn't give it to me." She squeezed his arm to stop him from telling her again why that sounded like a bad thing. She already knew it did. "It was one of the things he didn't want to lie to me about, and he asked me to trust him that in time he'd tell me everything. But right now, for his own reasons, he didn't want to share it. So he said he'd answer to anything I wanted to call him."

Wade wore a dubious expression. "Why *M?*"

She didn't want to share that with her dad because then he'd know how deep she was already in with M. "I actually guessed the first letter of his name."

"So it's probably something like Michael or Mark or Matthew."

"Maybe. The thing is, I don't really care what his name is."

"Why not? That seems like the least of what you should know about him."

"Because he's shown me he's protective, kind, gentle, and willing to say he's sorry and listen when I tell him how I feel and what I want. Rick showed up and didn't care about what I said or wanted. He just wanted what he wanted."

"And what was that?"

"To barge into my apartment and be with me despite the fact I told him the song wasn't for him. I didn't want to see him, and I wanted him to leave."

"Was M with you when Rick showed up?"

"Yes. But he didn't want anyone, including Rick, to see us together."

"And he didn't step in and kick Rick out?"

"He let me handle it, because I was handling it. If Rick hadn't left or had pushed his way inside, I have no doubt M would have stepped in to help me."

He eyed her again. "You're sure?"

It was easy to reassure him on this point. "M was not happy about Rick. At all."

"And you believe M is a good guy."

"He is to me. Whatever else is going on, he'll share with me when he can, but for right now, he's asked me to have some faith in him. I have no reason to believe that he's not a good man, other than people's perceptions about him. That's not based on any sort of fact. You taught us to go with our gut and always look for what's real and true, not gossip or rumor."

"You have a good heart, Lyric. I don't want to see anyone take advantage of that. I also know you're fair and not a pushover. So if M makes you feel this much for him, then I'll give him a chance. Rick is another story."

"You and I are on the same page about him."

Her dad looked up as Jax, Aria, and Melody walked out the kitchen door.

"What are you all doing here so early?"

Her dad stood up and faced her along with her siblings. "It's time you told them about Rick."

Melody grinned. "The guy from the bar last night, who couldn't take his eyes off you?"

Lyric saw the determined look in her father's eyes that she not do this alone. "You and someone else I know think alike on this."

Approval lit her dad's eyes.

"Is he your boyfriend?" Aria asked.

Jax eyed her, ready to go into protective-brother mode.

"No. He's someone who started off trying to connect with me online. Things got a little too personal and uncomfortable for me. I backed off from interacting with him and focused on my singing and songs. I hoped in time he'd get the hint that I wasn't interested. Then, while I was in Nashville, this guy showed up at the gig and approached me about writing songs together. He was pushy. I tried to get out of it without being rude, but he kept insisting, so I gave him a vague answer that we'd do something soon. I didn't know when I met Rick in Nashville that he was the same person from online who goes by the username LyRick." She spelled it out for them so they'd understand the play on her name and got three shocked looks. "And then he showed up out of the blue and found me at the ranch the other day."

Jax went on alert. "He followed you here?"

"Yes," their dad confirmed.

Jax swore under his breath. "How the hell did he know where you lived?"

She winced. "It actually wasn't that hard. He knew I worked at the Dark Horse Dive Bar and sang here. He looked up the bar, found the town, and flew here. Then a helpful person in town told him if I wasn't at the bar, he could find me at the ranch."

Aria pressed her lips tight. "Once he had Wilde Wind Ranch, all he had to do was look up the address."

"And now he's in one of the cabins," their dad added. "Hunt looked him up. He's got some minor infractions, but nothing to indicate he's aggressive."

Lyric didn't wholly agree with that. "He's persistent and determined to have my attention." Lyric wondered how the guy who looked so normal made her uncomfortable, while the guy who looked like a criminal made her feel secure, even when he kept so much from her.

Maybe it was simply that Rick's intentions were masked in his tenacious manner, and M refused to lie or say things just to placate her. He'd laid out the truth and given her a chance to decide if she wanted in or out.

Maybe that's what it was. One respected her choice, the other tried to impose his wants on her at every turn.

Her dad looked at her three siblings. "I want all of you on alert when this guy is around. I want you to watch Lyric's back. If you see or hear anything, make sure Lyric and I know about it. Hopefully this guy gets the message that she isn't interested and leaves."

"But you don't think that's likely." Jax eyed her again.

"No. He seems to think the things I say and do are all directed at him and that I want him."

"Why not just get Viper to smack him down?" Melody suggested. "The guy is always looking out for you anyway. He'd make an impression on Rick."

Lyric shook her head. "I don't need anyone to handle this for me. I can deal with Rick myself."

"I know you can, sweetheart." Her dad smiled to let her know he meant it. "I just want it known that this guy could go from nuisance to problem. I don't want you or them to dismiss something as nothing when it could become something dangerous."

Lyric understood her dad and siblings were looking out for her. And maybe she needed the help, because

Rick hadn't just crossed the line last night showing up the way he did, he hadn't respected her wishes when she stated them. And that was a problem perhaps she couldn't fix herself.

She didn't even want to think about what would happen if Viper saw Rick cross a line with her. Would he get jealous or angry and do something about it?

He'd let her handle it herself last night. He'd have stepped in if she'd needed him.

But he hadn't lost his head and gone all caveman, so she knew he'd help without making things worse.

Her dad gave her a quick hug. "Everyone is in the loop now about Rick. Anything else you want to share?"

"No." She was going to abide by M's request and keep their new relationship to herself and see where things went from here.

"Okay, then. I think it would be wise if you let at least one of us know where you are at all times. Just in case," her dad said.

"All our schedules are posted on the calendar system we use," she pointed out. "But if I go somewhere, I'll let someone know."

"Thank you." Her dad kissed her on the head. "I'll leave you all to it, then. Jax, a word."

Jax followed their dad around the building to the parking lot.

Aria and Melody stayed with her.

"How serious is this?" Aria asked. "Is this guy stalking you?"

"I don't know. But it feels creepy enough that I made sure Dad knew what was going on."

"I think you should use Viper," Melody suggested

again. "That dude is scary enough to make Rick back off."

"I'm not *using* him." She didn't like how that sounded or felt. "Do you really think Viper's scary?"

"Intense," Aria supplied. "Not mean, or anything. At least, I've never seen him be that way. I mean, he did throw Dan out the door when I caught him cheating, but he didn't rough him up or anything. He just forced him to leave."

"Yeah," Melody agreed. "He's just a big dude with attitude. But not in a bad way. Like I wouldn't want to cross him, but I also don't think he'd go out of his way to hurt someone. We've seen guys like that in the bar, who are just looking for a fight. He's not like that."

"No, he's not." And she was glad her sisters saw that, too.

Aria held Lyric's gaze. "You really like him."

"There's something there," she confirmed because they already knew it.

Melody bounced on her toes. "You two have been circling each other for a while now. You should do something about it, because he doesn't seem like he's going to make a move, but I can totally tell he wants you."

"We'll see." She left it at that because she couldn't tell them about last night. She didn't like keeping things from her sisters. They shared nearly everything. But she'd promised M.

For now, she'd keep that promise. And if later he still couldn't trust her with his secrets, then she'd have to decide if the relationship was worth it.

Chapter Seven

Viper was sitting at one of the tables in the back at the Wild Wolves clubhouse keeping an eye on Spike, who seemed unaffected that he was going to murder someone in a couple of hours.

They weren't the only ones hanging out today. A few of the guys he worked with on construction jobs were playing poker in the corner. The weather meant fewer jobs in the winter for them. He liked the work. Up early, done early, he had the evenings with his buddies here to work on their bikes in the shop out back, or just hang in the club playing pool, darts, poker, or pinball.

Some of the guys were married or had girlfriends, so the place was usually filled with people at night.

When he didn't need to be here, he preferred the Dark Horse Dive Bar. Good music, food, drinks. And Lyric.

He'd wanted to call her first thing this morning, but he'd had to meet up with his brother and tell him about what was going down tonight.

It took every ounce of willpower he had not to go and see her and kiss her again.

Last night had not gone as planned. He'd wanted to apologize for not showing up for dinner. He had no idea she'd thought it was a date. Like a real date. Dumbass that he was, he'd opened his mouth and poured out his feelings for her. Not in so many words, but enough that she got the point. He wanted to be with her, even if it wasn't a good idea right now. But he couldn't pass up this opportunity. Not when he had a shot at being with her.

Unable to hold off any longer, he texted her. He just wanted some kind of contact with her. He wanted to hear about her day, know what she was doing and how she was. Like, everything.

VIPER: Hey. How are you?

He sent the text feeling like an idiot. *Hey.* Nice opening.

LYRIC: Tired. You kept me up all night.

He grinned.

VIPER: If it's because you couldn't stop thinking about me, I'm not sorry at all.
VIPER: I couldn't sleep for thinking about you, Angel.

That was the truth. He was tired. Well, more than his usual drained self. But he was also amped about tonight and what it could mean going forward for him if he could pull all the pieces together.

LYRIC: I like knowing you're thinking about me.

If she only knew how often he did so.

VIPER: What are you doing right now?

LYRIC: Prepping for dinner rush and avoiding my shadow.

VIPER: He's back?

He didn't like it one bit.

LYRIC: Yep. But I've got it handled. I put him to work making the playlist for tonight.

VIPER: I don't like that he's with you and I'm not.

LYRIC: My dad made sure my siblings know what's going on. They're looking out for me. Melody is hanging in the kitchen with me right now.

VIPER: Don't ever let him get you alone. Please. I don't even want to think about what could happen.

It sent a cold chill through him and turned his good mood sour. If he didn't have to handle this thing tonight with Spike, he'd be there with her right now.

LYRIC: You're the only one I want to be alone with.

God, this woman. She didn't know what she did to him.

VIPER: I love that! I want that! But I mean it. Stay away from him.

He hoped she understood he was worried about her.

LYRIC: I'll be at the bar until I close the kitchen, then I'll be at my place. Alone.

LYRIC: Have fun doing whatever you're doing
tonight.
VIPER: I'd rather be with you.

And didn't that say everything about where his
head was at right now.

LYRIC: 🖤

He stared at the little symbol, hoping that one day
she really would mean she felt that way about him.

LYRIC: You know where to find me. I have no
idea how to find you. Maybe you'll divulge that
secret next time I see you.

He wondered if the secrets he was keeping were
already wearing on her.

"I don't think I've ever seen you look *that* intense.
And that's saying something."

He casually tucked his phone into the inside pocket
of his jacket and stared up at the one woman in this
place he actively avoided. Maria was the club's president's sister. And he didn't want Lobo on his case for
any reason, but especially for thinking he had a thing
for her. He didn't need that kind of scrutiny from anyone in the club.

Lobo could be extreme. He was a womanizer, alco-
holic, and sometimes quick to settle a slight with his
fists just for fun. He thought showing how tough and
unforgiving he could be made him look strong to the
others. Really, he was a bully who had command of
a bunch of followers who also wanted to look tough
and cool.

Viper had dealt with a lot worse.

He'd learned in any situation to keep his mouth shut, stay alert, and be ready for anything.

He stared at Maria and didn't say anything about her comment.

She put her hands on the table and leaned over, giving him a view of her curves. "Are you ever happy, Viper?"

He kept his gaze directly on hers. "Sometimes." He'd been happier than he could remember being in a long while kissing Lyric last night.

"What makes you happy?"

He picked up the glass in front of him. "A cold beer." Actually, he preferred the red wine Lyric had been drinking last night. And the food. And the company.

Maria shocked the hell out of him and sat down at the table beside him. Close. Too close.

More than one of the guys in the room glanced their way.

He barely looked at her.

"You've made some good friends here. These guys . . . they all speak highly of you."

He met her gaze, wondering where she was going with this.

"They all say you're quiet but focused. You're good at your job." Her gaze turned sultry. "I love a man who knows how to use his hands."

That was as unexpected as her sitting with him. "Are you flirting with me?"

"Not well, if you have to ask." She pouted. "I think I'm missing out on something. You and me, we could be good together. Unless there's someone else?"

He didn't dare mention Lyric. But he didn't want

to give her hope either. "I prefer to keep Lobo off my back."

"My brother has no say in what I do, or who I do it with."

He tried a different tactic to dissuade her from him. "I like this place and the people here. I don't want to do anything to mess that up."

"Including me." The raised brow and sexy pout didn't get her what she wanted.

"Excuse me?" Because he couldn't believe she'd meant that he didn't want *to do* her.

"You like me, too. Right?" The grin said she was messing with him.

"I hardly know you, but from what I've heard, everyone thinks you're nice."

"Is that all?"

Maybe a little flattery would get her to stop this. "A beautiful woman like you doesn't need me to shower her with compliments."

"That's only two. You think I'm nice and beautiful. That's something to build on."

He shook his head. "I appreciate the interest, but I'm not looking to get into anything right now with anyone."

"Seems to me you've been alone a long time."

Longer than she knew. And he was tired of his own sorry-ass company. But he had Lyric now and planned to do everything in his power to keep her.

"I like it that way. Less complicated." He really didn't need this right now.

"Did someone break your heart?" She put her hand over his.

He slid his hand free. "No." They usually just walked away with the same complaints. Everything came before them. He loved his job more than them. He was never around when they needed him.

And they were right.

But things had changed. He had changed. And now he wanted more.

Spike waved him over.

He stood and stared down at Maria. "Excuse me."

"You should know, I don't give up easily. Not when it's something I want."

He tried to let her down easy. "I've got other priorities right now." He hoped the abrupt brush-off would work and headed over to talk to Spike.

"Hey, man, I saw you with Maria. Everything cool?"

"Fine." He hoped.

"Good. Because you get in good with her, you'll be made like me."

Well, that got his attention. "What do you mean?"

"I can't talk about it now. You're not in the circle. Yet. But me and a couple of the others want you in on what we're doing."

This could be the break he needed. "Just tell me what's going on and what she has to do with it."

"I stuck my neck out yesterday taking you to that meet with those guys. You handled yourself. That counts. That matters. Just hold tight until me and the guys can talk you up enough to get you promoted."

Viper knew when to push and when to let things go. "Are you all set for your thing tonight?"

"Yeah. I'll be in and out. It'll look like she slipped and fell and hit her head."

"Are you nervous?"

"No. I've done this kind of thing before."

He tried not to sound excited by the confession, more surprised. "You have?"

Spike glanced around, then leaned in. "The first time, I kicked my girl's foot right out from under her when she was about to step down the stairs. She cracked her head open and died the next day. Stupid bitch was cheating on me."

"Damn." Viper seriously didn't know what else to say.

"The other two times were like this. Someone hires us to do a job. We get it done. One was this guy whose business partner wanted him out of the way before some deal went through. He wanted the money for himself, I guess. I rigged the heater in his hunting cabin. He died of carbon monoxide poisoning. Last month, that woman who disappeared mysteriously . . . They'll find her in her car in the lake in the spring after the thaw. Maybe."

He'd check those two murders out. "How many of these have you done?"

"Just those. Plus the one tonight." Spike looked thoughtful for a moment, then added, "You were with Bleaker the night he died. Those bastard feds killed him."

"Right?" Maria asked from behind him. "That's what happened, Viper?"

He schooled his features and turned to her. "Yes."

She eyed him up and down. "How did the feds know someone was coming for that woman?"

Viper glanced at Spike. "Maybe we shouldn't talk about this with anyone but Lobo."

"I'm not just *anyone*," Maria snapped, showing an aggressive side to her he'd never seen. She didn't like being dismissed. She wanted him to believe she had some power in the MC, though women took a back seat to the men who ran the club.

Spike looked nervous about agitating Maria, so maybe she quietly wielded power behind the scenes.

He let loose the exact same explanation he'd given Lobo after Bleaker died. "Fine. You want to know what happened? Bleaker fucked up. He got caught in that woman's house, killed someone, and left a witness."

"Things happen you can't plan for." She eyed him, expecting him to go on.

"Then, you don't go off half-cocked without thinking things through. If I'd known what he was getting me into, I could have helped him come up with a better plan than going in guns blazing at two trained feds."

"You weren't supposed to be there," she snapped, keeping her tone low and lethal.

"He asked for my help," he bit out, letting her know he was angry about the whole damn thing, because Bleaker could have gotten him killed. He still might, and the man was dead. "I didn't know what he had going with that lady. But when the shit went down, I backed him up the best I could. When he went down, I saved my own ass from ending up dead or in a cell."

"You disappeared shortly after Bleaker's death." Her gaze bore into him.

"That was some messed-up shit. Lobo didn't want the heat coming down on him or the club. I needed a minute. Plus, it was close to the holidays. I went home to see my family. Grandad's getting up there. I thought this might be my last chance to see him." His granddad was actually an ornery son of a gun, who'd probably outlive him. Especially if things here went sideways again. "Why the hell do you or anyone else care what I do?"

"Just making sure you're still a team player."

That got his hackles up, and he let her know it. "I've put in the time and paid my dues." He didn't think he needed to justify himself to her, but something told him she was working her own thing, and it had everything to do with Spike and the mysterious others in on it.

Maybe Lobo knew about it. Maybe he didn't.

Either way, Viper had just hit Maria's radar, and this might be the break he needed.

She held him in her considering gaze for a moment. "Spike has a job tonight. It's a solo mission." Maria eyed the other man. "Maybe next time you can assist. And if both of you perform well, maybe we'll make it a regular thing."

"Fine. Whatever." He shrugged like it didn't matter. "I've got to go bid on a job."

"What kind of job?" Her question sounded curious, but he thought it meant more.

"Bathroom renovation."

"Where?" Now he knew he needed to be careful around her.

"Willow Fork." He had all the info to back it up.

She raised a brow. "All the way out there."

"It's winter. I'll take all the work I can find, wherever I can find it."

"Will you be back here tonight? Or do you plan on hanging out at your favorite place?"

He didn't like that she knew he'd rather be at the Dark Horse Dive Bar than here wasting away hours with the guys. "It's too damn cold to be out tonight."

"I'll never understand why an Arizona boy like you came all the way out here."

"I hate the sweltering heat." True. He did. But,

though that was his cover story, he'd never lived in Arizona. He was born and raised in Montana and worked all over the northwest, but mostly in Idaho and Wyoming. "I just wish I could ride during the winter here." Everyone in the MC felt that way. His motorcycle, like everyone else's, was sitting in a garage.

He smacked Spike on the back. "Good luck." He headed for the door.

"If you change your mind, I'll be here tonight," Maria called after him.

He didn't turn or acknowledge that in any way, especially since the other eight people in the club heard her say that to him.

She was the last complication he needed in his life right now. But also possibly his way out of all this.

Chapter Eight

Viper did the last thing he should be doing and stopped in at the Dark Horse Dive Bar because he couldn't help himself. He'd taken a roundabout way to get here, making sure he didn't have a tail. He wouldn't rest easy until he knew Lyric was as safe as she could be when he wasn't around.

Because it was too dangerous for others to tie Lyric to him, he did a little lock picking to get in through the emergency exit in the back. The place didn't open for another hour, but he knew the Wildes and their staff would be here setting up for the night. Lyric was probably already in the kitchen cooking up some good stuff.

He got lucky coming in the back way, as he suspected he would with everyone up front getting ready to open the bar. He walked to the office door, hoping the man he'd come to see was there working.

He knocked on the door because he knew it locked from the inside every time it closed. Smart to keep people out of the office, unless they were staff and had a key.

The door opened, and Jax glared at him. "How'd you get in?"

Viper didn't answer. "I came to talk to you about Lyric."

"What about her?"

"Let me in, and let's talk."

Jax held the office door wide for him and closed it the second Viper stepped through. Jax started the conversation. "You're here about Rick."

"She told me he followed her here."

Jax sneered. "She told you before us."

Viper didn't mind the overprotective-brother thing. He appreciated it for what it was. Love. "He spooked her."

"It's too damn easy to know everything about everyone these days." Jax glanced at the computer, then the monitors showing the various security-camera feeds.

Viper focused on getting Jax to see him as an ally. "This guy started online. That wasn't enough for him. He showed up at her gig in Nashville. Now he's here. And I don't like it."

"Why?"

"Because I care about her." He had no problem saying that to Jax. He wanted to put the guy at ease and make him a partner and friend in this. Not someone who'd stand between him and Lyric.

"Does she know that? Because it seems like you spend an awful lot of time trying not to show her you care until you can't help yourself."

Yeah, he'd changed that last night. "She knows. But because of circumstances in my life, we're keeping it quiet for now. So keep it to yourself."

Jax stared long and hard at him for a moment, then seemed to come to a decision about him. "I get that. The people you hang with . . . not so nice."

"I would never do anything to hurt her."

Jax held his gaze, then nodded. "I know that. You always seem to be looking out for her."

"I always will. And that's why I'm here. We need to talk security for her and this place."

Jax pointed to the three monitors. One showed the bar. One the view from the bar out across the main room toward the stage at the back. One showed the hallway that led to the bathrooms and office. "I added extra security a couple months ago. That's how Aria discovered Dan was cheating on her. Plus, there was this groupie online who made Lyric nervous. He came into the bar a few times."

So Lyric had dealt with this before. "Not Rick, but a different guy?"

"Yeah. He tried to get Lyric to go out with him, but she wasn't interested. Probably because of you."

It surprised him Jax would so casually mention that, but he loved hearing that even a couple of months ago Lyric was thinking about him in that way.

"Anyway," Jax went on, "I had some words with him. He backed off and disappeared after that."

Viper appreciated that Jax had his sister's back. "She needs a better lock on her door upstairs. There's no cameras that cover the back of this place. She leaves the kitchen door unlocked and open all the time. I've even seen people come in through the kitchen to see her."

"It's well-known, especially among the people who really need it, that Lyric feeds anyone who needs a meal whether they can pay or not. In the winter, there's more need because people have to choose between heating their place or buying groceries. They come to the back to see Lyric, though they're always welcome in the bar. They just tell the waitress they'd like a Lyric Special, and they get a free meal."

Viper had no idea and liked Lyric and her family even more for supporting their community and caring in that way. "That's very generous."

"It started with our grandmother. Lyric carries on the tradition."

"Another reason we need to keep her safe. Add a camera to the back pointed at the door, so you can see who comes and goes. And one pointed up at her apartment door."

Jax readily nodded, then went quiet for a moment. "Do you think this guy is dangerous enough that he'd try to take her?"

"I'm not sure. But I'm not going to make it easy for him to do it if it comes to that. If you can conceal the cameras, that would be best, but otherwise, at least you can see anyone visiting her or trying to get into her place."

"I was already worried. Now you're freaking me out."

He understood Jax's feelings so well. "If I'm overly cautious, it's because I couldn't stand for something to happen to her if I could prevent it."

"I'm with you on that. Okay. Two more cameras and a better lock on her door. What else?"

"Any chance you can get her to stay at the ranch instead of here alone?"

"Lyric likes her place here for a lot of reasons. She spends a lot of hours working. What little time she has to herself, she writes and records her songs. Adding the long drive to and from the ranch, especially that late at night and on slippery wet roads . . ."

Dangerous. He didn't want to trade one worry for another. He didn't want to take something away from her that she couldn't live without. "She loves her music. I'd hate to take that time away from her."

"Right now, this guy is a nuisance. If things escalate . . . I'll do the big-brother thing and warn him away from her. Of course, if he saw you with her, he might think twice about whatever it is he thinks he can have with her."

"If I make it clear to *him*, then it will make it clear to *everyone* she's important to me. Then I have a bigger problem."

"Do you really think someone would go after her and risk you going after them?" Jax seemed to respect his strength and no-bullshit attitude.

"Desperate people do stupid things. I'd never forgive myself if someone went after her because of me."

"What if this guy goes for her because you didn't make it clear she's yours? If that's what this thing is between you two."

He thought about how she wanted to call him M. *Mine*. It still felt amazing and so unbelievable.

"I'll monitor the situation and do what needs to be done." It was the best he could do when trying to protect Lyric from Rick, himself, and the shit in his life.

Jax raised a brow. "You sound like my cop cousin, Hunt."

He ignored that. "How long until you can have the cameras up?"

"The guy who installed them is a friend. I'll get him out here tomorrow at the latest."

He'd have to accept that and hope Rick didn't lose his fucking mind and do something stupid. "Until then, keep a close eye on her."

"Where are you going to be?"

"Somewhere else tonight." He hated it, but he had a job to do. "If I could be here, I would," he assured Jax.

"Normally I'd ask a guy interested in one of my

sisters if it's real and not some hookup they're looking for. But with you, I've known from the moment you started showing up here that she was it for you, despite how you never did anything about it."

"Let's hope, for her sake and mine, you're the only one who sees it right now."

"Just make sure she feels it and knows it. Because if you're always pushing her away, she'll eventually leave."

"We have an understanding. This situation isn't forever, it's just what it needs to be right now, until I can change it." That was as much of an explanation as he could give.

Jax held his gaze. "Lyric is the one who takes care of everyone. Be the person who takes care of her."

"I want to be that someone more than you know."

"Okay, then."

Viper walked out ahead of Jax. He was late for his meeting with his brother and knew Nick was annoyed because of the number of texts his phone kept chiming at him.

But he couldn't leave without seeing her. "Before I disappear, would you mind asking Lyric to come back here to see me?"

"Sure. Hang on. I'll distract Rick while she's with you." Jax left, and a mere two minutes later Lyric walked down the hallway toward him.

"My mama told me never to meet strangers in dark hallways."

He grinned. "I'm not a stranger. I'm yours."

"Yes, you are." She walked right into his chest, wrapped her arms around his neck, and kissed him.

He broke the kiss but held her close. "How the hell did I get this lucky?" He dove in for another kiss, sliding his tongue along hers, holding her body crushed to his. Heaven. He didn't have a lot of time and regretted it deeply. "I have to go. I just wanted to see you, if only for a moment."

"Oh, well, never let it be said I wasted an opportunity to do this." She went up on tiptoe and kissed him again. Just a quick one.

"Anything worth doing is worth doing well." He kissed her back, this time sliding his tongue along hers, tasting mint and chocolate. "What were you eating?"

"My grandma's homemade thin mints. I love them. There's a couple in the bag for you." She drew her hand back over his shoulder and held up a take-out bag.

"What else did you make me?" It smelled divine.

"Two fried chicken drumsticks, some coleslaw, and a couple of biscuits I made this morning for breakfast."

"You really do love to cook."

"It's one of my things."

He heard Jax and Rick talking about their favorite beers down the hall. "We can't be seen together." He grabbed a handful of her hair and let it gently run through his fingers. "I'm sorry, Angel."

"No worries." Her bright smile said she meant it. "I'm just glad I got to see you today."

"Thank you for the food. What do I owe you?" He didn't want to presume she'd done this as a kind gesture, though it was that, too.

"You can pay up later." Lyric gave him a sultry look, letting him know she'd like something other than cash.

"Happy to. Anything you want." He swept his gaze down, checking out the curve of her breasts filling out the Dark Horse Dive Bar T-shirt and her hips curving in those tight jeans.

She blushed and gave him a bright smile. "But you'll also be explaining to me later why you met with my brother. Right?"

He held her gaze. "Because I want you safe." He held up the bag. "Thank you. This means a lot."

"Be careful. Be safe."

"Lock up this door after I'm gone." He left before he fell into another kiss with her and couldn't leave at all and climbed into his truck. He started the engine and kicked up the heater. His phone rang.

"You're late," Nick said, by way of hello.

"I had to make a stop." He opened the bag and pulled out one of the drumsticks. Still hot. He bit into it and moaned.

"What the hell are you doing?"

"Eating some really fucking good fried chicken."

"Lyric's chicken, I take it."

"I think I might have found the head of the snake on this job." As distractions went, that one was sure to refocus Nick.

"Who is it?"

"Maria." Just like him, Nick knew all the players in the Wild Wolves MC.

He started his truck and pulled out of the parking lot and onto the main road, headed toward Willow Fork. He'd double back down a side road once he knew he wasn't being followed.

"That's . . . unexpected. Are you sure?"

He filled Nick in on the conversation he'd had earlier with her and Spike.

"So Spike and some others want you on the crew who is working for Maria."

"That's my interpretation, but I still have no idea how the operation is run and if Lobo is in on it, or if his sister is running this out the back door."

"And what about tonight? Does Spike want you in on the murder?"

"No. I'll be with you and the team, making sure everything goes to plan."

"You're taking a risk."

"The last thing I want is someone to get hurt."

"I don't want your cover blown," Nick bit out, worried Viper would get hurt or killed.

He didn't want to risk it either, because then the last six months would be a waste of time and they'd have little to show for it. But it was his job. "We pick all the players up at the same time. I think Spike will talk. He likes to talk. This could finally be over." He wasn't being followed, so he took the shortcut back toward Blackrock Falls and headed to the meeting place where the FBI team would be getting ready for the arrests tonight.

"It's only over when we get them all," Nick reminded him.

"Working on it. Did you look up the cases Spike told me about earlier?"

Nick paused for a moment. Papers rustled in the background. "I've got someone looking into them. Since we have Spike recorded confessing to the crimes, it should be easy to open the cases back up, verify his story and how his victims died, and charge him."

"You'll want to hold off bringing up those cases until we have the other players in custody."

"I know. Not my first rodeo."

"I just want everything to go right." So it would be done, and he'd be free.

"It will. When will you be here?"

"I'm thirty minutes out."

"Did you get me some food, too?"

"I didn't expect to get this. She made it for me."

"Are you going to save me any?"

Viper bit into the second drumstick. "No. She made it for me."

"Asshole."

"Love you, too, bro. See you soon. We'll take down some bad guys, and you'll feel better."

"Is she worth leaving all this?"

"Who said I'm leaving?" He wasn't sure what he wanted, except for her. But he knew he didn't want to keep doing this and put her and his relationship with her at risk. Because he wouldn't like being away from her for months on end. He'd asked her to take a lot on faith already. He couldn't expect her to do it every time he went on an undercover assignment.

But that didn't mean he had to give up his job entirely.

"You're done with this. I know it. You know it. So let's not pretend that she's not the reason for it."

"You've got that wrong, Nick. She's not the reason I want out. She's the reward for doing all this for so long. I did my duty. I gave this job everything. Now I want to stop pretending I'm something I'm not. I want my life back."

"You've earned it, and then some. There's no one better than you at this. There's no one I trust more to do the job right."

He didn't want to let his brother down. But he deserved a life that was his. "I can't keep being two people and missing out on being with the family because I'm so deeply entrenched in another life that I don't get to live mine."

"I know. We miss you all the time. But you know everyone understands."

"That's nice. But it doesn't make up for the fact that I miss almost everything and have to hear about it secondhand from you. I don't want a relationship where my wife spends more time on the phone with me than she does in person. I don't want to just hear about my kids. I want to be there."

Nick's voice turned soft with wonder. "You really love this woman."

"I think I do, but we hardly know each other. I just had to hide in a hallway, out of sight of others just to spend a couple of minutes with her. I kissed her and had to let her go before we got caught. How do you think she feels about that when I can't tell her I'm one of the good guys, not some thug in a gang? She thinks there's something more to me. She's willing to find out. I want to show her who I really am. But right now, I can't."

"I'm sorry."

He didn't want the apology. "I want you to understand that I've changed. I still love the job, I just can't do it this way anymore. Not when I want the kind of life where I get to share it with the ones I care about more than anything. That includes you."

"I feel like I spend way more time being your boss than I do being your brother." The quiet admission held a lot of love and understanding.

Viper gripped the steering wheel tighter, feeling that all the way to his soul. "I don't mind that you're my boss. I resent that you forget sometimes that I'm your brother, too, and I need you on my side."

"I'm always on your side. I understand where you're coming from on this. We've both dedicated everything to the job." Maybe Nick was feeling as lonely as Viper felt.

"You'd like Lyric."

"I can't wait to meet her." Genuine interest.

"As soon as it's safe."

"You got it. We'll get this done tonight, then go after the rest of them." That was Nick. Always on his side, ready to help.

"Thank you, Nick. I know you hate to lose me in the field."

"You'll just have to train your replacement in all your sneaky ways."

He had some cool tricks. "I can do that."

Nick hung up on him, leaving Viper feeling a hell of a lot better about his decision and that he had his brother backing him up.

He didn't know what the next part of his life looked like exactly, but he was looking forward to getting to know Lyric much better, and himself away from this kind of work.

First, he had some bad guys to put away.

Chapter Nine

Viper loved this part of the job. He lived for taking down the bad guys. And in this case, they had three. Rich, the husband, who wanted his wife dead, so he could be with his lover and not pay out a divorce settlement. Aaron, the intended murder victim's brother, who Viper had learned was in deep debt and thought to blackmail his brother-in-law into paying him half the life insurance money to keep his mouth shut. And Spike, his MC buddy who was just doing a job and getting paid.

Sad, all the way around.

The greed of it didn't surprise Viper. People did a hell of a lot more for a hell of a lot less. Still, three men wanted to get paid for the death of one woman who hadn't done anything to deserve this kind of callous end.

Viper had a mask over his head, his FBI jacket on, a bulletproof vest, and gloves to hide the distinctive compass tattoo on his hand. He hung back and let the rest of the team do their job. They had the victim's house surrounded. Rich's wife, Kelly, had been questioned about her husband and advised of Rich's plans for her. Her reaction had been a loud string of expletives and a combination of shock and outrage. But when they told her about Aaron's involvement, she'd been quietly devastated.

He felt for Kelly. It was one thing for a marriage to fall apart. But it was another for your husband to not only want you dead but to pay to have you killed—while he was having an affair.

He thought about Lyric and how there was nothing she could say or do that would ever make him want to hurt her.

People weren't all the same. Some could sit at a business dinner while a man they hired killed their wife, and it didn't bother them.

Then there was Viper. He'd seen the worst humanity had to offer. He'd rather walk away than be like the scum he sent to prison.

He had a chance with Lyric, and he wasn't going to waste it. He was going to try to be his best self, the one he didn't often get to show others in his line of work, and hope they were happy together. And if for some reason they weren't as right for each other as he'd thought they were, then he'd walk away before he hurt her, or she hurt him.

It didn't have to be a fight. It wouldn't be that way for them.

"Something's wrong," Kelly announced, staring at her phone in the seat behind him.

"What do you mean?" Viper wondered if they'd missed something.

"It's Lynn. I told her not to come over tonight. I didn't tell her why." She turned the phone and showed him the text that pinged.

LYNN: HE KNOWS!!!

"What does that mean?" Viper glanced up and down the street, making sure all was clear, even though they were two blocks over from where the team was apprehending Spike.

"Oh God." Kelly pressed her fingers to her lips. "Aaron knows I've been sleeping with his wife."

Viper couldn't hide his surprise. "That's why he had no problem with Rich setting up the hit."

Kelly's eyes filled with tears. "You have to keep her safe."

He couldn't believe she'd kept this crucial piece of intel from them. "Do you think he'd harm her?"

"He's willing to kill me, his sister. Then, why not his wife, too?"

Viper swore under his breath and pulled out his phone to call his brother. "We have a problem."

"Explain." Nick, ever efficient with his words.

"Kelly and Lynn are having an affair. Aaron knows," he told his brother. "We need him in custody now."

"The team will move on him after we have Spike in custody," Nick said, just as the team leader announced over the comm, "Spike just arrived."

Viper checked his watch: 6:28 p.m.

Rich should be sitting down to dinner now in a crowded restaurant. What he didn't know was that there were also four undercover federal agents in the restaurant with him.

Viper glanced at Kelly in the rearview mirror where she sat in the back of the SUV waiting for all this to go down.

"What's happening?" she asked before he could get a word out.

"Our target just arrived. The team will have him in custody in a few minutes."

"Suspect approaching house from the rear," the

team leader announced, though only he could hear it. Kelly remained quiet and desperate in the back seat.

Viper waited for the call to go out that Spike was in custody.

"What about Aaron?" Kelly's anxiety filled the vehicle.

"One in custody," the team leader announced over the comm.

Nick sighed out his relief and gave Viper an order. "Get to the house. We'll regroup and go get Aaron."

He hadn't been their priority. Now they had a potential problem on their hands.

"I'm headed your way now. Gather the team." Viper hung up and started the car.

He turned to Kelly. "Call Lynn. Make sure she's okay, but don't tell her anything else. You're just calling because you're concerned." He sped off down the road and turned the corner coming to Rich and Kelly's house from the opposite direction all the other FBI vehicles had come from to take down Spike. He spotted something in a driveway across the street and two houses before his destination. And someone spotted him, too.

Luckily he had his mask to cover his identity. Even Kelly didn't know what Viper looked like, or his name.

But she spotted the man hauling ass through the side-yard gate of the house. "That's Aaron."

He slammed on the brakes and put the car in Park. "Stay here. Lock the doors. Do not get out of the vehicle." Viper ran after his target, announcing on his radio, "In pursuit of suspect across the street from your location. White male, black jeans, tan boots, dark green jacket over white shirt, black knit cap. He's climbing over the back fence from the light green house into a neighbor's yard." Viper ran through the gate and straight for the fence as Aaron dropped down. He heard a siren and knew the other agents were circling around to get in front of Aaron.

Viper was up and over the fence in no time, dropping down just as he spotted Aaron out of the corner of his eye. He got clocked in the head with a log and stumbled, pulling his gun as he steadied himself, but Aaron swung a saw with a short, thin blade, slicing through Viper's thin jacket, shirt, and skin from his shoulder down his bicep. Viper nearly lost his grip on the gun but had the presence of mind to swing the butt right into Aaron's face, breaking his nose and sending him to his knees.

Viper shoved him to the ground and pulled his hands behind his back so fast Aaron didn't have time to even touch his bleeding face. He slapped the cuffs on him and held him down with a knee in his back as he used his left hand to pull his radio. "Suspect in custody."

"Let me go. I didn't do anything," Aaron mumbled and wiggled underneath him as Viper tried to breathe and clear his vision. That blow had really rocked him. Adrenaline masked the pain, but it was coming soon. "Get off!"

Nick and two other agents raced into the yard, the homeowner staring at them from their back sliding-glass window.

Viper didn't move as the world spun around him.

Nick stared down at him. "You're bleeding."

"It's just a scratch."

Nick frowned. "Uh-huh. You can get off him now. We'll take him."

Viper closed his eyes as a wave of nausea hit him, and

he pressed his hand to the goose egg swelling on the side of his head. "I think I need some help."

"Help me. Get him off. I can't breathe!" Aaron wailed.

At a hundred and ninetysomething pounds, Viper kept Aaron practically immobile. Though he suspected most of Aaron's breathing problems were because his nose was gushing blood everywhere.

Nick spotted the log next to the saw someone had been using to cut up tree branches nearby. "How bad are you hurt?"

"He got the jump on me with that fucking chunk of wood, then tried to saw me in half."

Nick stared down at their suspect. "I'll add the assault on a federal agent to the assault on your wife and the murder-for-hire on your sister."

"Lynn deserved worse than a smack across the face for sleeping with my sister."

"She deserves better than you." Viper pressed both hands down on the guy's back in order to stand and move away from him.

Aaron groaned at the pressure, then rolled over once he was free and glared up at Viper. "Go to hell."

"You first. Enjoy prison." Viper tried to take a step.

Nick caught him by the arm and steadied him before he went down like a felled tree. "You've earned a trip to the ER and some pain meds."

"I always win the prize," he grumbled, because he'd been hurt on the job way more than Nick ever had: Viper spent his time in the trenches, and his brother spent most of his time behind a desk.

Nick was the brains, Viper the grunt.

His brother issued orders to the agents around them as he helped Viper out of the backyard and toward a black SUV. Not the one he'd used to keep Kelly safe until Spike was in custody. Blood had soaked his shirt.

"Great catch and takedown," one of the agents said. "Can't believe you spotted this guy so fast."

Viper took the smack on the back in stride. "He wanted to see his sister get killed for what she did."

Nick helped him into the front passenger seat of the vehicle. "He can keep hating her from his cell. I hope his sister and wife are very happy together."

"Me, too." Viper thought of someone who'd make him really happy right now, but he wouldn't get to see her anytime soon, and that was a damn shame because all he wanted was to be with her.

Chapter Ten

Lyric plated up an order while singing along to the song blaring in the bar. She knew all the words to Heart's "Alone" and sang them at the top of her lungs, thinking about how she'd like to get M alone tonight. She couldn't stop thinking about him and wondering what he was doing and what kept him busy and away from her.

She hit the chorus again and sang out the desperate lyrics when someone came up behind her and put their hands on her hips. Not M. She knew what his hands felt like on her now.

She jumped, the plate she'd prepared toppling to the floor. The dish shattered and the food went everywhere, including on her favorite work boots.

She spun around, her heart racing with the fear and shock that went through her.

Rick chuckled and raised a brow. "You are so jumpy."

"What the hell?" She didn't like the intrusion, interruption, or his assumption that he could put his hands on her.

He stepped into her. "You sing like an angel, even to classic rock."

She didn't like the *angel* reference coming from

him. She planted her palm on his chest and pushed him back a step so he'd have to release her. "What are you doing in the kitchen? I've told you it's not safe." She purposely looked down at the shattered dish and wasted food.

"I came in through the back and heard you singing that song." His gaze softened. "You don't have to be *alone* tonight. Let's get out of here. We'll go up to your place and—"

"No." She didn't want to hear how he would finish that sentence.

His gaze turned knowing. "Right. You're working. When you get off shift, then." He looked so hopeful. And sure.

She sighed, tired of this thing they kept doing. "What do you want from me?"

"I want to spend time with you, but you're always busy. Here. At the ranch. It's like you never have time for yourself. I hear what others don't. You recorded 'Come Over' last night, and now you're singing 'Alone' like you're desperate to have someone."

That irritated her. "I am not desperate."

"You're lonely. You want someone. Everyone feels like that sometimes. But I'm here. I can be that person. You and I—"

"There is no you and I!" She took a second to compose herself. "I barely know you."

He took a step closer, his body inches from hers. Way too close for comfort. "Is it too much to ask after I came all this way to be with you that you give me a chance? We have so much in common. Music. Songwriting. Food. You like cooking it. I like eating it." The grin was disarming.

And maybe she was being too harsh on someone

who seemed enthusiastically into her. He had some boundary issues, that was for sure, but maybe he was pushing because she kept trying to distance herself. "You said you came here because you wanted to write with me."

"Your songs are amazing. Everything you do is. You know how to put the emotion into the words. Just like you did a few minutes ago while you were singing. It's easy for you."

Not everyone allowed themselves to be vulnerable and let others see it.

She stepped back, and he let her have her space this time. "You have to tap into something deep and sing about something that matters to you."

"You can show me how to do that."

"Do you have some ideas you'd like to work on?" She didn't want to have to do all the heavy lifting.

"Yes. Lots of them. I get an idea, but then I can't seem to fill it out and finish it."

"That's why writing with others helps. You can try things out, see things from others' perspectives, and figure it out together. Some ideas work, others fizzle out."

His big smile returned, like he'd finally won her over. "So you'll help me."

"I don't have a lot of time, but yes, I'll help."

"Great. Thank you. You won't regret this."

She kind of already did, because this meant time away from her own writing and possibly M. She really wanted to spend more time getting to know him.

Rick took another step toward her, looking like he wanted to kiss her or something. She stepped back, slipped on the gooey cheese sauce from the chili cheese fries she'd plated, and landed on her ass. She threw her hand out to catch herself, and a sharp, biting pain in her wrist made her yelp.

She held up her arm and stared at the broken piece of plate sticking out of the side of her wrist. *Fuck!*

"What the hell happened back here?" Melody stood over her.

Rick squatted and reached for her arm.

"Leave it in," Melody snapped.

Lyric pulled her hand away from Rick and held it close to her chest. "Back up. Let me stand." Now she was really angry.

Melody glanced over her shoulder at the kitchen staff. "Can one of you clean this up while I take her to the ER?"

"I don't need to go to the hospital." But she did want to go up to her place and collect herself.

"That looks really bad." Rick cringed. "It's going to need stitches."

"Ugh!" This wouldn't have happened if Rick hadn't invaded her kitchen and her life. Again. "Fine. I'll go. But I can drive myself."

"I'll take you," Melody insisted.

The bar was packed. "I need you to run the kitchen. I'm already a worker short tonight." Lyric glanced at the order tickets piling up. "Please," she said to her sister.

Melody stared at the bleeding wound. "But your arm."

Blood trickled down her arm and soaked into her shirt sleeve at her elbow. "I'll be fine." She grabbed a clean towel out of the drawer by the sink and gently wrapped it around her arm to sop up the blood.

Rick helped her as the wound throbbed and hurt like hell. "I'll drive you."

She tried not to show how upset or angry she was

about what had happened. It was an accident. One he'd caused but not intended. Still, not his fault. "I'll take care of this myself. It hurts, but it's not bleeding that badly." Understatement, but if it got Rick to back off, great.

Aria rushed in. "Oh my God, what the hell?" She stopped short, her eyes glued to the blood seeping out of the wound and soaking the towel.

"I'm fine," Lyric assured her sister.

"That is not fine." Aria glanced at Rick, then at her. "Let me get my keys and purse. I'll drive you to the hospital."

"Good luck with that." Melody plated up a new order of chili cheese fries and put it on the counter under the heat lamps for the waitress to take out to their customer.

Aria glared at Melody, then her.

Lyric laid out the practical plans. "You need to run the bar. Melody will take over the kitchen. If Jax is here, get him serving. If not, call someone else in. I'll be back as soon as I can."

Aria took charge like she always did. "You," she snapped at Rick. "Out of the kitchen. Now," she barked. "I'm taking Lyric to the hospital. Melody, you've got the bar and kitchen. You know what to do." With that, Aria stared down Lyric. "Now, let's go."

Lyric grabbed her jacket off the coatrack by the back door and slid her good arm into it.

Rick helped her drape the other side over her shoulder. "I really want to go with you."

She turned to him. "Just . . ." *back off*, she wanted to scream at him. But she'd been warned not to antagonize him. It could make things worse. So she bit her tongue, took a breath, and found some calm in the chaos. "We'll talk later. Okay?"

"But I want to help." The puppy-dog eyes and plea didn't sway her.

The ER was bound to be busy. She already had little patience for Rick. She wished M was here tonight. She'd probably let him take her. He'd calm her.

Rick made her anxious and cautious, and she didn't need any more anxiety tonight.

"It looks worse than it is." She didn't admit that her fingers felt a little numb and that worried her.

"Let's go," Aria ordered, stepping in between her and Rick and herding her out the door to her car parked out back.

Rick stood and watched them go, his face a mask of frustration and anger.

Lyric found comfort in the quiet car.

Aria took the wheel. "Stubborn."

"Look who's talking."

Aria put her hand on Lyric's shoulder. "I don't like the way he looks at you."

Lyric didn't answer because she knew exactly what Aria meant.

Rick looked at her like she belonged to him. Not in a romantic way, but a possessive one that felt all wrong.

It didn't take long to get to the hospital. Aria parked. Lyric kept her arm close to her chest as they walked in. She spotted one of their frequent customers. "Hey, Drew, looks like there are more people at the bar than here tonight. My lucky day."

Drew gasped when she spotted the plate fragment sticking out of her arm. "What happened?"

She stopped in front of the reception desk but spoke to her nurse friend. "Kitchen accident."

Drew glanced at the person working the counter. "I'll take her to a cubicle."

Lyric answered all the receptionist's questions and did her best to sign all the consent forms before she dutifully followed Drew through a door and to a cubicle. Aria followed behind her. Lyric sat on the bed. Her area was draped off from the one beside it. She wondered what brought her ER neighbor in tonight. She hoped it wasn't serious.

She debated just yanking the piece of plate out of her arm and asking for a Band-Aid but thought she better let the professionals do it. She didn't want to cause more harm. The thick piece of ceramic was bound to cut her more on the way out. And she wouldn't mind some numbing stuff before they ripped it out. Although, she couldn't really feel anything but the throbbing anymore, and that scared her.

Drew helped her settle back on the raised bed. "Let me take your blood pressure and get a look at that wound before I call the doctor in here."

Lyric held her good arm out for the blood-pressure cuff.

Aria took a seat beside her, looking worried.

While Drew checked all her vitals, Lyric listened to the people in the next cubicle.

"Just sit still, and let them sew you up." The man's deep voice sounded both annoyed and concerned.

"I just want to get out of here." The familiar voice surprised her, and she turned and stared at the drape.

"M?" she called out.

There was a long pause. "Lyric?"

Someone opened the curtain between them, though they remained hidden behind it.

She stared wide-eyed at M, his chest bare, a bandage on his head, and a huge cut running from his shoulder down part of his bicep. A doctor sat beside him, sewing it up.

She threw her feet to the ground and went to him. She reached for him, but he stretched his free hand across himself and grabbed her arm at the elbow.

"What the hell happened to you?"

She stared at him in shock. "Me! Look at you. How did you get hurt?" Her heart hurt for him. The cut looked deep and bad. And she had no idea what happened to his head.

"Um, you're in my light," the doctor grumbled.

Drew put her hand on Lyric's shoulder. "I really need you to sit down. Once Dr. Thomas is done with your friend, he'll take a look at your arm."

She held M's gaze, tears gathering in her eyes. He looked so happy to see her, but also nervous. "Are you okay?"

"I'm fine." His fingers brushed against her skin where he held her.

She glanced at the other scars marring his bare skin, the wound to his head, the gash down his arm, the strained look in his eyes. "I don't believe you."

"I'm okay, Lyric, but I'd feel a hell of a lot better if you'd get that thing out of your arm."

"It doesn't hurt anymore."

The doctor glanced up. "Is your hand numb?"

She nodded. "I can't really feel it anymore."

The doctor set aside the needle and tools he'd been using to close up the worst of the gash on M's shoulder and stood up. "Please sit. I need to look at that." He turned to M. "I'm sorry. This could be very serious and time sensitive."

M waved his good hand. "Take care of her. I can wait."

Lyric shook her head. "No. It's fine. Finish sewing him up."

Drew pulled her away from M and back toward the bed. "Let the doctor assess the wound first."

Lyric lay back on the bed and let the doctor inspect the shard and her fingers. He pressed on the fragment, and she yelped.

"Hey," M said, looking like he wanted to get up and come to her.

The man with him ordered, "Don't you move."

M glared at the person behind the curtain and stayed put.

"Looks like this is pressing on the ulnar artery. It's a good thing you didn't pull this out. You could have nicked it and bled out. We'll need some imaging to confirm this hasn't actually cut the artery before we take it out and stitch you up. We need to hurry, though, because the blood supply to your hand is compromised. We don't want there to be any permanent damage."

"Are you saying I could lose function in my hand?" She panicked. How would she play guitar or piano or work in the kitchen?

"We'll do everything we can to prevent that." Dr. Thomas turned to Drew. "Get her upstairs. I'll put the order in now. Once we have the scan, we'll need to move quickly."

The nurse pulled a wheelchair into the cubicle.

Lyric glanced over at M. "Text me where you'll be later. We need to talk."

"I'm not leaving here without you."

The man behind the drape swore. "I can't stay. I have to go finish what we started."

M looked at the man. "Then, go. I'll be fine."

Aria stood. "I can take you home, along with Lyric," she volunteered.

The man behind the curtain glanced around it at her. "Who are you?"

"Lyric's sister, Aria."

The man stared at her for a long moment, then moved back behind the curtain like he didn't want them to get a good look at him. As it was, they barely saw more than his face because he had a black knit cap covering most of his head. "You need to go home and rest," he implored M.

"Not without her. I need to know if she's going to be okay."

The doctor sat down to finish with him. "She'll probably need minor surgery and be released in a few hours, unless there are complications."

M looked up at the man. "Go. I'll stay with them."

The man sighed. "I'll wait until the doctor is done with you, make sure you have your meds, then head out."

Aria looked at M. "I'll go with Lyric now, then come back for you."

"Thank you."

"No problem. I can't wait to hear what happened to you tonight."

The man behind the curtain poked his head out again. "It's best if you not say anything about seeing him here. It's safer. For him. Can you do that?"

Aria glanced from the man to M, then back again. "If Lyric says it's best, then yes."

Lyric didn't bother to look at either man. "Please, Aria. We never saw anything."

Aria gave her a nod, and Lyric knew that was a vow her sister would keep. "Off we go. No time to waste. See you soon, M."

Lyric stared at M until the nurse pushed her away and she couldn't crane her neck anymore to see his steady gaze as he watched her go.

The last thing she heard his friend say was "This is not good."

She didn't know what he meant by that, but she planned to find out when she was finally alone with M again.

Chapter Eleven

Viper sat through all the stitches, his mind on Lyric and not the poke and pull of the needle going in and out of his skin. He didn't care about his own injuries but worried about hers. "Her fingers were so pale."

The doctor cut the string on the last stitch. "I'm all done with you. Time to go see what the scan shows. I'll send the nurse back with your discharge papers and the prescription for your meds. You can get it filled at the pharmacy before you go."

Nick took the seat the doctor vacated. "You can't tell her what happened tonight."

Viper glared at his brother. "I know that. She knows I'm keeping things from her. This will either make her end this, or she'll trust me and wait until I can tell her something."

"I'm sorry. I was actually going to call her for you, see if she'd stay with you tonight because of that head wound. I'd do it myself, but I thought you'd want her instead."

It touched Viper that his brother would do that for him when right now wasn't a great time to have a civilian so close to him. Things were moving toward a conclusion with the Wild Wolves MC, and that meant things were volatile and dangerous.

"I have to know if she's okay. If she can't use that hand . . . it will change everything for her."

"And you want to be the one by her side through all this." Nick held up a hand. "You don't have to say it. You're more concerned about her than yourself. I saw the way she looked at you. She could give a shit about her own injury. She was more concerned about you."

"She's that kind of woman. She cares deeply about those she lets in."

Nick leaned in and spoke quietly. "And you need that after you've spent the better part of the last eight years pretending to be something you're not and lying to everyone around you."

"Yes, damn it. I want what we have to be real, not based on a lie. Or hundreds of lies. I'm so close to ending this. I want it so badly to be over and done, and I can finally move on with *my* life."

"Okay." Nick sat back. "She's got a gorgeous sister. What's she like?"

Viper grinned. "She's smart and tough. You don't want to fuck with her. She set her cheating boyfriend up to take a public fall. But she's not mean. She just called him out and exposed him for who he really is. She's loyal to her family and friends. She oversees the bar's whole operation, and that place is run well. And if I have my way, you'll definitely be seeing more of Lyric, and maybe that puts you and Aria in the same room again."

Nick's gaze dropped away. "I just think she's interesting."

"Uh-huh." Viper knew that look in his brother's eyes. "We finish this case, we can tell them both who we are and see what happens."

Nick kept his FBI jacket wadded up at the end of

the bed, their guns and badges concealed. "I need to get back to the office and see where we're at on the arrests tonight and if Spike will give us any new information about the rest of the Wild Wolves."

"I'll get back to it tomorrow, looking into Maria's connection and who else she's using in the MC. I'd also like to figure out if Lobo is in on the whole thing or completely in the dark." Thanks to cold temps, he could hide his injury underneath long-sleeve shirts.

"You can't save them all. Everyone who needs to go down for this will."

"M, you still in there?" Aria called out, because they'd kept their voices whisper-quiet, and she couldn't hear them.

Nick grabbed all the stuff and stood. "You good?" he asked on another whisper.

Viper nodded. "Go."

"I'll be in touch." He pulled the curtain back for Aria but kept his back to her as he ducked out the other side.

"Your friend shy, or what?"

"Yeah. How's Lyric? What did they say about her arm?"

"The scan showed that the piece of plate is compressing her artery. They'll need to be very careful taking it out. Which they're about to do once the numbing takes effect."

"They're not knocking her out?"

"The doctor said it wasn't necessary. He'll have the shard out and her stitches done in no time. Believe me, she's tough."

The nurse walked in behind Aria. "You're good to go, Mr.—"

"Thank you," he interrupted her, not wanting to

explain later that he'd checked in under yet another assumed name.

Aria raised a brow but didn't say anything.

"Your discharge papers and prescription. You can fill it on your way out." The nurse handed him everything. "Can I help you with your shirt?"

"I've got it, thanks."

The nurse nodded and headed off to her next patient.

Viper grabbed the ripped and bloody thermal. He slid it up his bad arm over the bandages, then stuffed his head through the collar. When it came to putting his other arm in, it got awkward.

Aria stepped in and helped him. "Are you going to tell her the truth about what happened?"

He held Aria's steady gaze. "I promised her I'd never lie to her. I've been as honest as I can without doing that. But there are some things she can't know right now."

"Because you're protecting her?"

"Always."

"Is that why you never acted on the attraction between you?"

"Yes. But now . . . She made it clear she wants to be with me despite some obstacles."

"If she's happy, I'm happy. If she's not, you won't be either. Get my drift?"

"Absolutely. Now, can we go see her?"

Aria glanced at the bandage on his head. "Are you really okay?"

"Nothing is keeping me from her." He stood, confirmed that he had his feet under him and his head on straight, then followed Aria to the elevator.

"So, um, I'm not great with blood," Aria reluctantly

admitted. "Or needles. Melody probably should have come instead of me, but I'm sure you can go in and hold her hand while they do the procedure. Right?"

He stepped onto the elevator with her. "I'll take care of her. Don't worry."

"Okay. Because your arm . . . that gave me the willies, and my stomach can't take much more."

Viper didn't laugh. He sympathized. "Once you show me where she is, find a soda machine and grab a lemon-lime soda. It'll help."

They stepped off the elevator on the second floor. "She's in room 210. That way." She pointed him to the left. "The waiting room is just there." She pointed to the right past the nurses' station. "I'll wait, then drive you both home."

Viper didn't wait to make sure Aria made it to the waiting room and took off to the left. He knocked once on the door, then walked in as Dr. Thomas called out, "Come in."

Lyric was sitting in a chair, her arm on a table draped in a cloth in front of her. The doctor sat on a stool, a nurse beside him with a tray of instruments, gauze, and other medical supplies at the ready. Lyric smiled up at him. "You made it just in time for the show."

He went to her, kissed her on the head, then met her gaze. "Are you okay?"

"It's all numbed up. The doctor is just going to pull it out carefully and sew me up."

Viper looked at her hand. "Your fingertips are tinged blue."

"Not for long." Dr. Thomas used a clamp to hold on to the plate piece and gently lifted it up and pulled it back toward him.

Viper watched the blue tinge change to white as blood began to move again. He slid his hand across Lyric's back and rubbed, hoping to give her comfort.

The doctor pulled the shard clear of her arm.

Viper swore the thing had stuck into her at least two inches.

"I'll just irrigate the wound, make sure there are no smaller fragments left behind, then I'll sew this up." The doctor pressed gauze to the wound to stanch the bleeding, then did what he'd said and began the first of many stitches.

"Does this seem familiar?" Lyric asked him.

"Yes," the doctor and Viper said in unison.

Lyric looked up at him. "How's the arm?"

"It's starting to hurt."

"And the head?" she asked.

He leaned down and kissed her on the forehead. "I'm·fine. I promise. We'll talk about all this later."

"Where's Aria?"

"In the waiting room."

Lyric scrunched her lips. "She hates blood."

"I hate seeing your blood." He brushed his hand over her hair, accidentally pulling out a few strands from her bun. He wanted to let it all loose and run his fingers through it.

Lyric watched the doctor tie the next stitch. "I prefer it on the inside, myself."

They all fell silent while the doctor worked on Lyric's arm and finally bandaged it. "You're all set. Try to keep the stitches dry. Make an appointment with your regular doctor to have those looked at in ten days, when they should be ready to come out."

She looked up at him. "We can do it together."

He shook his head at her but stopped because it

made his vision go wonky. "That's not the kind of date I had in mind."

"I'll take what I can get."

He hated that he couldn't give her everything. "Can I take her home?"

The doctor pushed the stool back and stood. "I'll write you a prescription for some pain meds."

"I'm good with ibuprofen." Lyric flexed her fingers. "The feeling is back." The relief he saw in her eyes told him how scared she'd been that she'd been hurt far worse than it seemed.

"If you feel any further numbness or nerve pain, get it checked out immediately, but judging by the scan and how well that came out without a ton of bleeding, I think you're in the clear. I'll have to come by the bar the next time you sing."

"I'd love that. And the food's on me."

"I'll have the nurse come back with your discharge papers. It'll be a few minutes." The doctor left, followed by the nurse rolling out the cart of instruments.

"Do you want me to go get your sister?"

Lyric stood up and held her hand out toward the chair. "I want you to sit down."

He was about to say he was fine, but she shook her head.

"Don't argue. Just sit."

He did so, and she brought the stool closer, sat on it, and put her hands on his knees. "How was your day?"

He understood she was trying to keep things simple. "Despite how it looks, it was actually good."

"Can you tell me what happened?"

"Not exactly. I can say that the person who got the jump on me won't be coming for me again."

Her eyes went wide.

"He's not dead," he assured her. "He's under arrest."

"But you're not."

"I didn't do anything wrong."

"He attacked you for no reason?"

He sighed. "It's complicated."

"Who was that guy with you?"

"I can't say right now, but you'll meet him again soon."

She smiled. "So he's a friend?"

"Yes. We're really close."

She raised a brow. "Why didn't he stay with you?"

"He had to get to work. I needed to be with you." He hated the frown that bent her soft lips.

"You should be at home resting. Do you have a concussion?"

"A mild one. I'll be fine in a few days." He took her good hand in his and squeezed it. "Don't worry about me."

"I can't help it. I don't like seeing you hurt like this."

He wanted to reassure her, but the nurse walked in.

"You're all set to go, Miss Wilde. Any questions?"

She took her discharge papers from the nurse. "No. I'm good. Thank you for everything."

"My pleasure." The nurse left them again.

Viper stood alone with Lyric. He immediately pulled her into his arms and held her. She wrapped her arms around his waist and laid her head on his good shoulder. "I promise you, Angel, this will all be over soon, and I'll tell you everything."

She squeezed him tighter. "I just want you to be safe."

He kissed her on the head again. "I know. I'm working on it."

She leaned back and looked up at him. "Hurry up."

He kissed her softly, wanting to take the kiss deeper, so he could show her how much he appreciated her.

But the door opened, and Aria walked in. "Oh. Sorry. Bad timing."

Lyric released him. "It's okay. Let's get out of here."

They all walked out together.

It was Lyric who took his hand. He squeezed hers back.

They walked onto the elevator, and Aria hit the button for the first floor. "So you two are really a thing now?"

"Yes," Lyric said. "Though, we'd appreciate it if you kept that private."

"What's going on with Rick?" Aria asked. "He was with you when you got hurt, but you didn't want him to bring you here."

"Did he hurt you?" Viper wanted every detail.

"No. Not exactly."

The elevator doors opened, and Lyric tried to walk off it, but Viper held her hand. "What does that mean?"

She tugged him to follow her out into the lobby area and across the way to the pharmacy.

Viper handed the lady at the counter his prescription. She entered it into the system, found his information, then went to fill the order.

While they waited, Lyric answered Viper's question about how she really got hurt. "Rick surprised me. I dropped a plate. We had a conversation. He was happy that I agreed to sit down and work on some music with him. He came at me. I stepped back, slipped on the spilled food, landed on my ass, and I got stuck by the plate shard."

Viper swore under his breath, picked up the meds from the counter, paid the small fee, then came back to her. "What do you mean he came at you?" He touched her back to get her moving out of the hospital and to the parking lot.

"I think he wanted to kiss me, but I stepped back so he'd know I was not into that, but then I slipped."

Viper glared. "So he did this to you."

Lyric stopped and put her hand on his chest. "It was an accident. That's all."

Aria hit the Unlock button on the key fob. "Why don't you just tell him to leave you alone?"

"I have. He's persistent. And Hunt told me not to antagonize him or it could make the situation worse."

Viper fumed. "I don't like it."

Lyric tugged on his hand to get him moving again. "I know. It's sweet. I appreciate it. But you have nothing to worry about. There's only one person I'm interested in. That's you."

He opened the car door for her and waited for her to get in the front passenger seat as Aria took the wheel. "Are you sure?"

"Who's here with me? Who am I going home with?" He went still.

Aria glanced over at them. "Where am I taking you? Rick's likely still at the bar waiting for you to return."

Lyric looked up at him. "My place or yours? Either way, I'm not leaving you alone with a head injury to-night."

He didn't really want to take her to his place, but he wasn't going to deal with Rick tonight either. "Mine."

"Do you have food?"

"Yeah. Some." It wasn't like he was a chef like her. "I'll make us something to eat, and we'll talk."

He had a hell of a lot better plans than that but closed her door, got in the back, and decided he'd take what he could get. Her.

She was all he needed today. Any day. Every day.

Chapter Twelve

Lyric stared out the windshield at the neglected apartment building with little hope the inside was any better than the outside. Cheap rent meant few amenities. Only two of the six outdoor lights worked and three of the many bushes out front were still alive.

But she didn't care where he lived, only that he had a place to rest, because Viper looked exhausted.

Viper squeezed her hand. "I can drive you back to the bar."

Aria had just left after dropping them off.

She glanced at the parking lot. "Where's your truck?"

"My . . . friend will have it back soon."

She didn't get why he paused before calling the guy he'd been with a friend, but she let it go. "Which one's yours?"

"Straight ahead. Second floor."

She walked up the steps ahead of him.

He stood next to her on the landing and pulled out his keys. "This place is like yours. It's just convenient for now." He put the key in the lock and let them in.

"It's fine, M. I'm not judging you on your"—she looked around the sparse but very clean apartment—"very tidy place."

"I like things in order," he grumbled like it embarrassed him or something.

She walked in and made herself at home by going to his fridge and opening it up. The contents were as sparse as his living space, but she found the basics and pulled out eggs, cheese, and a jar of salsa.

"You don't have to cook."

"I do if I want to eat. And you need to eat something so you can take your meds."

M dropped the bag of meds on the dining table, along with his paperwork, and the bag of additional gauze pads and wrap for his arm. "What I really want is a shower."

"I'll have this ready by the time you finish." She went to him and grabbed the cuff of his sleeve on his good arm. "But first, let me help you with this."

He pulled his arm free. She pushed the bottom of the shirt up his chest, then tugged the material over his head and gently down his injured arm. The bandage on his head came loose.

She pulled it off his head and tried to inspect the injury. "Bend down. Let me get a look at that."

"It's just a bunch of abrasions. No stitches." He leaned forward so she could get a look.

She gently brushed her fingers through his hair, pulling the strands away from the wounded area. "It's not bleeding. But it looks bad. How did that happen?"

"I got clocked with a log."

She hissed. "Ouch."

"The rough bark did the damage. It was a glancing blow. Hurt like hell. Definitely rang my bell. But at least I didn't get a bad concussion and have to stay in the hospital overnight."

She softly kissed his cheek. "I'm just glad you're alive."

He slid his hand along her waist to her back and pulled her close. "I don't know what I did to deserve you."

"It's not about that. I care about you. And seeing you like this . . . it kills me." She leaned in and kissed his hurt shoulder next to the edge of the bandage, then she gently started to unroll the gauze.

He stared down at her and brushed his hand over her hair. Before she knew it, the bun she'd twisted all her hair into came loose and it all fell down her back. His fingers combed through it.

She pulled the thick gauze pads off the long line of stitches and hissed again. "This looks really bad."

"The saw blade got caught up on the jacket I was wearing. It could have been a hell of a lot worse."

"Why weren't you wearing your leather jacket? That would have protected you."

He stared down at her. "You're not even going to ask about my being attacked with a saw?"

She raised a brow at his tone. "Are you going to tell me what happened?"

He sighed. "That's as much as I can tell you right now."

"And you can't tell me why you changed jackets." It seemed odd.

Another frustrated sigh. "No."

"Well, now I know basically how you got hurt. I'd like to know why, but you're not going to tell me that either."

"I'm sorry." Those two words held a lot of exhaustion.

"You warned me that your life wasn't your own right now."

"It's not. And having you here is a risk. I don't want anything to happen to you."

She held up her arm showing off her own bandaged

wound, a small wince, indicating the movement hurt. "Things happen."

He hated that she was in pain. "That was an accident. Right? Rick wasn't trying to hurt you." He eyed her, looking for any sign she'd downplayed or lied about what happened.

"I slipped and fell."

His gaze narrowed. "Because of him, but an accident all the same. What happened to me was no accident. What could happen to you because of me wouldn't be an accident." He ran his hand over his head and winced when he hit the wound without thinking. "You shouldn't be here."

"I want to be here." She put her foot down. "I came here to take care of you, and that's what I'm going to do. So go shower, we'll eat, and you'll tell me something real about you that has nothing to do with any of the stuff you can't tell me."

"Why?" He seemed genuinely bewildered.

She glared at him. "So we can get to know each other better."

"No. Why are you putting up with this?"

She walked right up to him, went up on tiptoe, wrapped her arms around his neck, and kissed him like neither of them were in pain and frustrated by the situation and everything that mattered was in her arms.

He immediately wrapped her up close, like he didn't want her to get away.

She was right where she wanted to be when she slid her tongue along his, tasted his desire as well as felt it pressed to her belly. She lost herself in the kiss, him, the moment, then pulled back and stared into his lust-hazed eyes. "Does that answer your question?"

"I don't remember what I asked. But I know you're the answer to everything for me."

She looked at him in wonder. "You say that to me, and I believe it, and I don't even know your name."

"Does it matter if you know that's how I feel and that it's true?"

"Apparently not. But one of these days, I will have your name."

"I like the way you said that."

She thought about it for a second. "Oh. I didn't mean—"

He kissed her so she couldn't finish that statement, then repeated, "I like the way you said that just fine. Don't change it. Just let it be here between us."

"You're serious." She couldn't believe he'd just put his feelings out there like that.

"It's the truth. It's how I feel. When I saw you tonight at the hospital . . . Since I got hurt, I'd been wishing that somehow I'd get to see you tonight. I wanted you with me to make all the bad go away. And then, there you were. My wish come true. I'd rather you not have been hurt." He took her hand, brought it up to his face, then kissed her palm above the bandage wrapped around her wrist. He held her hand against his wide, bare chest and warm skin. "I want you with me, and I know it's the last place you should be right now. But you opened the door, and I couldn't close it on you and risk losing you by asking you to wait."

"I waited long enough to acknowledge how I really felt about you."

"Then, always remember everything between us is real, even if I say or do something that contradicts that when we're around other people."

If he could tell her why it needed to be that way, he would, so she didn't ask.

"Okay."

Relief swept through him so profoundly she not only saw it but felt his body relax. "You seem to be under a great deal of stress and strain. I don't want to be someone who adds to that."

"You're not. Not that way. It's just . . . I couldn't take it if something happened to you."

That really did seem to be his biggest concern, and she appreciated it. "I'll follow your lead in public. But when we're alone, like we are now, let's let everything outside of us go."

"I can try to do that."

Which told her whatever was happening in his life wasn't easy to just set aside. "I'll get the food ready."

He kissed her on the head, then slowly stepped away and went to the only interior door, leaving her with a perfect view of his back and all the scars. He didn't turn to her, he just said, "I've had to endure a lot of pain to do the right thing. That probably doesn't make sense right now, but know that everything I've done was for the right reasons." With that, he disappeared into the room, and the shower went on a few seconds later.

It took her a second to move or think of anything else but the fact that she'd never met anyone so raw and honest and in need of understanding.

Maybe this wasn't the ideal relationship because of how much he was keeping from her. But she could try to give him the acceptance he was looking for by being open with her about what he could share. Those pieces of him were enough to make her care. Deeply.

And as much as he didn't want her to get hurt, she'd risk it to be with him.

Chapter Thirteen

Viper showered, made sure his stitches were dry, and pulled on a pair of boxer briefs and sweats. Getting a T-shirt on hurt like hell, but he managed on his own. He combed his too-long hair, wishing he could cut it, but keeping up appearances mattered, so he ignored it and the beard stubble.

Lyric hadn't complained about it scratching her, or that she hated it, so he assumed she was fine with it. Then again, if he was lucky enough tonight to make love to her, he'd leave her with a hell of a lot of beard burn, because he wanted to kiss every inch of her.

His achingly hard cock agreed with that plan, but he had a feeling Lyric wanted a hell of a lot more getting-to-know-you-time before she shared his bed. He didn't mind. He just wished he could tell her what she wanted to know.

Tired physically and frustrated with himself and his life, he headed back out to the kitchen. The second he smelled the food, his stomach rumbled.

Lyric heard the call and pulled a sheet of foil off the pan on the stove and dumped a huge omelet onto a plate. She added some fried potatoes and onions from another pan.

He went to her, slid his hand across her lower back,

pulled her close and kissed her on the head. "That smells and looks amazing. Thank you, Angel."

"You're welcome. Sit. Eat. Do you want a beer, water, or iced tea?"

She was drinking water and cracking eggs into the pan to make her own cheese and salsa omelet.

"I'm good with water." He needed to take his pills to stop the throbbing pain in his arm.

He took his plate to the table where she'd set out silverware, a napkin, and his meds. "Babe, if you need some ibuprofen, there's a bottle in the medicine cabinet in the bathroom."

"Thanks, but I had some in my purse and already took it." She flipped her eggs and sprinkled cheese over them.

He dug into the food and sighed. "This is so good."

She chuckled under her breath. "You're just really hungry."

"You're an amazing chef."

A couple minutes later, she sat in the chair beside him, her steaming omelet and potatoes piled high like his. "I'm just glad you had enough for both of us. I need to stock your fridge."

"I'd rather we didn't spend time here." He looked around his shabby surroundings knowing he could do much better by her. "Your place is really nice."

"You keep your place really clean."

"That's the only nice thing you can say about it." He'd lived in some real dives over the years. This place wasn't the worst. Certainly wasn't the best either. He thought about his cabin and wondered if she'd like it there. It wasn't here, so she'd never stay at it. He couldn't ask her to leave her life here. She was too much a part of her family, the bar, the ranch, this community.

She squeezed his hand. "Hey. Where'd you go?"

"I was just thinking about what comes next. You love it here, don't you?"

"It's home. I've had opportunities with my music to go other places, but this is always where I feel the most like myself. Why? Is this not home for you?"

"No. But it could be." He'd lived in several states over the years.

"Where is home?" She met his pause with understanding. "I promise, whatever you say, I won't repeat. I'll tell people you like to do lots of things with me and talking isn't one of them."

He chuckled. "I think I've talked to you more than I've talked to anyone in years."

She slid her hand up his forearm and back down again. "That's sad, M. People need people."

"Now you know why I need you so much." And maybe it wasn't fair to put that on her.

"I've wanted to be needed by someone for a long time."

Well, didn't that make them a pair? "My family is mostly in Montana. I have a small cabin there. It's quiet."

"Tell me about your family. Do you have any brothers or sisters?"

"I have a brother. We're really close."

"You have the same eyes."

His head snapped up so fast, he tugged at the stitches in his shoulder. "What?"

She gave him a knowing grin. "The guy at the hospital. He had your eyes. Same light brown color. Though, yours have flecks of green. His, flecks of gold. But they had the same intense look in them."

"Don't ever let on that you know he's my brother. In fact, don't mention that you ever saw me with him."

The smile died on her lips. "I won't."

"He's not happy I'm seeing you."

She took a bite of her potatoes. "Why?"

"Because you're a distraction."

She sipped her water. "You don't seem to mind that."

"I don't, but I also can't help myself."

"You shouldn't. You've warned me, and I'm still here."

"I know. And it baffles the mind." He dug into his omelet again.

"So it's just you and your brother and mom and dad."

"Yeah. Like you, we have some really close cousins. Dad's brother married my mom's best friend. They have three sons."

"All boys in the family."

"Mostly, yeah. We have some extended family who have a couple of girls, but the boys dominate the family tree."

"Did you spend the holiday with them?"

"I wasn't supposed to, but due to circumstances, it worked out that I could this year."

She didn't ask about that. He was relieved that he didn't have to shut her down once again. They were on a roll, and he wanted to keep sharing his real life with her. "What do your mom and dad do for a living?"

"Mom raises alpacas and has her own yarn company."

"Really? That's awesome."

He got up, went into his room, pulled the blanket off his bed, and brought it out to her. "She made this with her yarn." He hadn't shared anything this personal with someone in a long time. "I take it everywhere I go, so I have a piece of her with me."

Lyric stared up at him, tears gathering in her eyes. "That's really sweet." She grasped the corner of the blanket and rubbed it in her hands. "This is so soft. I love all the different shades of gray with the black. Your signature color."

He grinned about him wearing only black clothes. "It's easy to get dressed. Everything matches." It made him look tough. And at night, he could blend into the shadows and no one could see him. Very handy for his line of work.

He draped the blanket over the back of his chair, sat, and finished off his potatoes. "Those were so good."

"I'm glad you liked them."

He took his meds, downed some water, then worked on the rest of his omelet.

"What about your dad?" she prompted because he'd stopped talking.

"I grew up on the family cattle ranch. Dad still runs it, though it's a much smaller operation than when my brother and I lived there."

"Was he disappointed you didn't go into the family business?"

"Actually, we did. Sorta. We followed the previous four generations into the same line of work."

"I see. And is he proud of you both for that?"

"Incredibly, though he wishes I did more of what my brother does than what I do." He watched her face, looking for the frustration that he had answered but basically told her nothing.

"I'll fill in all the gaps and make sense of all this when you can finally tell me everything."

"You read my mind."

She grinned. "And your cousins?"

"Dad's brother is a lawyer turned judge. His wife, Mom's best friend, was a stay-at-home mom to her boys, but now she works for them at their distillery."

Lyric perked up. "Really? Which one?"

That would get her too close to his name and identity, and it was too dangerous for her to know that right now. "Ask me something else."

She looked at his hand. "Why a compass with no markings for direction? Did you just not have time to finish it?"

He stared at the tattoo. "No. I left it that way so I could fill it in later. My mom always tells me that no matter what I'm doing, no matter where I am, no matter what I've done or what has been done to me, I need to always remember that all roads lead home to the ones I love, who will always love me."

"That's beautiful."

"It's true. There are times I'm away far too long. But whenever I go home, there I am welcomed and loved like I was there yesterday."

"As it should be." She put her hand over his and the tattoo. "And the eagle soaring on your back?"

"A symbol of freedom."

"And the book he's holding in his talon?"

The rule of law. "I'll tell you another time."

"The scale on your shoulder seems easy. The scales of justice."

"I believe in being unbiased and fair and not judging people by their circumstances or background or the way they look but by what they do."

"Everyone starts with a level playing field. Balanced scales."

"And based on what they do, it's either in their favor or against." He needed to redirect this conversation before she guessed what he did for a living, though he suspected even if she already knew, like she knew about his brother, she wouldn't admit it to him right now because he'd asked her not to fish in that pond. "Thank you for the late dinner. You must be tired."

She stared at him, a slight smile tilting her lips. "One more question."

He hesitated but nodded for her to go ahead. "Do you prefer the right or left side of the bed?"

"I'll take whatever you don't want so long as you're in bed with me. And before you think you need to say it, I'll just tell you that I know tonight's not the night for us. I'm just glad you're here."

"It's not that I don't want you."

"I know. And it's okay to want to know more about me first."

She tilted her head. "It's not that I need more. I just so want to be right about you."

"You are. But not knowing my name, what I do, what and who I really am leaves you wondering if you can trust me and yourself."

Her mouth drew into a lopsided frown. "And now I feel like I've insulted you."

"Not at all," he assured her. "You've let me know this matters to you."

"I think we're building something."

"I think so, too. Which means we don't have to rush. You want more time, you can have all you want, and I'll still be here."

She stared at him for a long moment. "This is the most grown-up relationship I've ever had."

"Maybe it will be our best and last." He hoped so.

She stood and closed the distance between them.

"When you say stuff like that, I don't know why we're not naked in that bed right now."

It took everything in him not to touch and kiss her and convince her to go there with him right now. "You decide, Angel. I'm at your mercy."

"I just want you to want me, the way I do you."

"*Want* is too tame a word for how I feel." It took everything in him to be patient and not rush this, because he wanted her to be clear that, once they took this next step, there was no holding back on anything anymore.

She took a step closer. "If there isn't a word, then you should show me."

He didn't have to be told twice. He took her in his arms and kissed her.

Chapter Fourteen

It only took a second for Lyric to realize that, while M was all in with taking her to bed, his injured arm prevented him from taking charge of stripping her clothes away. She planted her good hand on his chest and pushed back from him, breaking their sultry kiss. He still had his hand up her shirt and back, the other at her hip.

She walked forward, pushing him back toward the bedroom. "I think you need to let me do some of the heavy lifting." Even though her wrist hurt, she had full use of her fingers. The bandage helped stabilize her wrist, so if she didn't bend it back and forth too much, it didn't hurt as badly.

"I want to help." He looked eager to please.

"You should probably just watch." To prove that to him, she crossed her arms over her waist, took the hem of her shirt in hand, and pulled it up and over her head, revealing a pale pink bra, her nipples tight and pressed against the thin fabric.

"Now, that's a sight I could get used to."

"Yeah? How about this?" She undid the button on her jeans, slid the zipper down so he could see the sexy lace-trimmed black panties she wore, turned her back to him, then pushed the jeans over her hips and down her legs, bending forward as she went so he got a good view of her ass.

"Damn, Angel."

Trying to save her injured wrist, she used her good hand to pull off her short boots and socks, then kicked off the jeans. When she turned to him, he stared in awe.

"So beautiful." The reverent words made her blush.

"Thank you." She stood before him in her bra and panties. "Dealer's choice. What comes off next?"

"Everything." He grabbed the bottom of his T-shirt and pulled it up and over his head.

She helped him get it off his hurt arm.

He reached behind her and undid the clasp on her bra with one hand.

She let it slide down her arms and tossed it aside.

His fingertips skimmed down her chest and over her breast. He molded the mound in his big, warm hand, and she sighed, slipping her hand inside his sweatpants and over the hard length of him.

He hissed with pleasure, hooked his hand at the back of her neck, and drew her in for a kiss, his tongue gliding along hers as her soft breasts pressed to the hard wall of his chest. He didn't use his injured arm too much: he simply put that hand on her ass and held her in place, while his other hand brushed up and down her back, then into her hair.

She squeezed his length in her palm and felt him harden even more.

"God, that's good," he sighed out. "But I want more."

She did, too, and used her hands to shove his sweats and boxer briefs down his legs. He sat on the edge of the bed, so she could pull everything off his big feet.

"There is nothing sexier than watching you nearly naked undress me."

"How about me riding you?"

"Yes." His eyes blazed with heat. He scooted back on the bed. "Come here."

She shimmied out of her panties, crawled up and over him, until he grabbed her with both hands and pulled her down on top of him. He kissed her so thoroughly and completely she lost track of time and place and reality and just wallowed in the feel of his big, hard body under hers, his hands holding her close, his passion pouring into her.

And when all that seemed to be more pleasure than she could take, he slid one hand over her rump to her dampening folds, and rubbed his fingers over her sensitive slit as he rocked his hips and cock against her belly. He slid one finger deep.

Fuck, yes!

He slid it out, slow and easy, then right back in as she pressed back into his hand needing more, her belly rubbing against his thick length.

She broke the kiss and spoke before they went too far too fast. "I, uh, have an IUD, so I can't get pregnant. I haven't been with anyone in forever and my last physical and labs . . . everything was clear. Not that I thought it wouldn't be."

He didn't stop touching her and trailed kisses down her neck. "The last time I was with someone was one night several months ago, before I met you. I used a condom. I always use a condom. Then I met you." He kept kissing her along her neck, her cheek, anywhere his lips found as his fingers stroked her and her body hummed. "I wanted you like I'd never wanted anyone," he whispered into her ear, then kissed her neck again. "So I went and got tested, even though I'd had a full physical and labs a month before that. I'm all clear."

She pressed up on her uninjured hand and stared down at him. "You did that specifically because you wanted to be with me?"

"Yes." Everything about him went still, but he held her gaze. "I thought because of the way I look and who I associate with you'd think I live my life a certain way. A little reckless. I wanted to be able to prove to you that you're safe with me. I have the results on my phone." He looked toward the bathroom where he'd left it in his jeans. "I can show them to you."

"They'd have your real name on them."

His eyes went wide, then he swore under his breath.

She reassured him. "I believed you when you said you'd never lie to me." Before he could respond, she rolled her hips and pressed her wet center to his thick dick, slid up it until the head met her soft folds, and she slid back and took him in.

His hands clamped on her hips. "Angel, baby, you feel so fucking fantastic."

She wanted to tell him he felt better than that, but she didn't have any words left as the pleasure took hold, and his warmth and strength and desire filled her.

She kissed him, long and deep, moving her hips up and down his hard shaft, his hands brushing over her skin, holding her close, amplifying every ripple of pleasure coursing through her.

She rose up and rode him, her head tilted back, her long hair brushing her ass as she moved. One of his hands was over her breasts, squeezing and molding the soft mounds in his palms, his fingers tugging at her tight nipple. She loved knowing he watched her as she took her time finding the right spot and thrilling to the feeling of him sliding in and out of her. His hand left her breast, sliding down her belly to the very spot where they were joined. His thumb brushed against her clit, and she moved against him until that ripple of pleasure became a wave that crashed over her and she came, rocking her hips against his as he thrust into her again and again, spilling himself inside her. She fell limp onto his chest.

She buried her face in his neck and tried to keep her weight on the other side of his injured shoulder and arm.

He held her with his good arm, his chest heaving as the seconds ticked by and they both calmed and settled into the quiet.

"Are you okay?" she asked on a whisper.

"I've never been better. Ever."

She laughed under her breath. "I mean, your shoulder?"

He hugged her closer. "I'm fine, Angel. Is your wrist okay?"

"All of me feels perfect."

This time he laughed. "Good. Then, you'll want to do this again sometime."

"Are you ready?"

He lifted his head to look at her. "For real?"

She shook her head. "I'll give you five minutes," she teased.

His head fell back on the bed. "After that, I need at least an hour."

"M?"

"Yeah, Angel?"

"This is perfect." She kissed his neck, right over his rioting pulse.

"It will be when I finish what I'm doing and I can give every part of me to you."

"I just want you to know that even this much is enough for me." She meant it.

He shifted so she was lying next to him and they were face-to-face. He put his hand on her cheek and stared into her eyes. "I don't deserve that. And you deserve a hell of a lot more than what I'm giving you."

"You've been honest. That's enough."

"Even when I'm keeping things from you?"

"I know you're doing it because you have a good reason. One that matters to you. One you believe in."

"I do, but it doesn't make me feel any better to be here like this, to start this relationship on uneven ground."

She brushed her fingers along his tense jaw. "I've got good balance. And so long as I can hold on to you for support until things are level, I know everything will be okay."

"You've put a hell of a lot of faith and trust in me. You have no idea how much I appreciate it. The people I deal with . . . It's all lies and manipulations and posturing. No one trusts anyone because everyone is lying and hiding something. And here I am, hiding a part of myself from you, the part that is who I really am."

"If you want to share it with me now, I swear I won't say anything to anyone. Ever."

"I want to so bad, but I can't. Not because I don't believe you, but because it could be very dangerous for you to know."

"They could use me to find out your secret."

He put his big hand over her cheek and looked her deep in the eyes. "They would hurt you to get it."

She kissed his chin. "I'm tougher than I look."

"I know how strong you are. I've seen it in the way you handle yourself and rowdy customers at the bar. But this is different." M kissed her forehead. "You are so special. I can't believe you're here with me."

She brushed her hand over his cheek, noting how tired he looked. "Before you fall asleep, let me wrap your arm."

"Leave it. I just want to hold you." He sounded groggier by the second.

"It'll only take a minute." She kissed him softly, then climbed out of bed. She quickly used the restroom, then went out to the kitchen to find the supplies he'd gotten at the hospital. On her way back to the bedroom, she heard her phone ping with a text. Probably one of her siblings checking on her. Or her parents, if her sisters told them what had happened tonight.

She pulled her phone out of her purse and stared at the twenty-three notifications. Three from her siblings. Twenty—her phone pinged again—make that twenty-one from Rick.

She scrolled through the first few.

RICK: I hope you're okay.
RICK: I'm sorry you got hurt.
RICK: I wish I was with you.
RICK: Are you okay?

They got progressively more insistent.

RICK: Why aren't you answering me!!!
RICK: Call me. Now!
RICK: You don't want to make me mad.

That one sent a chill up her spine.

RICK: I can't believe you're being so selfish and childish and holding this against me.
RICK: How could you do this to me????????

And by the end, he sounded unhinged.

RICK: You'll regret this.
RICK: I'm going to make it hurt.

"Angel? What are you doing? Come back to bed."

She silenced her phone and took it and the bag of medical supplies with her into the bedroom.

M was lying on his back, looking too good and tempting, despite how he rubbed his hand over his forehead.

"Do you have a headache?"

"Yeah. Would you mind getting me two ibuprofen from the bathroom?"

"Sure. No problem." She retrieved them for him, along with a glass of water and sat on the edge of the bed. "Sit up. Take these."

He did, and she used his new position to dab ointment along the long line of stitches before covering the worst portion of it in thick pads, then wrapping gauze around his arm and shoulder to hold it in place.

He cupped her cheek, met her gaze, then kissed her forehead. "Thank you, sweetheart."

She gave him a soft kiss, hating that he was hurt, and hoping to make him feel just a little better. "You're welcome. Lie back." She covered him with the blanket once he settled, then climbed into the bed on the other side and curled up next to him.

He immediately pulled her closer, until she pressed

along his side, rested her head on his good shoulder, and draped her leg over his.

"That's better." With that, his whole body relaxed.

She'd never felt safer or like she was exactly where she was meant to be.

They hadn't known each other long, but she felt like she knew him down to his soul.

She tried so hard to stay in the moment and enjoy their closeness, but those text messages spun through her mind, making her wonder whether Rick had just gotten caught up in his anger because of her silence or if he was unstable enough to act on his threats.

Chapter Fifteen

Viper came awake slowly to the wonderful feel of Lyric's hand stroking his head, her fingers brushing through his hair. It felt way too early for her to be awake.

She kissed his lips, his cheek, his forehead, then pressed her lips to his again. "I'm sorry to wake you, but I didn't want to leave without saying goodbye."

He opened his eyes and found her sitting on the bed beside him fully dressed. A sad disappointment, because he liked her naked and in bed beside him. "What time is it?"

"Just after six. Melody texted that she'd take my shift at the ranch, but I know she probably hasn't been to sleep yet since she closed the bar last night, so I asked her if she'd pick me up and take me to the ranch instead."

"Do you think you can manage with your arm? You don't want to pull your stitches."

"I'll be fine." She gave him another soft kiss. "Will I see you later?"

"I'm not sure. It depends . . . on a lot of factors." He hated to say the next part but had to do it. "Don't come back here unless I say it's okay. It's not that I don't want you here," he added quickly.

She pressed her finger to his lips. "It's fine. You've got your thing to do. I've got mine. You know where to find me, right?"

"I will always find you, Angel. I just wish it didn't need to be like this right now."

"I know. I feel that every time we're together."

"Be careful in the kitchen." He took her hand and brought it to his mouth and kissed the back of it above the bandage wrapped around her wrist.

She gently touched the bandage on his shoulder. "Stay away from whoever and whatever got you this."

"I wish I could." He reached for her and pulled her down for another kiss. "I want more of this. You and me together."

"Me, too. When you're with me, I feel safe."

He raised a brow and stared at her, seeing something cross her eyes and disappear. "What is it? What's wrong?"

"Nothing. I'm just . . . nervous about whatever it is you're doing. I don't want you to get hurt again."

He read something more in her eyes. "That's part of it, but there's something else. Tell me."

Her head fell forward, and she wouldn't look at him.

"Lyric, you need to tell me what this is about. If I did something to upset you . . ."

Her head shot up. "You've been nothing but good to me. Last night . . . it was everything and so much more than I expected. This is not about you and me."

"I hope to be free to spend time with you without all this other—"

She put her fingers over his lips and shook her head. "You've already explained you're doing something that is important and separate from me. And I'm sorry I'm making you worry that there's something wrong between us when there isn't. Not at all. I promise you that."

"Then, stop holding back on me, and tell me what has you upset or scared or whatever it is." And then it dawned on him. And he should have thought of it first. "Rick. You said he didn't hurt you. But?"

She pressed her lips tight. "I don't have time to explain it all. My sister is probably waiting downstairs."

He held her arms, his hold gentle but insistent. "She can wait. And so will I for however long it takes you to spit it out."

"He threatened me."

Viper shot up in bed. "What?"

"He's upset that I didn't return to the bar last night."

Fury stirred inside him. "So he threatened you."

"I'll fix it when I see him."

"*You* don't need to fix anything. *You* didn't do anything wrong. Don't let him make you think you owe him something. You don't."

"I don't want to deal with him at all, but I promised that we'd write together."

He soothed her with a soft stroke down her hair. "That was before he threatened you. What exactly did he say?"

She tapped her phone screen, then turned it to him so he could read the last several texts he left her last night. "Why didn't you tell me about this?"

"Because you seem to have a lot going on, and I didn't want to make my problem yours, too."

He stared at her in disbelief. "Did you not think I would help you? Or care that someone wants to hurt you?" It pained him to think she didn't feel like he cared.

"It's not that. I just knew that I'd have to take care of it myself because no one is really supposed to know we're seeing each other. And I didn't want you thinking about me when you're doing whatever you're doing."

Viper's heart sank and his throat clogged because she was right. He couldn't help her. Not in the way he wanted to help her. All he had to do was show up at the bar and make it clear to this asshole that he and Lyric were together, and if Rick went after her, he'd have to go through him. But he couldn't do that without putting Lyric in more danger. With Rick and the people he was trying to take down.

"M, it's okay. I can pull my family in if I need help. You've made it clear how you feel about me. And that's what really matters."

"Yeah. But right now is when you need me, and I can't do what I want and you need me to do."

"I can fight my own battles."

"This guy is unstable at best and dangerous at worst. I don't want to find out the hard way that he's worse than either of us knows."

"I'll be careful. And I want you to do the same. Because if you think I wouldn't stand between you and whatever danger you're facing that caused that to happen to you last night, you're wrong." She pressed her hand to his cheek. "I appreciate that you want to help. I really do. But I'll handle Rick. And if it comes to it, I'll call my cousin, Hunt. He can play bad cop and warn Rick to stay away."

"A guy like Rick doesn't listen to warnings."

"Then, he'll find I'm not meek. I will stand up for myself."

"I'm scared that won't be enough." Actually, he was terrified of something happening to her. "Do you trust me?"

"Yes. Absolutely."

He appreciated the instant and definitive answer. "Can I put an app on your phone that will allow me to track it? Just in case."

She handed her phone over to him.

He downloaded the app, put her information into his phone, then checked that he could find her phone, showed her on his, then handed her phone back.

Her brows went up. "Do I get to track you?"

"No. Someone else is doing that already." He gave her a second to object or voice her upset, but she didn't.

She swept her thumb over his bottom lip. "Do you feel better knowing you can find me?"

He did. "Do you?"

"Yes, actually."

He gave her the real truth. "It's not enough to know where your phone is for me. I need to know you're safe. You're the most important thing to me."

"But we can't be seen together."

"You're mad."

"I'm frustrated," she admitted, pressing her lips tight. "I want all of you. And it makes me sad that you seem to want to give me all of you, but you can't, and it makes you mad."

"I'm frustrated." He used her words because they were on the same page. "After last night, I hoped you'd leave feeling happy, knowing how deeply I care about you. Instead, we're talking about some guy who's making threats because you didn't go home last night and how you can't trust that I'll be there if you need me because—guess what?—I can't even make that promise to you."

She leaned in close. "But you want to, and that means everything to me."

"I just need a little more time." It felt like he'd been saying that too long, knowing that time was near, but also too far away.

"Take all the time you need. You know where to find me. And I'll be waiting for you. Impatiently. But always waiting." She kissed him like it was the start of something, even though they both knew it wasn't because she was headed out the door, away from him when all he wanted was to keep her close.

He poured everything into the kiss, trying to let her know he hated that it had to be this way for now, but giving her hope for the future he wanted with her.

If only he could finish this business with the Wild Wolves MC before her patience and understanding faded and all that was left was anger that he wasn't the man she needed him to be.

She ended the sultry kiss and brushed her hand over his hair the way he always did with her. "Be safe." She glanced at his wrapped and throbbing shoulder. "Stay away from people with saws and knives."

"You're usually holding one," he pointed out, thinking of her in the kitchen.

"I'd never hurt you. Ever." She kissed him again. "Besides, then I wouldn't get to sleep with you again."

"Is that what you want to do with me? Sleep?"

"I want it all." With that, she stood and walked out of his room.

"Me, too," he called out to her, just before the apartment door closed and his phone pinged with an incoming text.

LYRIC: Listen to this if you want to know how I feel about you . . .

He tapped the link to the audio file for Lee Brice's "Soul." He knew the song well, but he listened to the words, thinking of Lyric telling him how much she liked him in the sheets, that he didn't need anything but himself to impress her, and she liked everything about him. But most of all he liked the line telling him she'd love him forever because she just wanted to be his.

She liked his heart and his soul.

And maybe, she really did already love him.

He wanted that. But he needed to earn it. And that meant finishing this case so she could have all of him, not just the pieces he gave her when no one was looking.

Chapter Sixteen

Lyric leaned across the car and gave Melody a hug. "Thank you for the ride." They hadn't said much to each other on the way over to the ranch, both of them not really happy about the early hour.

"No problem." Melody yawned. "I'm happy you're happy with Viper. Or M. Whatever we're calling him now."

"Stick with Viper. He's M to me."

A soft grin made it onto Melody's exhausted face. "It's sweet you two have your own secret romance going on."

"*Secret* is the operative word there, so please don't say anything about it to anyone." She knew she could count on her sister but wanted it to be clear.

"I won't. But you should tell *him*, so he'll stop pining for you."

Lyric turned to the passenger window and spotted Rick walking toward the barn like a man on a mission. It didn't surprise her that he knew she'd be here this morning. He seemed to be keeping close tabs on her. "I'll handle him. You go get some sleep."

Melody's gaze sharpened. "Viper has a serious affection for you. Rick is seriously obsessed. There's a difference. You see it. We all see it. End it before this gets worse."

"I'm going to give him what he came for, then send him on his way." Lyric slipped out of the car and closed the door on Melody's objections to her giving Rick any more of her time. Lyric didn't want to make an enemy, she wanted Rick to go home. Peacefully and happy, so he'd leave her alone.

He barreled up to her, looking like he was ready for a fight. She cut him off. "Rick. So good to see you. I'm so sorry about the miscommunication last night and that you got upset with me. That's the last thing I wanted."

Rick's eyes went wide with surprise and whatever he was going to say sputtered out.

She kept going, not giving him a chance to talk. "I have to work out the horses this morning, but after that, I hoped you'd drive me to the bar. I'll get the barbecue going, then you and I can spend some time working on a song. I can't wait to hear your ideas. How does that sound? Say in like, three hours?"

He stood there dumbfounded.

She took his lack of speech as affirmation that he agreed. "Great. I'll work as fast as I can and knock on your cabin door when I'm ready to go." She walked toward the barn, thinking it best to just keep on the move so he'd just go along.

He followed her. "How's your wrist?"

She held it up but didn't stop walking. "Eleven stitches. No big deal." The pain had decreased significantly, but she'd be careful today.

"Where did you stay last night?"

She reached the barn and turned back without answering the intrusive question. It was none of his damn business. "Lots to do if you want to get in a couple hours of songwriting. I'll come find you as soon as I'm done."

"Do you want some help?"

"It will go much faster if I do it myself." With that, she walked into the barn hoping he took the hint this time and gave her some space.

She felt him watching her as she made her way toward the tack room and waited as long as she could before looking back to see if he'd left. Alone, she breathed a sigh of relief.

"Lyric," her dad called out from one of the stalls.

She found her dad checking out one of the horses. "Is everything okay?"

"He scratched his hind quarter on something." Wade rubbed salve over the small wound. "How is the arm?" The casually asked question came with a very serious look in her father's eyes.

She pulled back her sleeve and showed him the bandage. "Eleven stitches. Nothing to worry about."

"Except there is *someone* to be concerned about, especially when he was with you when you got hurt."

She glanced back down the stable's alleyway, found it clear, then looked at her dad. "I'm going to do the song with him after I'm done here. Then I'm going to make it clear that he got what he wanted and I don't have time for anything more."

Her dad gave her one of those looks like it was a good plan but missing some key details. "Do you really think he'll just leave?"

No. She didn't. But she had to try. "I've been wholly resistant to spending time with him. Maybe if I do this one thing that he asked me to do, he'll stop trying so hard to force himself on me."

Her dad ran his hand over the horse's back. "I'm concerned that what you're seeing on the surface with him is much more sinister on the inside. Are you really prepared for what he might do?"

"I'm hardly ever alone except for when I'm at my place after work."

"I'm not one to interfere in your personal life. I try really hard to remember you're all grown and living your own lives. But it would be nice to know that you're not alone at night."

"I wasn't last night," she confessed without details. "I hope I won't be for long, but things are complicated right now, so I have to rely on myself and friends."

"Does he know what's going on?"

She knew he wasn't talking about Rick, but M. "Yes. But he's got his thing, and I've got mine. Overlapping our lives isn't going to happen until he finishes whatever he's working on. But I know the future he wants is with me. That's enough right now. It's something to build on when he's free to live his life the way he wants to live it. Finishing his thing is important to him, but it is also something he knows he has to do so that he can be with me. He's concerned about Rick, just like I am, but he trusts me to take care of myself and ask for help when I need it. He also made sure he can find me if I get into trouble."

Her dad's eyes lit with interest. "How so?"

"He put a tracking app on my phone."

His eyes narrowed. "What happens if you don't have it on you?"

She sighed. "Yeah, it's not foolproof, but it's something."

"I appreciate that he's trying to take care of you. What can I do?"

"Same thing you always do. Have my back. You taught me to be careful and do the right thing. Rick came all this way for a song. I'm going to give it to him. After that, if he can't accept that I don't want a personal relationship with him, then I'll have to be aggressive about keeping him away."

"But first, you want to be nice."

It was her nature. "I have to live with my choices, and being mean just because I don't like this guy feels wrong to me. If he can't accept my honesty, then he leaves me no choice but to be more forceful."

Her dad stroked his hand over the horse's long neck. "You could just tell him you're seeing someone else."

She'd thought about it. "I think that might escalate things."

Her dad nodded. "You may be right." He came out of the stall. "I'll help you with the horses today." He notched his chin toward her wrapped wrist.

She knew he meant to stick close to her while she was here because of Rick. He'd rely on her siblings while she was at the bar. She appreciated her family so much. She was lucky to have all of them both on and by her side.

She wished M could be with her, too, and wondered what he was doing today.

Chapter Seventeen

Someone knocked on Viper's door. He hoped like hell it was Lyric but knew she wouldn't return, not unless he asked her to come. He felt like a dick about it—she should be able to come and go as she pleased—but for now it was the way it had to be. He'd love it if she was in his bed every night.

He checked his place for anything of hers, his gut souring at the fact he had to do so to keep her safe. He wished she'd left more than her fading scent on the sheets and an indelible memory of their night together.

But thank God she didn't, because the second he opened the door to his surprise guest, he wanted to be sure Lyric wasn't linked to him. "What's up?"

"That's how you say hello to me?" Maria touched her fingertips to her chest and brushed her hair back in what was intended to be a sexy move but did nothing for him.

He didn't respond to her question and waited to see what she was doing here. He had no idea she knew where he lived and wondered which one of his MC brothers gave her his location. Few had ever come here. Spike was in lockup, and Bleaker was dead. Which left only Lobo, her brother. He didn't think she'd asked him. Scratch or Cueball were always at the club playing pool and flirting with Maria, so it was probably one of them.

"How'd your bid go last night?"

"What do you care?" He'd nearly forgotten about the cover story about him doing a bid on a renovation job. He didn't have to wonder if his brother had taken care of covering his ass.

"Have you heard from Spike since you left yesterday?" She studied him closely.

"No."

"Are you going to invite me in?"

He stood his ground. "Why?" He didn't want her in his place. But he also couldn't get rid of her, because he had a feeling she was behind the murder-for-hire business.

"So we can talk. And maybe get to know each other better."

He'd used a lot of women in the past on jobs to get information or give him cover. But this felt wrong, even if it was necessary. He inwardly cringed at having to do it, disregarded his personal feelings, and held the door open wider to let her pass.

"What's going on with Spike?" He hoped to uncover more of the plot and get her to confess to being the ringleader.

She took her time looking around the tiny apartment, then stared into his bedroom at the unmade bed. "Looks like you had a restless sleep."

"I slept like a baby," he corrected her, thinking he'd slept like a very satisfied man with the woman he loved by his side.

It didn't even shock him that he thought that about Lyric. His feelings for her had been growing for a long time. But finally being able to talk to her and be with her over the last few days, and especially last night, solidified it for him. He didn't just care about her. He didn't just want her. He loved her.

It was a new and strange feeling for someone like him who pretended to be something and someone else all the time. But he liked having this living thing inside him that wouldn't let him ignore it.

"Alone?" Maria asked, interest and something else in her eyes. Jealousy?

They didn't have that kind of relationship. They'd barely spoken up until now. But he'd caught her eyeing him now and again.

"Alone," he confirmed.

Her gaze swept over him. "A man like you doesn't have to sleep alone."

He didn't know exactly what she meant by that, except that she thought he could find a woman anytime he wanted. Maybe, but he'd never been that kind of guy. For good reason. His job hit number one on that list every damn time. It came above all else, including his loneliness.

"Sometimes I prefer it." Not anymore, though. He'd take Lyric in his bed any day of the week. Every day would be amazing. "So why are you asking *me* about Spike? He did the job for you last night. How'd it go?"

"You don't know?" She tried to seem casual, but he felt the intensity coming off her.

He folded his arms over his chest hiding the pain that shot through his shoulder when he pulled the stitches. "No."

"It went to shit." She didn't deny Spike was working for her.

He slowly unfolded his arms. "Did the husband get

cold feet? That guy didn't seem to have the balls to go through with it."

She huffed. "Someone talked. The FBI showed up and took Spike, the husband, and the brother-in-law into custody."

"For real? How do you know?" It hadn't hit the news yet.

"I have my sources."

He wanted to know if those sources were in law enforcement. "The brother-in-law's a hothead. I bet he spouted off about it to the wrong person. I warned Spike about that guy."

"It's the second time the FBI interfered and I lost a man."

Bingo. Thank you, Maria, for that very nice confession. "*You* lost a man?" He gave her a sly grin. "I knew you were running the show. You're smart, even if Lobo doesn't give you enough credit for it."

She preened at the praise.

"You know those guys want Lobo, the badass, running things, but behind the scenes you're working all of them."

She grinned and did that hair-flip thing again. "A man with a brain. I knew I liked you."

"I assume Spike won't rat you out."

"If he knows what's good for him, he'll keep his mouth shut."

He prodded her some more. "But he's facing some serious charges. What if he gives you up in some deal?"

"He won't. I take care of my people. His new lawyer will be there to see him today."

Viper was starting to catch on. "What do you have on the lawyer?"

She gave him a sly grin. "Stuff." She winked, flirting with him by showing off that she could be the bad girl and blackmail a lawyer into doing her bidding.

"You are so not what you seem." He let her think he was impressed. "I mean, you were taking care of that kidnapped baby not that long ago, but you had all this other stuff going on, too."

"One has nothing to do with the other. I wanted to keep that baby. Lord knows I'd be a better parent than her father any day. Beating up women just because you're stronger doesn't make you right. But Cyn, the baby's aunt, was tied to that cop, Hunt, so I couldn't hold on to the baby. Maybe I'll have one of my own." She held his gaze.

He did not respond to that in any way and dumped the suggestion in the never-going-to-happen bin in his mind. Not with her. With Lyric? Whole other story.

She kept talking. "And Officer Hunt Wilde . . . he's tied to the Wildes that run the Dark Horse Dive Bar. One of your favorite haunts."

He didn't even try to deny it. "Good food. Good music. Lots of women. What's not to like?"

"Oh, I think there's one particular woman you like most."

He did not like where this was going. "If that was true, I wouldn't be sleeping alone."

"Really? Because I've heard you have a thing for this particular dark-haired Wilde chef." The intensity of her gaze warned him to tread carefully.

"You should always appreciate a woman who can cook. But that one wants nothing to do with me." The lie tasted sour on his tongue. But he had to protect Lyric at all costs.

Her gaze sharpened. "But you want her."

"I'm not looking for anything serious. And that woman is a wedding gown, picket fence, and babies waiting to happen." God, how he wanted a life with her.

"And you're just a lone wolf."

He didn't even blink. "I like it that way."

"Me, too." She seemed to relax. "But a warm body in bed doesn't hurt once in a while. Unless I want it to," she added, letting him know she was up for some kinky shit if he was into it.

"Live and let live."

"Which is why I'm here."

He raised a brow. "What did you have in mind?" He could lead her on and hope she confided more of her dirty secrets to him. He preferred the illegal ones over sexcapades, but he'd take what he could get right now if it got him what he ultimately wanted down the road.

"You. Me. A rope."

He maintained his neutral tone. "Go on."

Her sultry gaze didn't quit. "I have a job. If you're interested."

"It's never a chore," he teased, keeping the innuendo going, so she'd have to spell it out for him.

She shook her head and rolled her eyes. "I mean a job like I gave to Spike."

He paused, so she'd think he considered it for a moment. "Exactly what are *you* and *me* doing with a *rope*?"

"Enough of the games, Viper. Flirting with you is fun, but this is business." The steel in her voice showed him exactly why the others followed her down this dark road. She drew them in with sex appeal and held them in her grasp with her strength and their shared misdeeds that could take them all down. She also had the threat of taking them out and using one of the others to eliminate them if they got out of line.

He bet Spike was sitting in a cell right now wondering if she'd kill him for getting caught. Through the MC and her brother, there were contacts and connections to be made in the jails and prison. It was a matter of knowing the right person and having the money to pay them off.

He let her catch a glimpse of his annoyance. "Then, stop teasing and show me the goods."

Approval lit her eyes. "The job is simple. Go to the address I provide at the time I say. You'll find your target and hang them in the garage, making it look like a suicide. I can give you tips for this. I'll pay you two grand."

"Spike's job came with a twenty-grand payday. I do the job, take all the risk, and you want ninety percent of the take. You can fuck off with that bullshit."

"I bring in the job, vet the person paying, insulate you from the transaction, and will have your back if you're stupid enough to get caught."

He appreciated how she laid that all out for him. "Ten grand."

"Five."

"Let's just settle on eight. For now. Or you'll have to get one of the others to do your bidding." He wondered why she had come to him and not one of the others in the club who were more . . . malleable.

"The others aren't like you. Spike saw how calm and collected you were with the mark and the unexpected addition of the brother-in-law the other night. He vouched for you. I know you served time for assault and other nefarious things."

Viper had been a bad boy. At least on paper.

"But you also got off on an attempted-murder charge."

He gave her a smug look. "They didn't have any evidence I did it."

She raised that brow at him again. "Exactly. You only got caught for that assault because of a hidden camera."

"Fucking technology."

"Do we have a deal?"

He stared at her for a long moment, then nodded once. "Yes. When does this have to be done? I've got a small job going in Willow Fork."

"You're going to have to cancel it. This job is in Salt Lake. You need to leave today. You can scope out the place tonight, do the job tomorrow night, then drive back."

"Are you coming with me?"

She gave him a sultry grin, then shook her head. "You'll meet the client, collect the money, do the job, then come back."

"With twenty grand, I could afford not to come back."

"Who said it's twenty?" The *gotcha* look didn't become her.

But he took it in stride. "How much is the job?"

"Fifty. Unlike the last guy, this one has money and wants the job done fast." She handed him a burner phone and headed for the door, smugness written all over her face. "I know this is the last time you won't get the details up front before we negotiate, but God it feels good to best you." She turned back before she opened the door. "I'll text you the details. The only communication I want back is a text saying it's done. When you return"—she glanced at the bed behind him—"we'll celebrate."

The second the door closed he breathed easier, then glanced at the shelf by the window and the hidden camera recording everything. He picked up his phone off the table and stopped the audio recording on it, too. Ever cautious, he liked to have a backup just in case.

He sent the audio to his brother, then went to the linen closet, pulled out the folded blanket on the bottom shelf, pried open the panel at the back, revealing the hidden compartment and the laptop connected to the video feed. "I love technology."

He pulled up the video file, cut it to show Maria's arrival and their conversation all the way to her leaving him, then sent it to his brother, too.

He pulled out the cell phone he kept hidden with the laptop and texted Nick.

> VIPER: I just got hired to do a job. Meeting client for payment tonight. Salt Lake City.
> VIPER: I'll make contact once I'm on the road.

He hated to leave now, but he didn't have a choice. He'd collect the payment, arrest the asshole who wanted someone killed, have the FBI make it look like the victim bit the dust tomorrow, then show up back here with the money for Maria and find out how she was setting up the jobs and shut her down. This would finally be over.

Three days. Maybe a week.

Then he could have his life back. He could be with Lyric. Everything would be normal again. No more hiding. No more lies. He could be himself once more.

He could give Lyric everything she wanted and have everything he wanted with her.

All he had to do was leave her for a few days.

She'd understand.

She'd be okay.

He'd make it up to her when he returned.

The unsettled feeling in his gut didn't bode well. He usually listened to that warning, but this time he didn't know if it was the job ahead or Lyric's worrisome shadow that made him uneasy.

He worried about her, but she could take care of herself. She had her family watching out for her.

Nothing was going to happen to her. It was just his overactive imagination and protective streak making him apprehensive about leaving her.

After this job, he could focus on her. On them.

She could handle one overzealous guy.

If anything happened, her family and the bouncers at the bar would help her. She'd let him know if she needed him.

He wanted so badly to be the guy she turned to when things got bad.

Chapter Eighteen

Lyric's phone rang the second she walked into the bar with Rick, threads of a song already coming together in her head thanks to their brainstorming session in the car.

Rick eyed her, annoyed by the interruption.

She shrugged. "Why don't you set up on the stage? I'll just be a minute." She checked the caller ID and hid a smile, turning to the hallway next to the bar to turn on more lights as she answered. "Hello."

M didn't waste time or words. "I'm going out of town for a few days. I won't be in touch."

"Do I get to ask any questions?"

"I can't answer them. I'm sorry."

"Okay."

Neither of them said anything for a long moment.

"That's it?"

It seemed he was either spoiling for a fight, or more likely upset he had to go and he wanted her to be upset about it, too. She'd miss him. "I'm disappointed I won't see you for a few days. But I hope you have a good trip. I'll see you when you get back."

"I hate disappointing you." The grumbled words made her grin.

"Then, you'll make it up to me when you get back."

"How?" The suggestive tone in that deep voice tightened her belly.

"Sounds like you've got a few days to figure that out. Lucky for you, I'm easy to please. Think naked thoughts."

"Well, now I am." Humor erased the sour note he tried to put in his tone.

She grinned. "I mean it. I'll miss you."

"I missed you the second you left this morning."

She sighed, her heart melting. "A few days seems like forever right now."

"If I didn't have to go . . ." So much regret and remorse in those few words.

"I know. It's fine. I'll be here when you get back."

"You really are an angel."

"I want this to work. And I know you do, too."

"More than anything. And I know that sounds hollow when I'm leaving to do something that's important, but not more important than you."

"I don't want to start a fight here, but it does feel like whatever you're doing is more important. And maybe if I knew what it was, I'd understand better. Right now, though, all I know is you're leaving and I want you to stay. And maybe that's not fair to say. I'm not asking, because you've made it clear this thing you're doing needs to be done. I'm taking it on faith that it is and you are doing it for the right reasons."

"Do you believe that?"

"Did you listen to the song I sent you?"

"Yes."

"You have a good soul. I have enough faith right now to believe this will all make sense someday."

He let out a heavy sigh. "You have no idea how much I appreciate you."

"Maybe you'll tell me all about it when you get back."

"I hope so. I would really like to tell you everything."

"I look forward to that day. And seeing you again."

"One of these days, the real me is going to show up for you." It sounded like a promise.

"You already did the night you came to see me at my place and you opened up about how you feel about me. You were enough then. You're enough now."

"I don't deserve you."

"I don't believe that at all."

Rick stood at the edge of the stage. "Lyric. We doing this, or what?"

"Who's that?"

"Rick. We're setting up to write a song at the bar, then he's got what he wants, and I'm done."

"Be careful, Angel. Guys like him, who think others should just give in to what they want, always want more."

"He can't have what I won't give."

"He's forced you into this."

She hated that he was right. "Yeah, well, it's not like I can tell him I have a badass boyfriend and to leave me alone."

The quiet on the other end of the line made her gut flutter. "Sorry. I overstepped." She'd spoken without thinking.

"No, you didn't," he assured her. "You have no idea how much I'd love to claim you as mine, too."

"You mean the way I did, M." She gave him another few seconds to absorb that. "We're both hiding this relationship."

"You told your family."

"Your brother knows about me," she shot back.

"But I can't walk into that bar and kiss you in the middle of the crowd."

"One day, you will. Until then, when it's just you and me, we get to be us, like this. And if you were here, I'd sneak away to a private spot and kiss you goodbye."

"You make me wish I was with you every second of the day."

"You are," she assured him. "I think about you constantly."

"It's the same for me, Angel. I'm sorry I won't be in touch. I'll miss you like crazy."

"Me, too. Be safe."

"I'll see you soon."

Lyric's heavy heart sank in her chest. She really did miss him already.

Her phone pinged with an incoming text from him. She clicked the link, and tears gathered in her eyes when Aerosmith's "Angel" began to play.

M: When everything seems dark, you're my Angel. You make everything bright. ♥♥♥

The man knew how to speak to her in her love language. Music didn't just convey the words, it evoked emotion. And M sent this song right to her heart.

If her presence in his life saved him from whatever was taking such an emotional toll on him, then she'd be the one to bring the light for him.

"Lyric!" The irritation in Rick's voice made her wonder why she was doing this favor for him at all.

But an hour and a half later, the smile on Rick's face said it all. She'd delivered on taking the snippets of ideas he'd had and turned them into a cohesive song that had a great hook and that sing-along feel that lifted the spirit.

He had a decent voice and played guitar well. But it would take a lot more than that to make it in the country-music industry with all the competition.

Rick set his guitar aside. "I knew we'd be great together. This is just the first of many hits we'll write."

She stood and put her guitar back in its stand. "I'm so glad you like the song."

"It's perfect. I couldn't have done it without you. People are going to love it."

"I hope so. You can play it for your friends, record it when you get home, and send it out to record labels and agents, share it on social media. Whatever you want to do with it."

"What are you talking about? I'm not leaving."

"You have your song. What else is there?"

"But I have a ton of ideas. You said you'd help me."

"I did help you." She gave him a smile. "Now I have to get to work."

He glanced around the bar and grimaced. "This isn't what you want."

She narrowed her gaze, taken aback he'd speak to her that way. "You don't know what I want. You don't know me."

"You're a gifted singer and songwriter. You're wasting your time here."

She raised a brow, insulted by his words. "Is that what you think?"

"Yes."

"That just shows how little you know me and what I want for my life."

He cringed. "You can't seriously want to stay here in this dinky little town working in a bar."

She held her arms out to encompass the place. "And yet, here I am."

He shook his head. "No. You're made for bigger things. Let's go to Nashville. We'll write more songs. We'll sing them together. We could be the next great duo."

She shook her head and stepped back. "If that's your dream, go for it. I wish you lots of success. While I love playing in Nashville when I go, this is home."

He stood and took a step toward her. "Why are you being like this?"

"Like what?"

He leaned in. "Difficult."

She held her ground. More than annoyed, she let her anger fly. "Why can't you accept that I did you a favor and now we're done?"

"You don't mean that."

"Why do you insist on telling me what I want and what I mean? Do you think I'm stupid and unable to make decisions for myself?"

"No. You're just wasting your talent."

She folded her arms over her chest. "It seems to me you benefited from my talent. Take the song I practically wrote myself, and get out."

He raked a hand through his hair, frustration in the lines on his forehead. "You are so dismissive."

"You get what you give," she shot back. "From the moment you got here, you have insinuated yourself into my life with little consideration for me. I was just supposed to go along with *your* plans, despite the fact I have my own life here."

He stared at her wide-eyed. "I thought you wanted to help me."

"Based on what, exactly? Did I invite you here? No."

"You said we'd write together."

"Because you wouldn't stop asking. Instead of working with me to set up a convenient time, you just showed up and demanded my time. And now I've given it to you. I wrote you a song. Now we're done."

"I need more than that." His desperate look didn't sway her.

"Then, write more songs. Work with other songwriters if you have to. It doesn't have to be me."

He reached out to touch her face, but she immediately stepped out of his reach. His gaze turned hard, then softened. "You're what makes it special."

"You have no idea if that song will be the one that breaks out. It's definitely worth a shot if you work hard and get it out there. But that's on you. Not me. I do what I do because I love it. I do it the way I do it because of the way I want to live my life. I have family, friends, commitments that are important to me. All you see is my talent and how you can use it for yourself. Well, I'm not your puppet. You don't get to pull the strings and make me do what you want."

He looked around the bar. "Can't you see that you could be so much more?"

She was what she wanted to be, where she wanted to be. "You may think I live my life small, but I'm happy. Can you say the same?" She didn't think so.

"You're wasting yourself here. We could be so good together."

She put her foot down. Again. "There is no *we*. You came here for a song. You got it."

"I came here for *you*. Don't tell me you're not interested, because you've been flirting with me the whole time we wrote the song. All those smiles when we got a line just right. The way you looked at me when we created the story of two lovers finally coming together. And the title. 'Love Is You.' You looked me right in the eye when you came up with that."

She'd been thinking about M. "Rick, it's a song. A story. It's real to those who relate to it. I gave you the words, the lines, the title. But I don't feel that way about you. If I smiled, it's because I enjoy writing and finding the perfect rhythm and rhyme in a song. I feel the most special kind of joy when a song comes together and conveys emotions and meaning that others will feel. But that has nothing to do with how I feel about *you*. I don't know how else to say it, but I don't have any romantic feelings for you. I don't even know you." That was one sentence too far. She should have stopped when she dropped the hammer that she didn't have feelings for him.

But that last sentiment put a light of hope in his eyes.

Fuck my life.

"We had fun today. I saw it in you. You loved working with me."

She liked playing music and working on the song. "Rick, you've seen how busy my life is. I don't have time to work with other people even part-time. And truthfully, I don't want to, because I have my own stuff I'm working on, plus the writing I do with my partner. While I occasionally write with other people, I'm loyal to Faith."

"Why won't you give me a chance?"

"I have. I did. I enjoyed today." Right up until he pushed for more. "Now it's over."

"No. Let's make it a regular thing. Faith will understand."

"I just told you I don't want to, nor do I have the time."

"Your family can cover for you." He looked pleased he'd found a solution.

She shook her head and walked toward the edge of the stage.

He took her by the arm and spun her back toward him, his fingers digging into her bicep. "Don't turn your back on me."

She pointedly looked at his hand on her arm. "Let go."

"Say you'll do this again. A couple more songs. You and me spending time together." A desperate, angry edge to his tone warned this was escalating to a bad place.

"Right now, I don't even want to see you again. Take your hand off me."

"Do it now." Jax closed the distance, fury in his eyes.

Rick released her and held his hands up. "We were just talking."

"Use your mouth, not your hands." Jax stared Rick down, coming up beside Lyric, ready for a fight.

"What are you even doing here? You work at the ranch today," Rick pointed out.

It disturbed her that he knew Jax's schedule. And hers. And maybe everyone else's around here. Having two members of her kitchen staff tending the smokers and doing the prep in the kitchen mostly out of sight hadn't been enough protection.

Jax glanced at her. "I heard you were working here with him. Thought I'd come down and make sure everything's okay." He glared at Rick. "I'm so glad I did."

"We're done for today," Rick announced, picking up his guitar and the papers detailing the song. He put both in his guitar case. "We'll talk more about this later, Lyric."

"I've said all I have to say. Now, excuse me. I have work to do." She dismissed him and headed for the kitchen.

"I'll walk you out," Jax said, letting her know he'd lock the door behind Rick, giving her some peace of mind that he wouldn't sneak up on her in the kitchen again.

She was just coming out of the walk-in fridge with several pounds of drumsticks when Jax walked into the kitchen. "Don't start. I wasn't alone here."

"And yet, that didn't matter. He still put his hands on you. Thank God Viper texted, asking me to check on you."

That surprised her. "Really?"

"Yeah. Looks like his instincts were spot-on. Who knows what might have happened if I hadn't shown up."

"I'd have screamed for help." She pointedly looked to the two people standing outside the back door.

Jax frowned. "You okay?"

"Fine. Rattled," she admitted. "He doesn't see me. I'm just something he wants. Someone who can give him what he wants."

Jax huffed out his frustration. "I don't like him."

"Neither do I. I thought he'd be happy with the song and leave."

Jax sneered. "But he wants more."

"Yes. M—Viper said the same thing."

"Where is he? Why didn't he come check on you?"

She wished he was here. "He's out of town on some job."

Jax nodded. "Construction is hard to come by this time of year. I guess he's got to take work wherever he can get it."

"Yeah." She thought it was more than that. Something to do with the Wild Wolves MC, not a renovation or building project. But what did she know? He wasn't really one to share.

Jax read her mood. "You're pissed about something."

Rick had a way of doing that to her.

"He wouldn't listen to me. He thinks I can't make up my own mind and decide what I want. He thinks I'm wasting my life here."

Jax sneered. "Seriously? Dump him."

"What? No. Not M—Viper—whatever. I mean Rick."

"You've made it clear to us that you want to work at the bar and do your music thing your way. Has that changed?" He waited patiently and openly for her answer.

She appreciated so much that Jax asked. "No. I like my life. It's looking even better with M in it, even though we're kind of complicated right now."

"Something is definitely strange when the so-called normal guy who's into music like you seems more of a threat than the biker dude you're hiding a relationship with."

"M is honest. He appreciates me. Rick . . . he wants to control me."

"I'm liking Viper a lot better now, especially since he gave me the heads-up about how he feels about you. If he worries, it means he cares."

"I know he cares. I just wish whatever is holding him back ends soon."

"I want you to be happy. If he's it, great. But Rick . . . you need to stay away from him."

"I'm done being nice. I'm done trying to spare his feelings. I'm just done." She rubbed her hand over her sore arm.

Jax frowned. "He lays a hand on you again, kick him in the balls and put him down just like I showed you."

Sounded like a plan to her.

Chapter Nineteen

Lyric had closed the kitchen nearly an hour ago and had taken the stage with the local band they'd hired for the weekend. She played with them often and enjoyed the set, getting out of her head and lost in the music.

Rick had spent most of the night drinking at the bar and glaring at her.

She preferred another broody man and wished he was here instead. Wishful thinking.

But her conscience pricked, and she felt bad for leaving things the way she had with Rick. Her soft heart didn't like being mean and wanted to make amends. So when the song ended and the band's lead vocalist announced they were taking a break, she grabbed her acoustic guitar and went to the mic, knowing this was a huge mistake, but impulsively making it anyway, so she could live with herself.

"Hello, Dark Horse Dive Bar."

The crowd raised a glass and shouted, "Hello." It was a thing they did.

"I haven't shared a new song in a while, but I've got something special tonight." She waited for the cheers to calm down. "Rick Rowe, do you want to join me onstage to share your brand-new song?"

Rick's eyes went wide, and the crowd followed her gaze to the bar where he sat.

"Come on. They're waiting." She caught the shocked and angry look Aria sent her from the bar.

Her sister probably thought she'd lost her mind throwing this particularly obstinate dog a bone, but Lyric didn't like feeling guilty, so why the hell not? The defiant voice in her head was a lie. She knew she shouldn't be doing this, but she couldn't get out of it now that reason wanted to override her conscience.

Melody appeared in front of the stage with a loaded tray of drinks held up in one hand. "And they say I'm impulsive and stupid."

Lyric leaned down, away from the microphone, and said, "Anyone says that about you, I'll kick their ass."

"This is a bad idea," Melody warned, walking off with the drinks just as Rick took the stage with her.

Don't I know it?

She notched her chin toward the second microphone. "I'll play and back you up, you sing. Ready?"

"Um, this is the first time I've ever sung to this many people."

"Then, make it good." No pressure. They just had about a hundred and fifty people waiting on them.

She didn't let Rick overthink it and started playing the song. He missed the cue to start, so she replayed the intro, held his gaze, and sang him into the song. Once the lyrics started flowing, she let him take it on his own, backing him up just like they'd done today when they wrote the song.

It wasn't flawless by any means, but people were listening, dancing, and caught onto the chorus and sang along to it. She played the last few notes and let the music fade. With a smile for Rick and a job well done, she announced, "Rick Rowe, everyone!"

The crowd gave them a round of applause, and they took a bow.

Rick pulled her into a hug, the guitar between them, keeping him from crushing her body to his. She gave him a second, then pushed back and away from him.

"Thank you, Lyric. What a rush! That was awesome!"

Lyric set the guitar aside and let the crowd get lost in the recorded playlist she'd already set up for the break. She waved her hand out for Rick to precede her offstage. They accepted a bunch of appreciation for the song from a ton of people as they made their way to the bar.

Aria handed her a bottle of water and a fresh beer to Rick.

"Seriously, that rocked. Oh my God, I can't believe I just did that." He had that mad rush of a high she got when she played onstage.

"You need to do it more, so you're comfortable in front of a crowd," she suggested.

"Yes. Let's do it."

Fuck. She really wanted to say that out loud but held her tongue.

Of course he thought she meant he could play the stage with her here.

She shook her head. "No. I mean you need to do that back home. Or wherever. This was a one-time thing."

"You say that now, but when I'm big, you'll beg me to play here in Nowhere, Wyoming."

She wouldn't beg him for anything, least of all to play at her bar. "The crowd enjoyed the song." They were already primed and riding the high from the band playing for them the last hour.

Rick needed to work on his confidence, his pitch and tone, and his engagement with the audience. You only got that last one by performing for people. Yes, there were nerves, but you had to use that energy to pull the crowd in, then you could feed off their vibe.

There was nothing like it when the crowd was into the music and amped. She loved it.

And right now, Rick was riding the high of it.

It could be addictive.

She downed her water.

"Let's do another song," he coaxed.

"The band will be back in ten minutes. I need a break, too."

"Come on. One more."

She shook her head. "Look, I did you another favor, letting you see how everyone reacts to the song we wrote. You got to sing for a crowd. Be happy with that."

"You get to play whenever you want." The bitterness dimmed his excitement.

"I own the bar," she reminded him.

He perked up. "Which means you say who gets on stage."

"Exactly. I let you have a turn. Now the band *I'm paying* will finish out their set before closing."

The enthusiastic vibe disappeared under a wave of anger she could feel coming off him. "You really get off on giving just a little, then shutting me down."

Anger pressed her lips tight, then she let it out. "It's no small thing to get to play for a packed bar when you're a no-name artist to them. It's also no small thing for me to rearrange my schedule today to write with you. But if you don't appreciate those things, there's the door." She pointed to the entrance where the bouncer kept watch on who was coming in and anyone who needed to go out.

He backed off, but she knew he only masked the anger simmering inside him. "I guess I owe you a thank-you."

Yet he didn't actually thank her. She let it go, because what was the point with him. "Enjoy the rest of your night." She walked away and headed for the one place he couldn't follow her. The restroom had a line, so she backtracked to the kitchen, out the back door, and up to her place.

When she reached the landing and went for the doorknob, she stopped, her fingertips an inch from the busted handle and lock. The frame had some splintered wood, and the door stood open about six inches.

Motherfucker.

She pushed the door open wide and stared into the dark interior making out little at the back of her place, but seeing the disarray and destruction littering the floor in front of her.

Fuck. Fuck. Fuck.

One good thing about owning a bar, she had the cops on speed dial.

"Hey, Lyric. Trouble at the bar?" Officer Bowers always sounded ready to help. He was a good cop and a nice guy, not one of those people who'd gotten jaded by dealing with the worst in society day after day. He cared.

"Not the bar, but my place upstairs. Someone broke in and wrecked everything. Mind coming and taking a look? I'll explain more when you get here. And if you don't mind coming around the back, instead of through the bar, I'd appreciate it."

"You don't want me to spoil everyone's good time."

No, she didn't. "I appreciate the understanding."

"On my way. Be there in a few, unless I get an emergency call."

"Thanks, Officer Bowers." She hung up and ran downstairs and back into the bar.

She found Aria in the back office. "Hey. I thought you were going to play with the band? Where'd you go?"

"Upstairs to pee. Someone broke in and trashed my place."

Aria's gaze sharpened. "Rick?"

She shrugged. "Don't know. But that's my guess." Especially after he'd left her those text messages last night. Because she'd showered and changed at the ranch this morning, then worked with Rick and in the kitchen, she hadn't been up to her place all day. "Bowers is on his way to check it out. I don't want to go inside until he gets here. Can I borrow a jacket? It's frickin' cold out."

Aria notched her chin toward the jacket hanging on the peg on the wall by the door. "Let me know what he finds."

"Everything broken and trashed."

Aria frowned. "It's that bad?"

"Someone is really pissed at me."

"Maybe they trashed the place to cover up what they stole? At least until you inventory?"

"But if they were looking for quick cash, why not wait until the end of the night and rob the bar? There's a lot more money in here than upstairs."

Aria stood, walked around the desk, and pulled her into a hug. "I'm sorry. This is the last thing you need right now."

"Like you, I think my two problems are tied together."

Aria released her. "How's your wrist?"

"Hurts still, but better." Like a deep bruise, it would take time to heal, but it didn't really impair her ability to use her hand.

"Well, we have surveillance of the back now, so we can pull that up and give it to Officer Bowers. Maybe we got whoever did this on camera."

"Wait. What? Since when do we have cameras out back?"

"Today actually. They were installed early this morning. Viper came to see Jax about making sure you were safe."

"When?" She remembered him coming to the bar during the day. "Never mind. I remember him showing up when we were closed."

"I like that he's looking out for you and including Jax in that."

"Yeah. Me, too. I better get up to my place and meet Bowers."

"Want me to call Jax or Mom and Dad to come help?"

"I've got this. You and Melody have the bar tonight. I'll help close, once I've got this settled."

"Where's Rick now?"

"I didn't see him in the bar, but he could still be here. Maybe he finally took the hint and left." Lyric grabbed the jacket on her way out of the office and pulled it on. By the time she exited the back of the kitchen, she spotted Officer Bowers coming out of her apartment.

He stared down at her from the landing as she made her way up the stairs. "Who'd you piss off?"

"They didn't take anything, did they?"

"Doesn't look like it. Your laptop has been smashed.

TV, too. Jewelry box is turned over, stuff scattered everywhere. If you have a stash of cash somewhere, you can check for it, but this kind of destruction looks personal."

"I'm not saying he did it for sure, but I'd appreciate you having a word with Rick Rowe. He came to town about a week ago. I met him briefly in Nashville recently. He's pushy and insistent that we could be so good together. Writing songs and more. I've made it clear I'm not interested. Last night, I cut myself in the kitchen. Mostly it was his fault. He came up behind me. I toppled a plate of food. When he moved in to kiss me a bit later and I stepped back, I slipped and ended up on my ass, a piece of the broken plate in my wrist." She held it up to show him the bandage. "I got fixed up at the ER, then went home with a friend. Rick sent me a bunch of texts that grew increasingly angry, to the point he threatened me."

"Let me see."

She pulled out her phone and showed him the texts.

"Why didn't you report that he threatened you?"

"I thought I could handle it by giving him what he wanted."

The officer raised a brow.

"A song," she clarified. "I met with him today. We wrote a song. I even played it with him onstage tonight. I thought that would appease him."

"But he wants more?"

She nodded. "And he's not taking *no* for an answer."

"Where is he now?"

"In the bar," Melody called up to them from the bottom of the stairs, her breath fog on the wind. Melody must have come out of the bar when Lyric had been talking to the cop. "Aria told me what happened. Rick's at the bar. Left side."

"He's also staying in one of the cabins at the ranch." She wanted the officer to know everything.

"Go inside and look around. Don't touch anything. I'll dust for prints. But see if anything was stolen. I'll go talk to our person of interest."

Melody waited for the officer to descend the stairs before she came up and looked at Lyric's place. "Oh my God."

Now that the lights, at least the ones that weren't smashed, were on, it looked worse than Lyric originally thought.

"Mind gathering some supplies downstairs for me to clean this mess up once Officer Bowers is finished?"

"Sure." Melody met her gaze. "I'm so sorry. It looks like everything is ruined."

Yeah. Nothing survived this guy's rage. Stuffing was pouring out of the chairs by the fireplace. The two small tables were broken into pieces. She could so easily picture M sitting there eating his dinner, enjoying the warmth of the fire, talking to her in that deep voice she loved to hear.

She missed him so much.

She wished he was here.

She didn't want to be alone in this mess. Her place felt violated.

The bed had gotten the same treatment as the stuffed chairs. She'd have to replace not only the sheets and blankets but her mattress, too. She mourned her beautiful and expensive chenille blanket. It had been cut or torn into multiple pieces, threads pulled into long strings and snippets of them all over the floor. Anything glass or ceramic, including her dishes in the kitchen had been smashed. The pretty lighted birch tree behind her bed had more broken branches than intact ones.

She mourned the destruction of all her photos of family and friends.

The upstairs apartment was at the back of the bar. With the music blaring and the parking lot out front, no one would have heard the destruction going on up there. And if it had been done after-hours, there were no close neighbors to hear anything either.

Whoever did this would probably get away with it if they didn't have them on surveillance.

The tears didn't register until Officer Bowers stood beside her and said, "I'd want to cry, too, but the truth is most of this can be replaced. You know what can't? Your sense of safety. That you'll have to rebuild over time. And I can tell you, it takes a lot of time to get that back."

She appreciated his commiseration and kindness. "What did Rick say?"

"That he didn't do it. He'd never do anything to hurt you."

"Right. I don't believe that now. Not after he grabbed me in the bar. Not after seeing this."

"You never said anything about him putting his hands on you."

"He was angry. I let it go." She had kept letting things slide with him. No more.

"Do you want to press charges?"

Her gaze fell on a broken wineglass. Maybe it was the one M used, maybe not, but it felt like she'd lost a piece of that memory. "I just want him gone."

"He's actually waiting to talk to you downstairs."

"I have nothing to say to him. Now. Or ever."

"That's your choice. Aria showed me the surveillance footage. There's nothing there."

She turned to him, shocked. "What do you mean?"

"Looks like the camera was installed this morning after this happened. No one came up to your place, or left it, until you came upstairs tonight."

"You're sure?"

"The picture is clear. The camera shows the stairs and door. So unless they came in through a window . . ." They both looked at the two windows at the back of her place that were closed, locked, and intact. The one in the bathroom was too small for anyone to climb through.

She sighed, knowing this had been done sometime last night while she was with M and Rick was furious with her for not coming home. "Nothing is missing, so far as I can tell right now."

"Then, I suggest you stay with someone and never be alone. Whoever did this is sending you a message."

She assured the officer she understood with a nod. "I hear it loud and clear."

"Don't give this guy a chance to do worse. If he tries to contact you, ignore it and document it. If he hurts you, report it. Don't be nice. Don't even argue with him. He wants your attention, good or bad. Don't give it to him."

She nodded that she understood.

He looked around her place again. "Give me some time to take pictures of the damage and get some prints. I'll need yours to exclude you from whatever I find."

"I'll take some pictures, too, while you do that."

"Go for it."

She took several of the main space, and a couple of the bathroom that wasn't hit as bad as the living room and kitchen area.

M said he wouldn't be in touch, but she texted him a pic of the living space and a message anyway.

LYRIC: Your day was definitely better than mine. ☹

She tucked her phone in her jeans back pocket and searched the mess on the floor for a notebook. She found one, then spent ten minutes looking for a pen to make a list of what needed to be replaced.

It dawned on her that she'd left her purse in the kitchen downstairs. "I'll be right back," she told Officer Bowers as she headed out the door and down the steps.

She wasn't surprised to find Rick lurking on the patio area. "Go back to wherever you came from, and never contact me again," she ordered, not stopping on her trek to the back door.

"I didn't do this."

She spun around to confront him, even though the officer had just told her not to engage. She'd make herself clear one last time. "I don't believe you. And even if you didn't, I don't want you anywhere near me ever again. I'm tired of you lurking in my life, showing up unexpectedly all the time, telling me how I feel and what I should do. Every time I try to be nice to you, you bite me in the ass with your assertion that you know what I want. I'm done. Is that clear enough for you?"

His gaze went soft with sympathy she didn't believe at all. "You're upset. I get it. I would be, too."

Frustration was ice in her veins. "You were upset last night and threatened me. You said you'd make it hurt. Well done. It's not just that you destroyed my place, it's that you tainted it."

"I didn't do it," he snapped.

"Right. Like you didn't break into that other place and take things."

His eyes went wide. "How do you know about that?"

"My cousin is a cop. You should think about that next time you think about coming after me." She turned and headed to the kitchen door.

"Lyric, you need to listen to me."

She spun back around. "That right there. You telling me what to do. I don't need to do anything where you're concerned." She glared hard at him. "Leave me alone. That's the last time I'm telling you. Next time, I'll get a restraining order. Pack up your stuff and go. You are not welcome at the ranch or the bar anymore. I mean it. Don't. Come. Back." She walked into the kitchen and pulled the door shut behind her, locking him out. She breathed hard, her emotions so raw and overwhelming she didn't know what to do with all her anger and disappointment and frustration mixed with sadness.

"Lyric, you okay?" Aria asked from across the room.

"I will be." But right now, she really hated that her place was a wreck and M wasn't here. One made her mad, the other sad, and it piled onto everything else.

"What can I do?" Aria asked.

"Nothing. I've got it. I just came down to get my purse. I should probably grab the toolbox from the office. I need to repair the door the best I can until I can get it fixed properly."

"I'll get it and bring it up."

"Thank you."

Aria rubbed her hand up and down Lyric's arm. "Did you call him and tell him what happened?"

"I texted him, but he told me before he left that he'd

be out of touch, so I don't expect to hear from him anytime soon."

"I'm sorry. I know at times like this, it's nice to have your guy around."

Yeah. It would be. But he was MIA.

But she could handle this on her own.

And while her sisters took care of the bar, she would let the person who'd destroyed her place know how she felt.

* * *

SHE SAT ON the floor in the middle of the destruction in her apartment, her phone in front of her recording, the opening piano notes playing from the soundtrack she'd sing to. For the first and only time, she sang to Rick. Alanis Morissette's "Uninvited" perfectly captured her feelings and said everything she wanted him to know. She didn't want him. He'd come uninvited and unwanted into her life. And while she—anyone— would appreciate the interest in her, he was not allowed to cross the line and assume she wanted his attention.

And though the song ended with a line that conveyed she needed time to think, she changed it, reiterating that he was not welcome.

The song was dark and filled with her anger and her decisive message.

She posted it without any words to her followers about why she'd chosen it. They'd know. Because minutes later, *he* was the first to respond in the comments.

LyRick: I see right through this. You don't want to want me. You just can't help yourself. You say go away, but then you invite me to write and spend time with you, and you look at me and I know you feel something. You just don't want to admit it. Next time you see me, it will be the same. You won't be able to help yourself. You'll be nice. You'll pull me in. Next time, I won't let go.

Sonya22: Dude! Get over yourself!

Songwriter4life: Beautifully haunting rendition. Luv it!

BrazilBabe10: Epic! And if you're actually sending a message to someone . . . RUN! You don't want someone like this in your life.

LyRick: Fuck off. You don't know me or what Lyric and I have together.

More wonderfully appreciative comments about the song and her singing came in after Rick's comment to @BrazilBabe10. Lyric usually stayed online and chatted with others, but tonight, she sent one last message to Rick and blocked him, then closed out of the app and went to work on cleaning up the mess he'd made of her apartment long into the early morning light.

Unable to sleep, she threw out all that was broken and salvaged the pieces of her life she'd bought and collected as she had grown into her independence and made a home for herself in a cozy space she called her own.

Until now it had been her sanctuary. A place where she made music and her life.

Now it felt stained by the person who had violated her privacy and home.

No, she couldn't sleep, so she made a fire, sat on the floor, her knees pulled to her chest, and stared at the flames waiting for another day to begin, hoping it would be better. Praying M would come home and ease her weary mind and heart.

Chapter Twenty

Viper walked out of the interrogation room with a lot more answers than questions this time around. He'd successfully completed the first part of the job. He'd met the husband who wanted his wife killed, accepted payment for the job, and arrested the guy for hiring him to kill his wife. Now all he had to do was wait for tomorrow when they set the scene to make it look like the wife had been killed. He'd send Maria a fake picture along with links to fake-news reports, showing her he'd successfully done the job, uncover who all the players were in the scheme back at the Wild Wolves MC, arrest them, and be done with this for good.

It was nearly dawn. He was tired. All he wanted to do was call Lyric and hear her voice, but she was probably sound asleep after her shift at the bar ended hours ago.

"Good work in there. You got him to tell you everything about how he set up the meeting." Nick looked pleased.

Viper felt drained but also excited that this was almost over. "We'll get the rest done tomorrow—which I guess is actually today at this point. How's the wife?"

"Devastated. Angry. Hurt. I think she'd like to set up a hit on her husband."

"I would, too, if I was her." He held out his hand. "Do you have my phone?"

Nick pulled it out of his pocket and handed it over.

Viper tapped in his code and saw the text notification from Lyric. He smiled and pulled it up.

"I take it that grin means—" Nick cut the teasing comment short at the face Viper made when the picture she'd sent shocked him.

"What the . . . If that asshole hurt her . . ."

"Is Lyric hurt?" Nick asked.

Viper quickly showed Nick the photo of her destroyed place, then called her.

Nick kept close, a worried look on his face.

"You're up early," Lyric said by way of hello.

"I haven't slept yet."

"Me either." The weary words made him even angrier.

"Are you okay? What happened?"

"The picture doesn't do justice to what he did to my place."

"I take it you weren't there." He breathed a sigh of relief.

"Best we can tell, based on the surveillance footage, which I didn't know existed until my sister told me you went to Jax and asked him to set it up—"

"Because I was worried that asshole wouldn't leave you alone. And look what he did."

"It was very sweet. I appreciate it. But it didn't help in this case because he had to have done it while I was at your place."

Thank God she'd been safe in his bed with him. "You're sure?"

"Yep. Cops think so, too."

"Good. You called them. Then, this is documented and on the record. Did they arrest him?"

"No. He claims he didn't do it. There's no evidence yet to support my claim that he did. We'll see if the cops get any fingerprint matches. Doesn't really matter, though. After the threatening texts he left me last night and my interactions with him today, I know he did it."

He went eerily still. "What happened today?"

Nick frowned. He could hear everything, since they were standing so close, even though Viper hadn't put the phone on Speaker.

Lyric sighed but didn't say anything for a second before she admitted, "I tried to be nice."

He completely understood. "You're too nice sometimes."

"Yeah, well, it bit me in the ass again." She told him about her day with Rick and how he reacted to her not wanting to write with him anymore or let him perform at the bar. "You know what I like about you? You never tell me what to do or how to feel."

"You've got that covered, Angel. Where are you?" He needed to know she was safe.

"I just finished cleaning up my place about half an hour ago. There's not much left. It's going to cost a small fortune to replace my bed and furniture, all my dishes." The words were so filled with grief and heartache he felt his chest tighten in sympathy.

"Who's there with you? Aria? Melody? Jax?" He hoped one or all of them had stayed with her.

"Aria and Melody agreed to keep this quiet until the morning. They closed up the bar, helped me, then went home."

"You're alone." He didn't mean to raise his voice or sound angry, but it scared the hell out of him to think of her as a sitting duck.

"Me and the cop in his patrol car downstairs."

He breathed a sigh of relief. "You shouldn't be alone."

"That's what the first cop said, so he left another one with me."

"Why didn't Aria or Melody stay?"

"Because I don't like to cry in front of anyone, and I needed some time alone to be angry without anyone seeing it."

He felt that like a punch to the chest. "Are you mad I'm not there?"

"That goes in the sad column. But I understand. You're busy. I'm glad you called. It helps."

"Not enough. I hate that I'm not there."

Nick squeezed his shoulder, then walked away, leaving Viper alone to talk to Lyric in private.

Viper ducked into an empty conference room at the police station they were working out of and sat at the table. "I'm sorry, sweetheart." He meant that more than he could express. "What do you need? What can I do?"

"Tell me the truth."

His heart jackhammered in his chest. "About what?"

"I have to buy all new stuff, so maybe you can help me decide what to get. What's your favorite color?"

His adrenaline rush waned and he smiled. She wanted the truth about him, but in a different way than he thought. "Blue and green."

"I should probably upgrade to a king-size bed if you're going to be in it."

He liked where this was going. "We definitely need a big bed."

"Do you like white dishes or colorful ones?"

"My mom has white dishes, but they have different

patterns. Some have waves or lines or textures around the edges. They're classic. Colored dishes sometimes make the food look weird to me."

"Okay. I'm learning a lot here. Sheets. Super soft or crisp?"

"I like you on top of me best, but otherwise, it better be soft."

"Do you sleep hot or cold?"

"Can we get off the bed thing? It's getting uncomfortable here." He adjusted his hard length but didn't bother to wipe away the images of her in bed with him. He liked them too much. "As long as you're in bed with me, I'll be the happiest man alive."

"I've been thinking about buying a house. Maybe now is the time to do it. What kind of house would you like?"

"I told you I have a cabin near my family," he reminded her. "It's got this great river-rock fireplace and all this wood. I like it, but sometimes I wish it was lighter and brighter. It's also small. A house should be big enough for a family."

There was a short pause before she asked, "Do you want kids?"

"Yeah. I do. I sometimes feel much older than my age and wish I had a wife, kids, a home." He could picture her, their kids, a house full of laughter and love and music.

"Do you want to know why I never moved to Nashville and pursued a singing career?"

He'd like to know, because it had crossed his mind that she might want to do that someday, and what would that mean for them? "Why?"

"Because I like a simple life. I want it centered around family and love and music."

"I think about that kind of life all the time now."

"Are you a cat or dog person?"

"Both, I guess. I grew up always having a dog in the house. We had barn cats, but I didn't spend much time with them. Why? Do you want one?"

"Of each? Yes."

He chuckled. "What kind of dog?"

"A sweet one. But I want a black cat. I'll call her Pepper."

"If we get a white dog, you could call it Salt."

"Maybe Sugar," she suggested. "I think it would be sweet to hear you call the dog that all the time. 'Come here, Sugar.'"

She always found a way to make him grin and laugh.

"How about I save that one for you?"

"You don't have to call. I'm always being pulled to you."

"You've got this hold on me I can't explain. And I like it."

"Yeah. Me, too."

"You sound tired."

"I am, but the sun's up now, and I can't sleep. Not here. Not without you."

It killed him to hear her say that, but at the same time he loved it that she wanted him there. "I'm sorry, Angel. If I could be there, I would."

"I know. Stop apologizing. It's not necessary. I just want you to know that's how I feel. I want us to always be honest."

"Then, tell me what you're really feeling and thinking about what happened at your place."

"I'm scared."

He knew it but didn't like hearing it one bit.

"Mostly, I'm mad. Why do this to me? What did I do to deserve this? I never asked him to come. I never gave him any signal that I wanted him in my life. I tried to be nice. But look what that got me."

"It's not your fault. And being nice got you a family who loves you, friends who are there for you, and me."

"I like you. Him, I want gone. For good. You should have seen him last night, telling me he didn't do this and that I needed to give him a chance."

"It sounds like you already did." Viper didn't like the situation at all and knew that it could quickly escalate. "Please don't go anywhere alone. If you feel threatened or scared, call the cops. I'll be back as soon as I can. I hope you know I'm always thinking about you, and I want to be there more than anything. If something happened to you . . . I can't even think it."

"I keep reminding myself, it's just stuff. I can replace it. I'm still here. I'm fine."

"That's what's most important."

"I'll be really happy to see you when I see you."

"Same. If I can speed things up here, I will."

"Do what you have to do. I'll be here when you get back."

He didn't want her to know how scared he was that she wouldn't be waiting for him.

"I think I'll go out to the ranch, ride my horse, and talk to my parents and brother about what's going on. Maybe do some online shopping while I'm cooking for tonight's crowd."

"Friday night at the bar is always packed."

"Busy is good. I won't be in my head. Time will go by quickly, and I'll be closer to seeing you."

"You're off on Sunday. If I'm back, let's spend time together."

"Sounds good to me."

He yawned, the long night catching up to him.

"Go get some sleep. Be safe." She always said that to him, even though she probably thought he was doing something shady.

"You be safe, Angel. I'll never forgive myself if something happens to you and I'm not there to stop it."

"You can't be with me all the time. Bad stuff happens when you least expect it. At least in this case, I'm expecting it. I'll be on guard. I promise."

"I feel like if I let you get off the phone, I'll spend every second worried about you."

"I can't help that, but if it helps, all you have to do is look at the tracker on your phone and you'll know where I am."

"Yeah, but not how you are."

"Lonely without you."

He heard something more in those words. "Isn't that a song?"

"If it's not, it should be."

"I want you writing happy songs."

"I'm working on one inspired by you."

"Yeah? What's it called?"

"'What's Your Name?'"

He chuckled. "I can't wait to hear it."

"Are you going to answer that soon?"

"I like that you call me Mine. But yes, I'll tell you everything soon."

"Something to look forward to. Have a good day, M."

"Have a good day, Angel." Seconds after he hung up, she sent him a text.

LYRIC: It feels like you were always meant to be mine.

He clicked the link on the Maddie and Tae song "Strangers" and listened to the words that fit them so well, grinning that he knew exactly what the duo was singing about. It felt like he and Lyric had always known each other and were meant to be. That everything in their lives had simply been leading them toward each other.

He'd never believed in such things. And then he met her.

He texted her a link to one of his favorite songs. "You Make It Easy," by Jason Aldean.

VIPER: I never thought I'd find someone like you.
LYRIC: You did. And I'm not going anywhere.
See you soon.

He hoped he could hold on to her long enough to finish his business so he was free to be with her. So he could be the man she saw behind the face he showed the world right now.

He didn't want to lose her because of his job.

Or someone's obsession.

Chapter Twenty-One

VIPER: Your talent blows my mind
VIPER: That song Uninvited
VIPER: Haunting powerful
VIPER: Dangerous! ☹
VIPER: You sent him a message but he's not listening because it's not what he wants to hear
VIPER: He deserved it absolutely.
VIPER: But now I'm really worried. And you should be, too.
VIPER: And that's our thing! I don't want you sending musical messages to anyone but me
VIPER: Be careful. You poke a bear, they bite.
VIPER: I miss you like crazy

Lyric read the messages, knowing M wanted her to be prepared for the repercussions of what she'd done last night. Maybe it was stupid, and yes, she'd let her anger override good sense, but she'd earned a little retaliation after what that asshole had done to her place. Okay, stupid, yes. Her life wasn't worth the damage to her place.

Reading between the lines of those text messages, she appreciated that M hadn't gone ballistic on her for doing it. Though, it was clear he didn't like it or that she'd used a song to communicate with Rick.

That was their thing. And she hated that M thought she did that with everyone. She'd set him straight on that.

LYRIC: I miss you like crazy
LYRIC: I'm done with him and all about you!
LYRIC: You get all my good musical messages and my heart with them
LYRIC: Be safe
LYRIC: I can't wait to kiss you again ♥

She finished off her third cup of coffee and tried not to think about Rick. If he'd tried to send her any online messages or texts after she posted the song, they were blocked.

She was done with him. At least, she hoped so.

But hoping wasn't reality, and she needed to remain on alert for whatever he had planned next.

Chapter Twenty-Two

Today was not Lyric's day. Her parents were upset about the break-in and destruction of her property. They wanted her to skip work and move back in with them. At the same time, they wanted Rick out of the cabin. He'd apparently not returned last night or this morning. When she went into the cabin to check the place out, she found several odd things that belonged to her. Things she hadn't noticed were missing. A hair tie. Her favorite pen. One of her notebooks filled with songs and ideas, along with some personal musings.

She hated that he had seen her private thoughts. Even worse, some of them were about M.

She didn't like him knowing she had feelings for M. It could set him off. Again.

To send a clear message, she'd packed up his stuff and left his bag outside the cabin door.

When she got back to the bar and started the barbecuing and cooking for the big Friday-night crowd they always anticipated, she found that both barbecues and the smokers had been filled with trash from the dumpster. A raccoon had gotten into one of the barbecues and didn't want to leave. It took her an hour to clean it all up and get the meat cooking.

It didn't take a genius to wonder who'd vandalized her stuff.

She sent the pictures she took to Officer Bowers and told him she'd be by to file a report.

Then her mom texted that Rick had been by the cabin, taken his stuff, and left without anyone seeing him.

The band she'd hired to play tonight came down with a case of food poisoning from the place where they'd had breakfast, so she had to scramble to find a band available and near enough to get here on time. She did it, but it was a lot of calls and groveling on short notice. Plus, she had to pay the band extra for gas since they were coming in from Colorado.

She was so happy when the bar opened and she could focus on serving up orders. And since it was Friday, she had a few people in need who stopped by to pick up groceries for the weekend when their kids didn't get school meals for free and they needed the extra help.

But when she spotted Mindy sporting a black eye and busted lip at the back door and not wearing a coat or even a sweater over her stained white T-shirt, she got mad, but she didn't let it show.

She rushed to Mindy and pulled her in the back door. "Hey, you look like you could use something hot to eat and drink. Take a seat at the table. I'll get you whatever you'd like, plus a hot coffee or tea."

Mindy bit her lip, winced, and shook her head. "The kids are in the truck. I just . . . I hoped . . . They're hungry."

"Okay. No problem. You know you can always come to me for help."

Mindy kept her gaze on the floor, her arms wrapped

around her middle, not to get warm but in a protective way that crushed Lyric's heart.

"Let's get the kids. They can warm up, eat something good while I pack up some food for you to take home."

"He wouldn't let me bring them in. Can you hurry? He's not in a real good mood. We couldn't pay the heating bill. Again."

"Okay. Sit down. Get warm. I'll be right back." Lyric turned to her staff. "Grady, would you take over for me? I need to do something." She turned to Christie. "Can you get Mindy a hot tea in a to-go cup and two hot chocolates for her kids?"

Mindy shifted from one foot to the other. "You don't have to do that."

"It'll only take a minute." She rushed out into the bar, grabbed one of their large glasses, then went to the sound system and cut the music.

Everyone stopped at the sudden absence of the blaring song.

"Listen up," she shouted. "We have a family with two small kids who needs to pay their heating bill. Who's got a few bucks they can spare to help out?"

Melody came by, grabbed the glass, then made her way through the bar, collecting the money people pulled out and held up.

"Thank you, everyone, for your generosity!" Lyric went back to the kitchen and found Mindy pacing by the back door.

"You didn't need to do that."

"These are your neighbors. They want to help. So let them." She went into the pantry and grabbed the cash out of her purse to add to whatever Melody had collected. Then she snagged a plastic bag and started filling it with food, enough for a couple of days, maybe more. She set it down beside Mindy. "Let me get you some meat to go with all this. Plus, I made mac and cheese. I know your kids will love that."

Mindy suddenly reached out and grabbed her arm. The intensity rolling off her made Lyric's heart race.

She stilled and gentled her voice. "What is it? You can tell me."

Mindy's eyes filled with desperation. "I'm pregnant again."

She wanted to congratulate Mindy, but the utter shock and fear on her face made that seem inappropriate right now. "What do you want to do?" Lyric had no judgment for the poor woman, only understanding that she was doing the best she could and that she was brave to come to Lyric and ask for help.

"I don't want to go back out there. I don't want to keep doing this. I don't want another child, not when I know what's happening to me and my kids will happen to them." Mindy shook her head, silent tears streaming down her face. "I can't. But what am I supposed to do?"

"You say the word, I will go out there and get your kids. I will call the cops, and you can press charges against him for hurting you and your kids. I know it doesn't mean he'll be gone for good, but it will be enough time for me to get you the help you need. There are places you can go, with your kids, that will help you start over. I have the names and numbers ready for you. We've talked about this before. I will help you. If you want it."

Mindy didn't move, she simply let the tears fall as she thought about her decision.

Lyric held her breath, hoping this time Mindy took the hand offered to her.

The agreement came with a single nod, Mindy's gaze still on the floor, but her answer clear.

"You stay in here. I will go and get the kids." First, she went back out to the bar and got John, their bouncer. Two hundred and twenty pounds of muscle, a man no one wanted to mess with.

"What's up?" John asked as she approached him.

"I have a situation."

"That asshole back?"

"No. A different one. Mindy's in the kitchen. Her husband and kids are in the truck out back. Call the cops. She's ready to file charges. I'm going to get the kids. He won't see me as a threat. I don't want him using the kids to get the cops to back off and Mindy to back down again."

"I'm with you. But he starts anything, I'm going to bust him in the mouth like he does his wife."

"Let's try to do this in a calm and rational way. The kids have seen enough violence."

John waved her on, pulled out his phone, and called as he followed her back to the kitchen.

Lyric caught Mindy's fearful look and reassured her with a smile. "I'll be right back with the kids. No matter what, stay in here. He sees you, he'll know something's up."

Mindy nodded, backing into the wall and sinking to the floor, wrapping her arms around her legs.

John stood next to her, keeping a distance so she didn't get spooked by his presence.

Melody walked in just before Lyric walked out the back door. "I collected two hundred and forty-seven dollars."

Lyric smiled. "I've got thirty-two to add." She

handed the money over to Melody, then whispered, "I'm going for the kids. Back in a minute."

"Be careful."

Everyone knew about Mindy's situation. The cops wouldn't be surprised to get a call about her.

Lyric took a deep breath and walked out the back door ready to face off with a guy who thought he could get away with hitting his wife and kids. Well, not tonight. She walked right up to the truck and opened the back door. The two little ones, five and seven, stared at her wide-eyed and nervous.

"What the fuck do you think you're doing?"

She smelled the booze and felt the hostility coming off Tim. She ignored him and focused on the kids. "Hey, you two, your mom is waiting inside for your order to be ready. I thought you might want to come in for some hot chocolate." She didn't wait for an answer and pulled the five-year-old little girl out of the truck. She wasn't even buckled in.

The boy slipped out the other side like a lion was after him.

By the time Lyric turned with the little girl to set her on her feet, her brother was already there to grab his sister's hand and pull her toward the bar.

Lyric met Tim's icy glare. "Can I get you some coffee while you wait?"

Tim opened the truck door.

She backed away, glancing over her shoulder for just a second to whisper "Run" to the kids.

They took off.

She squared off with Tim.

"Where is my wife?"

She kept calm. "Getting the food."

"What's taking her so damn long?"

She shrugged. "We're packing it up so you have enough for a few days."

He took a menacing step closer. "You think you're better than me because we came here for food. I don't need your judgment when I'm trying to feed my kids."

Lyric was so happy to hear the kitchen door slam. The kids were safely inside.

"You've got great kids." She tried to keep things positive, because she was the one facing off with a predator.

Tim glanced at the closed door, then her. "What did you say to her? Get her out here. Now!"

"She'll be out in a minute."

A look came over Tim that didn't bode well for her. "You can't keep me from her or my kids."

She held up a hand. "I just wanted to know if you want a cup of coffee."

"I'm getting my wife." He barreled toward her. "You can't stop me."

Lyric held up her hands, thinking she could try. All she needed was just a little time for the cops to show up. "Tim, come on. She'll be out in a minute. Let her finish her tea."

"Fuck that." He rushed her.

She grabbed onto his coat sleeves as he took her by the sweatshirt and tossed her aside. She fell onto her hip on the cement and spun around from the momentum, scraping up her hand as she pushed up and ran forward to block his path again. "Stop. You can't go in there."

Tim just kept moving. "The hell I can't."

Lyric stepped right in his way again and held her ground.

He grabbed her with one hand and backhanded

her with the other, but she saw the blow coming and moved to avoid it, ending up with a cut on her cheek from his ring. Warm blood trickled down her skin. Her face throbbed from the glancing blow that could have been a hell of a lot worse.

He shoved her aside again with a low growl.

Fucking asshole. She lost it. As he passed her, she kicked him in the back of the leg, sending him to his knees. The second his hands hit the pavement, she shoved her foot into his side to send him over onto his back. She stood over him. "Stay down, or I'll make you."

He swiped a hand out to grab her foot.

She jumped back out of his way.

Jax and John came out the kitchen door.

Tim saw them, scrambled up, and rushed her again.

She waited, knowing this could go very wrong, but bided her time until he was close enough to duck and use her legs to launch herself in a crouched position into his midsection, she then lifted with her legs and sent him over her shoulder and back, flipping to the ground.

She'd done it with Jax a dozen times when they were kids. They didn't roughhouse like that anymore, but it paid off now.

Adrenaline gave her strength and masked the pain in her face and sore wrist.

John quickly grabbed Tim and rolled him onto his stomach. He pulled the guy's hands behind his back and held them between Tim's shoulder blades. Every time Tim struggled against John's hold, it hurt Tim's shoulders more.

"You're going to dislocate your arm if you don't be still," she warned, brushing her fingers against her wet cheek.

Jax cupped her face and checked out the cut. "Damn it, Lyric. Why didn't you just wait for the cops?"

"Because I wasn't going to let him near Mindy or those kids. Not after she asked for my help. She needs to see that someone will stand up to him."

Jax shook his head. "You need to go to the hospital."

"I'm fine."

The cops showed up.

"Please take care of that," she begged Jax. "Let me go check on Mindy."

"I don't think the kids should see you looking like this."

She hadn't thought about that. "I'll go around the front and clean this up in the bathroom before I see them."

Jax raised a brow. "You sure you're okay?"

"A little shaken," she admitted, her heart pounding in her chest. Mostly from adrenaline, but there was still some fear in there, too.

"Take the rest of the night off. You need to rest and get some sleep."

"I'm fine. The buzz will keep me going for a little while longer."

Jax didn't look convinced but left her anyway to deal with the cops and a very loud drunk.

"I didn't do anything," Tim bellowed.

The cop just kept reciting his rights to him as they led him to the patrol car, his hands shackled at his back.

"This is your fault, you bitch."

She grinned at him. "I'll add my charges to your wife's."

"We need to get your statement," the cop called out to her.

"I'll be back in a few minutes." She made her way

around the side of the building. Distracted by her aching face, she pressed her hand to her throbbing cheek and wasn't really paying attention to her surroundings, until she was suddenly spotlighted in the headlights of the car beside her, the engine revved, and the car sped forward. She had only a split second to think and try to jump out of the way, but she mostly ended up with her butt on the hood, momentum throwing her back into the windshield as she slid and fell off the side of the car as it turned out of the parking spot and sped off.

She landed at a weird angle, wrenching her back and hitting her head on the running board on the side of a truck. Her head swam and her vision blurred as she sank into the ground, her body going limp.

Voices rang out, some close, others far off.

And then Aria's face, her eyes filled with horror, came into her watery view. "Lyric? Can you hear me?"

"Hmm." It felt hard to think, let alone talk.

"Call an ambulance," she ordered someone. That was Aria, always taking charge.

Which meant Lyric didn't have to do anything, so she let the dark swallow her.

Chapter Twenty-Three

Viper adjusted the gun on his belt and scratched at the mask covering most of his face, impatient to be done with this case. The wife he was supposed to kill tonight stood on a chair in the garage, her head bowed forward, a rope around her neck and draped over the beam the automatic garage-door opener was secured to.

"Try not to move," the crime-scene guy instructed as he snapped another photograph getting most of her in the picture, except her feet on the chair. "That'll do it."

They'd spent the last ten minutes setting this scene with the wife's enthusiastic help. Brave lady. Still, all this for one picture.

The tech handed him the phone. Viper checked the picture, thought it looked legit, and texted it to Maria with the message *Done*.

He slipped the burner into his pocket and glanced across the garage at Nick. "We good?"

"The husband is in custody. Ambulance is on the way. The fake-news report links are all set. Maria clicks on any of the ones you send her, or googles the victim's name and suicide or hanging, she'll see what we want her to see."

"Great. Then, I'm heading back."

"To meet Maria, or someone else?" Nick asked just as Viper's phone pinged with an incoming text.

He ignored his brother's pointed question and pulled out the burner. No message there, so he pulled out his cell and saw the text notification from Lyric. He was about to put his phone away and look at it later, but something set off an alarm inside him and Rick popped into his head.

He pulled up the text.

LYRIC: I know for sure your day was better than mine.

It took a second for the picture to pop up.

"Holy fuck." His heart stuttered, then kicked into high gear as his adrenaline and fear surged. He couldn't believe the bruises and cut on her beautiful face.

LYRIC: It looks bad, but I'm fine. Nothing broken. Mild concussion. A drunk and a car. 2 separate things.
LYRIC: Hell of a day.

Nick, concerned, came over and read over his shoulder. "What the hell does she mean, two separate things?"

"That's what I'd like to know. I need to get there. Now."

"Yeah. Whatever you need."

Viper knew Nick would get the ball rolling on that, and sure enough he pulled out his own phone to make it happen, while Viper called Lyric.

"Hey, this is Melody."

Viper's heart sank and panic rose when Lyric's sister answered instead of her. "Why can't she answer?"

"She asked me to text you because she's a little out of it right now. In fact, she just drifted off again."

"Tell me everything," he ordered.

Melody told him the whole story about the drunk wife-beater and the subsequent car accident that had happened not more than an hour ago.

"Was it just a random accident as she walked around the bar to go in the front?" He didn't think so.

"No. The video is clear. Someone intentionally hit her."

Rage swept through him. "I want to see that video."

"I'll send you the one of her kicking the drunk's ass I took, but the other . . . I'll have to get it from Jax."

"Fine. Can you put the phone to her ear so I can say something to her even if she is out of it?"

"I think she'd really like to hear your voice. Go ahead."

"Angel, baby, it's me." His chest ached with all the sorrow he felt for her and not being there. "I'm so sorry I'm not with you, but I'm on my way. I'm leaving right now."

"Mmm. M. It h-hurts."

"I know. I'm sorry. I'll be there soon." His throat clogged with emotion.

"She's asleep again," Melody informed him. "But she heard you. That's good."

"What did the doctor say?"

"The worst of it is a mild concussion. They think it will be gone by morning. She's pretty banged up, though. She rolled up on the car hood, hit the windshield, and bounced off onto the pavement. It left a lot of bruises. And that drunk deadbeat smacked her hard."

"Yeah, the asshole's been practicing on his wife." Viper would like to get his hands on the guy and show him what it feels like to be hit like that.

"I hope they throw the book at him for what he did to her and Lyric. I don't even want to know what he's done to his kids. But I'm so proud of Lyric for standing up for them."

"So am I. Are you going to stay with her?"

"Jax and Aria are covering the bar. Mom and Dad are here, too, though they stepped out to get some air. They were really panicked when they got here. They needed a minute after seeing her."

Viper felt for them. He needed more than a minute to get over seeing Lyric's face. "I'm on my way back. It may be a few hours until I can get there. If she wakes up again, tell her I'm coming. I'll be there as soon as I can."

"You're a good guy, Viper. She didn't want to worry you. I convinced her to tell you what happened, mostly because I could see in her eyes that she wanted you."

"I'm more than worried. I hate being away from her."

"Is it going to be a problem if someone sees you with her?"

His gut knotted. Their relationship was becoming the worst kept secret, even if he trusted her family to keep it quiet. "Don't tell anyone I'm coming."

"Okay."

"I don't know what she's told you . . ."

"If she thinks you're worth all this, then we know you are."

He appreciated the benefit of the doubt when he hadn't yet been able to prove to them he'd treat Lyric right. "If I didn't have all this other stuff happening, I could be what she sees in me."

"Then, finish whatever it is and be with her." Melody made it sound so simple.

And he was so close.

"The nurse is here to check on her. Gotta go." Melody hung up, leaving him feeling helpless.

Nick didn't waste words. "Plane will be ready when you get to the airport. Once you land, Hawk will be there to helicopter you right to the hospital."

"For real?" He couldn't believe his cousin, Hawk, would do that.

Nick's gaze filled with concern. "She looked really bad."

He didn't need the reminder. The image of her was burned into his mind.

His phone pinged with an incoming text. He tapped the video and watched the scene play out between Lyric and the obviously drunk and belligerent man who was taller and heavier than her.

"Damn." Nick winced. "She took his ass down."

"Not before he hit her."

"I think she might be able to take you." Nick grinned and smacked him on the back. "I like her."

"I'm in love with her," he admitted to his brother, knowing it like he knew his name. Feeling it like a living thing inside him.

"Yeah. I got that already. Go. There's an agent out front ready to take you to the airport."

"Thank you, Nick, for understanding and making this happen."

"Nothing you wouldn't do for me."

Viper gave his brother a bear hug, then turned and sprinted out of the garage to the waiting car, leaving his brother with the confused, distraught, and angry wife, who had to fake her own death to keep his cover intact.

He should have thanked her for her cooperation.

Nick would do it for him. His brother always had his back. Same went for him with Nick.

Now all he had to do was prove to Lyric that he had hers.

He desperately wanted to see the video of her getting hit by the car. He wanted to know if Rick was behind the wheel. It could be just some drunk leaving the bar, but he didn't think so. Their bouncer was good at spotting the ones who shouldn't be driving and stopping them.

And the way Melody described things, it sounded intentional.

Which meant whoever did it could come back and try again.

Chapter Twenty-Four

Viper saw the hospital helipad and breathed a sigh of relief they'd finally made it. He waited for his cousin to set the helicopter down before he turned to him, talking through the headsets they both wore. "Thank you for doing this."

"You're family," Hawk said simply. "You need anything else, you let me know."

"This was huge." Viper leaned over and gave his cousin a hug and a hearty smack on the back. "You need me for anything, *you* let me know."

Hawk nodded. "I can't wait to meet your girl."

"I hope it's sooner rather than later. But I've got to finish a job first."

"I know. But at some point, you've got to put yourself first." Hawk knew what he was talking about. He clamped his hand on Viper's shoulder. "Go see her. You'll feel better. Then get the fucker who did this, and you'll know she's safe and you can breathe again."

Of course Hawk understood exactly how he felt.

Viper didn't waste any more time and rushed out of the helicopter, ducking from the rotor wash as he ran for the door where someone from the hospital greeted him. He bet Hawk had to get clearance to land here and made sure they knew he was coming.

"She's stable and resting comfortably in room 311." The woman led him into the back of the ER and right to the elevator.

Entering it, he thanked the woman, then hit the third-floor button. Two floors felt like an eternity. As the elevator doors opened, he rushed down the hall, toward the nurses' station.

A nurse stood up. "For Lyric Wilde?"

He nodded.

She pointed to the room across from her.

He rushed in and found Jax in a chair next to the bed, his arms folded over his chest, head bowed forward as he slept the wee hours away.

But it was Lyric who held his attention. She looked so fragile and still, a bandage on her cheek, the other side of her face swollen and beginning to bruise. The stitches on her wrist from the cut she'd gotten before weren't covered anymore. Whatever other injuries she sustained were either covered by the gown and blanket or weren't visible at all.

He ached for her and rushed to the side of the bed and took her hand. He wanted to wrap her in his arms but wasn't sure where or how badly she was hurt, so he restrained the overwhelming desire to hold her, felt the loss of that opportunity, and blamed the person who put her there for taking that from both of them.

He leaned over her, so she'd feel him close, and whispered in her ear, "I'm here, Angel."

She immediately turned her face and pressed it to his cheek.

It had to hurt, so he kissed her on the forehead, pressing his lips to her skin for a long moment and brushing his fingers through her hair. "I'm here, baby. You rest."

Her fingers closed in his jacket and she held him close. "Stay. Please stay." The plea in her eyes intensified his guilt.

"I'm right here." He kissed her on the lips, softly and with everything he wanted her to know. She was precious to him. He didn't want to leave her ever again, but he'd have to, far too soon.

She looked up at him. "You look tired."

"You took ten years off my life, then the trip here seemed to take forever."

"I think I heard a helicopter. Someone must be really hurt."

He stared down at her. "You are."

Confusion clouded her eyes. "You came by helicopter?"

"Yes. My cousin flew me, so I could get to you faster."

Tears filled, then spilled over her lashes. "That's really sweet."

He brushed his thumb along her temple. "I should have been here."

"You're here now." Lyric pushed herself up, making him move out of her way.

He sat on the edge of the bed, her hand in his. "Maybe you shouldn't move so much."

"Maybe you should shut up and hug me."

"I don't want to hurt you."

A tear slipped down her cheek. "I really don't care. I just want to be close to you."

He pulled her to him as she maneuvered her way into his lap. He wrapped her up and held her. It didn't surprise him that she clung to him, letting the tears fall for all she'd been through tonight. Some of it he was sure was relief that he was finally here. He'd seen a lot of victims hold it together, until they just couldn't anymore.

Jax put his hand on Viper's back. "I'll be in the waiting room down the hall. Take all the time you want. Come get me if you have to leave. She won't be alone, ever, until we get who did this."

"Thanks." Viper would talk to Jax later about protecting Lyric going forward. Right now, she needed him to be her boyfriend, not an FBI agent. He wanted to be so much more for her.

Alone, he held her until the tears faded, her breathing evened out, and she sat content in his arms.

"I don't know what happened." She sounded so confused.

"We don't have to talk about it right now." He wanted her to rest and feel safe. But he knew both those things would take time to come, because right now she was locked in the trauma of it all.

"I just wanted to help her."

"I know you did. You got the kids away from him. You kept them all safe. You called for help. You did everything right." And that asshole would pay for hurting all of them.

"I knew I needed to be careful. I saw it coming."

"And you stopped him." He held her tighter, seeing that man hit her all over again.

"Melody showed me the video. It felt like that was someone else."

He understood that, too. "Nick thinks you can take me."

She looked up at him. "You would never give me a reason to defend myself like that."

"Never." He kissed her softly to seal that promise. "All I want to do is take care of you."

"You're doing a really good job right now."

He found a grin. "You make it easy."

"I liked that song you sent me. It's one of my favorites."

He hadn't even realized his words were the song title. But he loved that she knew it and found comfort in it. "I like our song thing. It makes it a little easier for me to tell you how I feel. You're better at it than me."

"It says a lot that you rushed back here to be with me. I'm sorry I took you away from whatever you were doing."

"Don't be. I'd rather be with you."

"How did it go? Did you finish, or do you have to go back?"

"It went as planned. I don't have to go back, but I'm not done. Yet."

She snuggled closer. "What happens after it's over?"

"I tell you everything. And hopefully we stay together, only without all the secrets and subterfuge."

She eyed him, serious and concerned. "Do you think telling me the truth will make me break up with you?"

"No. It's not that," he assured her.

"Then, what is it?"

"I don't know. You've known me one way for months. I guess I'm not sure you'll like the real me."

"I know the real you. You're right here. *I* get the real you. Everyone else gets someone else. Viper is another part of you, but not the real you."

He didn't want to talk about it. "You need to get some sleep."

"Are you leaving?" Her body trembled.

"No." To prove it, he held her closer. "I'm not leaving. Not yet." He hated that he couldn't drop everything and stay with her indefinitely.

Someone knocked on the door, then pushed it open.

Viper nearly went for his gun hidden at his back, but relaxed when he saw a nurse.

Her eyes landed on them, Lyric in his lap. "Oh, sorry. I, uh, need to check her vitals."

Viper stood with Lyric in his arms, turned, laid her back in bed, and pulled the blanket up over her bruised legs, but not before he pulled the gown up and checked out the horrible bruise blooming on her hip and thigh. "Can we get some ice for this?"

"I didn't want to do it while she was trying to sleep, but since she's awake, it would be best to ice it again." The nurse checked Lyric's heart rate and blood pressure and asked her a bunch of questions to make sure she was oriented. Satisfied all was well, the nurse left to get the ice pack.

Lyric stared up at him. "I've never been in a helicopter. Was it fun?"

"It can be. The view is usually spectacular. But tonight, all I could think about was you and how long it was taking to get here."

"Does your cousin fly for a living?"

"Hawk is ex-military. He doesn't like to talk about his time overseas. Now he flies for fun and part-time doing search and rescue."

"Why were you in a helicopter the other times?"

"Uh . . . for work."

The nurse came back in, thankfully, giving him an out for having to tell Lyric he couldn't elaborate on that. At least, not right now. But he bet she was wondering why a guy who did construction would need to ride in a helicopter.

The nurse pulled the blanket back and gently placed the ice on the worst of the injury and used a rolled-up blanket to help keep the pack in place. "If you can take it, leave this on for about twenty minutes."

Lyric nodded, though she looked really uncomfortable and in pain.

The nurse left them alone again.

He sat next to her on the bed. "What can I do?"

She took his hand. "Tell me something real."

That was easy. "I'm seriously worried about you."

She squeezed his hand. "Tell me about you and Nick when you were little."

He loved that she was always trying to get to know him better. "He always thought he was the boss of me back then. He still thinks it now, though, technically, he is actually my boss."

"Really?"

He ignored that land mine and went on. "Nick is smart. Like, brilliant. He always did well in school without even trying. Me, I had to work at it, mostly because I was bored in school. I liked being in the action, so I played a lot of sports."

"What was your favorite?"

"Oddly enough, volleyball. Not on a team, but one-on-one."

"You like to win." She grinned.

"I like to strategize and beat my opponent. That's not to say I didn't do well on team sports."

She grinned, checking him out. "I bet you did better than well."

He tried to hold back a smile. "It made me popular."

"I bet you never had trouble getting a date."

He kissed her hand. "I really want to take you out on a real date."

"Dinner at my place was a real date," she reminded him.

He appreciated her so much for enjoying whatever time they spent together. He went back to their original topic. "Nick had a single-minded mission in life. He knew what he wanted early. I came into it later and discovered a skillset I didn't really know I could use."

"And what was that?"

"I'm a good liar."

She cocked an eyebrow. "Why would you need to be a good liar?"

He didn't like the thoughtful way she looked at him, like she was putting pieces together. "Never mind about that for now. The thing is, Nick and I, we're close. Always have been, even though we're not really alike. I irritate him. A lot sometimes. Because he likes to stick to the rules. And I sometimes color outside the lines."

"Aria is like Nick, I think. Smart. Logical. She likes things to add up. Routine is her best friend. Melody is a live-for-today-not-what-could-happen-tomorrow kind of person. Jax is as steady as they come. But he can be fierce when there's a threat to someone he loves."

"What do you think I am?"

"You're Jax on steroids. You have conviction. Truth matters to you. You don't tolerate people who hurt other people, yet you don't seek retribution, you want justice." She'd nailed him.

"You don't think I want to punish the asshole who hurt you?"

"Do you want to hurt them?"

"I'd like to, very much." Even though he knew it wouldn't solve anything.

"But would you?" she asked but knew the answer, because she really did get him.

"Not unless I had to."

"One look at you, what you'd like to do to them written all over your face, they'd know better than to take you on."

That gave him pause. "Do you think I'm scary?"

"Not to me. I don't think there's anything in you that could hurt me."

"I think you could take me down with a few words." *I never want to see you again* came to mind.

"I'd need a damn good reason to ignore my heart and say something to hurt you. And if I ever did, I'd be lying. Or have a really severe head injury. I'd pretty much have to be insane."

He chuckled, and she smiled. It felt good to sit and talk like this.

"So you're thinking about keeping me." He hoped forever.

"I decided I wanted you long before you stood me up for dinner."

He frowned, feeling incredibly sorry about that. "I didn't know it was a date. I apologized. And I've wanted you since the moment you caught me staring at you and you smiled at me."

She grinned again. "Because you looked so intense, and I thought if I smiled, you'd smile back, but you looked even more disgruntled that I smiled, and I thought, *he doesn't want to like me, but he does.*"

"I did. I do. In fact, I more than like you."

"I felt that when we made love. I feel it when you kiss me. I feel it even when you're not here and I know you want to be here."

He brushed his hand down her long hair. "You can't be this perfect."

"I appreciate that you think I am, even though you know I'm not."

He leaned in and looked her right in the eye. "You're perfect for me."

She put her hand on his cheek, and he leaned into her touch. "That's the nicest thing you've said to me."

"I want to be everything you need me to be."

"You are, and more. I can't believe you're here. And I also knew that if you could be, you would find a way. And you did."

"I need you to know that I will always be there for you."

She brushed her thumb across his cheek. "People can't live up to *always*. I don't expect you to."

"You should be able to expect me to show up when you're hurt."

"You know that thing you're keeping from me? Is it a good reason why you wouldn't come to me if I needed you?"

He didn't know how to answer that for her, except that he truly believed she'd understand. "I already know you'd accept it."

"Okay, then. Relax."

"I don't know how you're taking this so well and in stride."

"I'm a songwriter. Words have meaning to me."

"I get that."

"Which is why you've been so careful about what you say and how you say it." She had a point.

He knew she'd pay attention to what he said. She listened. She looked for the meaning and feeling in everything.

She grabbed her phone from the bedside table and scrolled to a song.

"This is one of my all-time favorites. I always wanted this song to be what I had in my life. And then you walked into my bar, and I couldn't take my eyes off you. Then you walked into my place and told me that you wanted me, and I knew I didn't want to ever lose you and the way you made me feel. Happy. Loved. Safe."

She showed him her phone.

"Safe," by Katie Armiger.

And then she played the song and it became one of his favorites, too, because every line felt like his heart speaking to her.

When the song ended, he wrapped her in his arms, held her close, and said what he couldn't hold inside anymore. "I love you."

She turned and faced him, her gaze steady and filled with everything he felt inside for her reflected back at him. "I love you, too."

They shared a kiss that was soft and warm and so filled with love that it enveloped them like a cocoon.

He leaned back and looked at her beautiful face, amazed she loved him the way he loved her.

"I wish we were somewhere else," she whispered.

"Me, too. But you need to rest now." He brushed his hand over her head. "Sleep. I'll be here when you wake up."

"Promise."

"I swear."

The second he finished speaking, her eyes drooped shut. He kept her hand in his and managed to put the bedside bar down, lie on his side next to her, and enjoy being close to her.

He must have drifted off, because the next thing he knew someone was gently nudging his shoulder.

"Wake up, man. You need to go." Jax sounded urgent.

Viper came awake all at once. "What is it?"

"My parents will be here any minute."

He didn't see the big deal, but then he realized he was in bed with Lyric lying halfway on top of him.

He gently rolled Lyric to her side and slipped out from under her.

She woke up, reaching for him. "Hey. Where are you going?"

He leaned down and kissed her softly. "I have to go, Angel. Your mom and dad are on their way up. And I can't have people knowing we're together."

She gave him a pouty face, then said, "Okay. Call me later."

"I will." He took a step away, then turned back to her, meeting her sleepy gaze. "I love you."

She smiled so big and bright his heart felt fluttery in his chest. The feeling surprised and delighted him.

"I love you, too."

Jax looked from him to his sister, then back again. "Then, why are you leaving?"

"Because if I stay, I put her life and mine in jeopardy." Every word held the frustration and anger building inside him, though he tried to contain it. "All I want is to be with her, but I can't. Not right now. Not the way I want to be."

"If you're married—"

"It's not that. It's the MC. That's all I can say." He stared at Lyric. "Are you feeling better?" The bruises looked worse in the soft morning light.

"Yes. Go. I'm fine."

He rushed back to her, kissed her quickly, then went to the door, found the corridor empty except for one nurse at the workstation typing in notes, and made his getaway.

He had things to do today. Plans to make to take down Maria and the others in the club helping her. He couldn't wait to be done but knew this was the most dangerous part of the job when he exposed himself for who he really was after he'd deceived so many dangerous people.

Chapter Twenty-Five

Lyric's parents vetoed her going back to her place and drove her out to the ranch after she was discharged from the hospital. She'd showered and changed into the clean clothes she kept in her old room because she often needed to change after working at the ranch with the horses.

Today, though, her mom kept following Lyric around to see that she really was all right. And Lyric had to admit, being pampered by her mom wasn't at all bad. Sitting in the kitchen, her mom at the stove flipping pancakes, country music playing like it always was, Lyric sipped hot chocolate with whipped cream because her mom thought she needed a treat.

What she needed was some peace, like the kind she found last night with M holding her while she slept. She wanted time to process what had happened with Rick, with Mindy and Tim, and whoever had tried to run her over. Right now, none of it seemed real.

She wondered how Mindy and the kids were doing, too.

"Lyric!" Her mother hardly ever raised her voice, which meant Lyric had been locked in her head long enough to get such a reaction from her mom.

She focused on her mom's concerned eyes. "Sorry. What?"

"Eat. You'll feel better."

Lyric stared down at her plate filled with two stacked pancakes and a mound of fluffy scrambled eggs. The smell was divine, and her empty stomach rumbled. The rest of her ached. She felt like one big, throbbing bruise, her joints stiff.

Her mom sang along to the ballad playing and sipped her coffee. It felt like so many unremarkable but cherished days of her childhood.

Lyric dug into the food, knowing her mother would give her that time before she said what was on her mind.

"I saw him leaving the hospital when we arrived." The words came in a rush, like her mom couldn't hold them in any longer.

Lyric chewed her food, washed it down with hot chocolate, then looked at her mom and played dumb. "Who?"

"That guy who's always at the bar."

"You'll need to narrow that down. There are a lot of guys at the bar." She hid a grin, knowing she really wasn't getting away with stonewalling.

Her mom pressed her lips tight. Robin Wilde did not suffer fools or obtuse children. "Is he good to you?"

She met her mother's concerned gaze. "Better than anyone I've ever known."

Her mom's gaze softened. "Why didn't he stay with you?"

Lyric didn't really have a good answer to that but knew there was one coming when he was ready. "It's complicated."

"Is he married, or with someone else?"

"No. But thanks for thinking I'd be a home-wrecker."

"I don't think that at all. People don't always make clean splits, even after a relationship is over, for all kinds of reasons." Her mom gave everyone the benefit of the doubt. Once. Then, all bets were off.

"He's not like that. He's in the middle of finishing something with the motorcycle club. Once it's done, it won't matter who sees us together."

Her mom raised a brow. "Why does it matter now?"

"He says it's to protect me and him."

Her mom leaned on her forearms on the counter. "Somebody might not like you two being together?"

"I don't know. Yes. I guess."

"What's he finishing?"

"Not sure." But she had her suspicions. She stuffed another bite of pancakes in her mouth, despite the fact she was quickly losing her appetite.

"So you can't be seen with him and you don't know why? You don't even know what he's doing?"

"Mom, I trust him. He's given me no reason to doubt that what he says is true and what he doesn't say is to protect me."

"Is he a criminal?"

"No." She didn't really have anything to back that up, except his word, but she knew it to be true in every cell of her being. "He works construction jobs with a few of the other guys at the club. But I think whatever he's doing now is separate from that. I also think it's important and something he believes needs to be done."

Her mom looked thoughtful. "Like he's helping someone?"

"Maybe. I don't know. What I do know is that he's

honest and kind and he loves me." Lyric stared at her plate, taking that in, knowing it was true but also so thrilled and in disbelief that it was real.

It took her mom a second to say anything. "Are you in love with him?"

She met her mom's gaze. "It makes no sense but all the sense in the world. We're still getting to know each other, and yet . . ."

Her mom's eyes softened. "It feels like you've always known him."

Lyric adored her mom for understanding and not telling her she was going too fast. "Yes."

"That's how it felt when I met your dad. I was like, *Oh, it's you.* From that moment on, we spent all our time together. We just wanted to spend every second of the day with each other."

"That's how I feel. I hope, soon, we'll be able to spend all the time we want together."

"It'd be nice to know he's around in case . . . you know."

"He felt terrible for not being there last night. But the man took a helicopter to get to me, so . . ."

Mom stood up straighter, her eyes wide. "He did?"

She liked surprising her mom and seeing the approval that M had made a huge effort for Lyric when she needed him. "His cousin flies them and picked him up wherever he was and dropped him right at the hospital."

"Wow. He really went all out to get to you."

She stared at her mom. "I couldn't ask for more."

"Except maybe that things were simpler between you two?"

"Yes. But it's not forever, it's just for right now." His words to her.

Her mom leaned on her forearms on the counter again. "Right now is when you need him most."

"And he showed up."

Her mom frowned. "And then he left."

"Mom. Please. Don't make it harder for me to deal."

"That's just it, honey. I want you to be happy."

She held her mother's gaze. "I am when I'm with him. More than I've ever felt. And that makes the in-between worth bearing. It hasn't been that long. And he's working on ending whatever he's doing. I need to give him a chance to do that."

"And in the meantime, someone, most likely Rick, is trying to kill you."

She shoved her plate away, her appetite gone. "It's not M's job to keep me safe. I'm perfectly capable of doing that myself." She needed to believe she could stand on her own, that the violation of her home and sense of security hadn't made her so scared she'd stop living her life the way she had always done.

"You were nearly killed last night."

Not M's fault, even though she knew he felt guilty as hell for not being there to stop it. "Even if M was there, he couldn't have stopped that car."

Her mom ran her fingers over Lyric's arm. "I just want you safe."

She softened. "He wants the same thing. He knows I'll take every precaution. He can track my phone if something happens."

Her mom's eyes went wide. "He can?"

"Yes. He thought it would make me feel better to know that he can find me."

Her mom planted her hands on the counter and narrowed her gaze. "Tell me the truth, Lyric. Are you afraid Rick is coming back for you?"

"I'd be stupid not to think he is," she hedged. "Now I see how obsession makes people act crazy. He doesn't see reason where I'm concerned. He wants me to do what he wants and be what he wants. There is no consideration for my feelings." She slumped in her seat. "I tried to be kind to him, but then I had to stand up for myself."

"Of course you did. Don't blame yourself for what he's done."

"I don't. Not really. It's just . . . sad. And all I want to do is live my life without worrying about someone attacking me at work."

"Please tell me you're not thinking of going there tonight."

She felt the guilt even now, letting down her siblings and the others who'd have to cover for her. "It's Saturday. Our busiest night."

Her mom shook her head. "I'll take your shift. I don't mind. I want you to rest."

"Maybe. I'll see how I feel later." She didn't want to give in to the fear, and her body had had enough and needed rest. Her dad and Jax were already at the bar doing the prep work for tonight, including barbecuing and smoking the meat that took hours. They could handle things.

Her phone rang. She hesitated to check it, fearful it would be Rick, calling from a different phone. But she made herself do it. The unfamiliar number with only *Blackrock Falls* as a caller ID gave her pause, but she answered it anyway. "Hello."

"Lyric, this is Officer Bowers. I'm calling from the station. I was wondering if you could come down and give your statement about what happened last night. Also, Tim would like to speak to you. If you're up to it."

She didn't much care what that abusive asshole had to say.

"I'm on my way."

Her mom raised a brow and frowned. "What?"

Lyric hung up. "The cops need me to come down and make a statement."

Her mom relaxed. "I'll drive you. After you finish your food."

Lyric took a few minutes to eat as much as she could, but in the end only managed to make it through half the plate.

Her mind was on last night and thinking about what Tim could possibly want to say to her. She'd find out soon enough.

Chapter Twenty-Six

Viper arrived at the Blackrock Falls police station a few minutes earlier, asking for an update on the case, which led to him also having to inform the lieutenant that he was FBI and working an undercover case.

"Why the hell weren't we informed that you're working in our jurisdiction?"

Viper had ignored that question the last time the lieutenant asked it. "Need-to-know. And I'm not here to talk about my case, but the two you're working."

"I heard about the FBI making an arrest recently in Willow Fork."

He ignored that, too. "Lyric will be here shortly, so let's talk about what you know about her case."

"You still haven't said what your involvement in it is."

"I'm interested in what happened to her." He hadn't been there to keep this from happening in the first place, and he couldn't put Rick in his place and let him know Lyric was his, so he was left with doing this the roundabout way. No matter what, he was going to make sure she was safe.

"Why? Is she connected to the case you're working?"

"As I said before, I was never here, you know nothing about me, and you certainly don't know about any connection between me and her." He stared down the lieutenant until he got the nod of acceptance he wanted. "Look, I know it sucks that I'm asking you for information on these cases and giving you nothing in return. My case is sensitive. The wrong person hears the wrong thing and it's my ass." It could be his very life. "I'm sure it's not hard for you to link me to the MC, but other than that, I can't tell you my focus on the case."

The lieutenant settled into the conversation with less hostility and more cooperation. "We've been watching the MC for a long time. There's never been any red flags that suggested guns or drugs or anything illegal going on there besides some drunk driving and minor assaults—petty stuff. Certainly nothing that warranted the FBI."

Viper held his tongue.

The lieutenant sighed. "Okay. Fine. You've seen the video of the car hitting Lyric. The car was stolen from the local-diner parking lot after the owner left her purse open on the counter and someone snagged the keys right out of it."

"That was brazen." The premeditation worried Viper.

"Yes, it was. The diner had approximately thirty people in it at the time. Some paid cash and weren't regulars that the staff could identify, so it's hard to say who took the keys. We're still talking to people we identified as being there at the time the car was stolen. No one recognized Rick's picture so far."

That didn't mean he wasn't there. "So it looks like no one saw anything," Viper guessed.

"So far, but we'll keep working the case. We found the car but it had been wiped down and there was nothing left in the vehicle that didn't belong to the owner."

Viper couldn't help but wish for something, one small piece of evidence to nail the bastard who'd hit his girlfriend. "What about Rick Rowe? Have you found him yet?"

"He picked up his belongings from the cabin at the Wilde Wind Ranch without being seen and hasn't returned. We don't know where he's staying now or if he flew home."

Viper had information the lieutenant didn't. "He didn't fly anywhere. At least, we didn't find him listed on any outgoing flights in the past forty-eight hours." Viper had used his resources to check that out, because if it wasn't Rick, he had to assume it was someone linked to his case, who knew about him and Lyric. Right now, his instincts told him this was Rick.

The lieutenant sighed. "Thanks for checking that out."

Viper would do anything to keep Lyric safe. "Is there anything else you need?"

"No. This is a priority. All my officers are looking for this guy and doing routine checks at the bar and out by the Wilde ranch. We want this guy behind bars before he tries to hurt Lyric again."

No matter what they wanted, they'd need some evidence first or Rick would walk.

Viper held on to his anger by a thread. "Did you get all the messages and background from Lyric about their interactions? I want this guy to go down not only for the hit-and-run but stalking, too. I want it on the record, so that when he gets out it follows him, and the next person he obsesses over can see that he's done it before, and law enforcement takes it seriously."

The lieutenant planted his fists on his hips. "We are taking it seriously."

Viper shook his head. "I know you are. I'm just saying, stalking cases can be hard to prove."

The lieutenant gave him an indulgent look, because Viper was acting like a boyfriend, not law enforcement. "When Lyric gets here, we'll get a record of everything from her."

"Okay. Thank you."

"If it was someone I cared about, I'd want to nail the asshole with everything that would stick."

Viper didn't acknowledge that in any way.

Someone knocked on the door but didn't open it. "She's here," Officer Bowers called out to them.

"Send her in here," the lieutenant said back through the door.

Viper went to the blinds, pulled one louver down so he could find her, then frowned when she walked away from the office and went to Tim, the guy who'd beaten his wife and hit Lyric. Viper wanted to rush out and protect her from the asshole, but the guy looked up at her as she approached him, and Tim's eyes softened with an apology and a plea. Lyric hesitated and stood away from Tim, closer to the officer at the desk, and listened to whatever Tim had to say to her. She nodded her agreement to whatever he'd asked her, then turned and headed for the office Viper was in.

A second later, she opened the door and stepped in. She spotted him, glanced at the lieutenant, walked in acting like they weren't together, and closed the door.

"How are you?" Viper asked, desperate to hold her in his arms.

The bruises on her face looked worse, the swelling better. "Okay."

She eyed him, then the lieutenant. Another knock on the door.

The lieutenant went to answer. "Let me see what they want." He stepped out, leaving Viper alone with Lyric.

"Are you here as my boyfriend, or something else?"

He paused, then gave her the truth without adding any additional information. "Yes."

She smirked, a knowing coming into her eyes. "I thought so."

Smart woman. "Keep it to yourself."

Her grin remained. "Fine. So what's going on?"

He wanted some answers of his own. "You tell me. What was that with Tim?"

She cocked her head at his tone. "Well, he's sober and facing some serious charges and the loss of his wife and kids, so he's remorseful. I accepted his apology and agreed to his request."

He didn't like that at all. "What request?"

The lieutenant walked back into the office and closed the door.

Lyric finished explaining. "That I continue to look out for Mindy and the kids while he's away."

The lieutenant added on, "Everyone in town, including everyone who works for this office, knows that the Dark Horse Dive Bar is a safe place for domestic-abuse victims and families in need of food. Lyric gives them all a safe space and the resources they need."

"With the help of everyone in the community," Lyric added.

"She raised enough money last night with donations from all the patrons to pay Mindy's heating bill. She supplied Mindy and the kids with enough food for a week."

Lyric stepped toward him but caught herself. "Mindy will be working at the ranch part-time for a while."

Viper wanted to take her in his arms but resisted, hating the need to keep distance between them. "I take it so you can recuperate."

She rolled her eyes. "That's what my mom and dad told me this morning when they drove me home from the hospital."

He studied her face, worried that she wasn't her vibrant, sweet, happy self today. Not that she should be after what happened, but he didn't like seeing the bright light in her dimmed. "Are you upset about it?"

She scrunched her lips. "I like to pull my own weight."

"You do, and then some," Viper assured her. He'd seen it. And the more he learned about her extracurricular activities, the more he understood how connected she was to this town and her family.

He needed to consider that when he had time to think about their future.

The lieutenant nodded his agreement as well. "Officer Bowers will take your statement about what happened last night. We have statements from all the witnesses at the bar, so it shouldn't take long for you to fill in anything we're missing. As for Rick, there's been no sighting."

"Let's hope he's gone." She pulled out her phone from her purse and tapped the screen. "But he's not gone-gone. He posted on my YouTube channel under a new user ID that wasn't even an attempt to hide his identity." She turned the phone to Viper and showed him the message.

YourRick: Why can't you see we're meant to be? I missed you. See you soon.

Viper thought about how he worded the message. "He *missed* you."

Lyric nodded. "You caught that, too."

"As in, he won't next time?" the lieutenant asked.

"He'll see me soon," Lyric answered. "So I guess this isn't over."

The lieutenant opened the door, stepped out, then turned back to address Viper. "I'll keep you posted." To Lyric, he said, holding out his hand, "Bowers is waiting for you."

"Give us a second."

The lieutenant hesitated because they'd finished with business and there was nothing more for them to ask Lyric about the case but left anyway.

Viper waited for the door to close again, then pulled Lyric into a hug, wishing that having her close eased her mind and kept her safe, even though he knew it wouldn't be that simple. "I'm sorry, Angel. I wish there was a simple way to end this. I wish I could be the one who keeps you safe."

She held on tight, her nails digging into his back, but she looked up at him, understanding. "But you've got somewhere else you need to be."

He traced her beautiful face with his fingertips. "I'm sorry."

She shook her head. "I understand. And trust me, I won't be alone. I won't make it easy for him to get to me."

"Stay out at the ranch. Your family, plus everyone who works there, will look out for you."

"Officer Bowers said he'd drop me at the bar after

this. I'll be there until closing, then I'll spend the night at the ranch. We'll see what comes tomorrow."

"If I can get away, I'll let you know." Viper wished he could take her to his place. If only it was safe. But he had a job to finish. And if all went according to plan, maybe he'd get it done before Rick even had a chance to come up with a new scheme to get to Lyric.

Until then, he needed to be sure she was safe.

He dipped his hand into his pocket and pulled out the round object and held it out to her. "Keep this on your person at all times, even when you sleep."

She held up the disk. "What is it?"

He frowned, not liking this one bit. "A tracking device."

Lyric eyed him. "You're tagging your girlfriend?"

He shot her an irritated look. "You have a better idea of how to find you if this guy succeeds in taking you?" He hated the scared look in Lyric's eyes.

She kissed him softly. "I was only teasing. Thank you. This is . . . sweet."

"It's disturbing," Viper acknowledged. "I know that. But it's the only way I can go do my thing and know that if something happens, I can find you."

"You can track my phone," she pointed out.

Not good enough now that Rick had escalated to attempted murder. "First thing he's going to do is make you ditch your phone. He won't want you to have a way to contact help. Put the tag in your sock or somewhere he won't find easily."

She put her hand down the front of her shirt and tucked the tag into her bra, under her breast. "Good enough."

His mind went to a dark place and thought of how Rick could find it there, but he didn't say anything.

"Yeah. That works. Promise me, you'll never go anywhere without it."

"I promise."

"It works like a cell phone's GPS, so I can find it anywhere." He didn't want to think about what would happen if it was underground or the signal was somehow blocked. He pulled out his phone, tapped the screen, then showed Lyric. "See? The tag, and you, are right here with me. When you're not, it will show me on the map where you are and how far away you are."

She looked up at him, complete trust in her eyes. "But what if you don't know I'm gone?"

"I've given the lieutenant my number. If anyone reports you missing, he'll alert me, and I will come for you."

"Okay." Lyric's voice sounded sure and strong, but he knew she was feeling anything but.

He cupped her cheek. "I promise, Lyric, I will come for you."

"I know. I just don't want to think about you having to do so."

"Trust me, Rick does not want me to have to find you. He tries something, you should tell him that. Remind him, you've got me and a lot of other people who will scour the earth for you."

She sighed. "I know that. I hope, after what he did, he realizes that he's in trouble, and coming for me again is the last thing he needs."

Viper couldn't count on Rick to listen to the little voice in his head to save himself, because that voice was playing only one tune. It was telling him Lyric belonged to him.

Viper could relate to how that felt. Everything in

him said she was his. But he'd done things the right way and proved himself to her. She trusted him. She loved him. And that was a gift, not something you could take or force. It just happened.

"Never stop being optimistic and hoping for the best." He kissed her forehead and brushed his hand down her hair. "You're a light, Angel. That's why so many of us want to be near you."

"Yeah, well even I can't brighten someone like him. He's a void that sucks everything in and gives nothing back. He can never be filled or satiated. He thinks I will make everything better in his life, but that's not my job or responsibility. I can't be that for someone."

"No one can," he added, letting her know he understood. As much as he needed her in his life, he had to be okay on his own, because she couldn't do that for him. And while his troubles stemmed from being alone and wanting her in his life, it wasn't that he needed to be fixed, he simply wanted more for himself. A partner. Someone to make memories with. Someone he could talk to and count on and love. Someone who was there for him as well.

Lyric glanced toward the door. "Well, I better get this done. I've got lots to do today, including checking on my apartment." She squeezed his hand. "And you have someplace to be."

He tilted her head up so he could look her right in the eye. "With you is where I always want to be." He kissed her, letting her feel how much he meant that, then released her.

"M?"

"Yeah, Angel?"

"If it was you, nothing would stop me from coming for you, too. Be safe."

Those words, that vow, hit him right in the heart. He kissed her again, wishing he could stay, but knowing he had to go and he had her blessing. "I'll see you soon." He kissed her one last time, then left the office and went out the back way like he'd come in without being seen, on a mission to finish his business so he could be with her.

Chapter Twenty-Seven

It was getting harder and harder to be away from Lyric. She was all he thought about. All he wanted. And being tied to his job and away from her when she needed him ate away at Viper's already-bruised soul.

He parked his truck in the lot at the Wild Wolves clubhouse. A handful of cars were in the lot, including Maria's. Surprised she wasn't at work at the hairdresser next door to the diner downtown, he headed inside hoping to get what he needed to end this once and for all.

The second he walked into the club he caught the excited vibe. Lobo and Maria were at the bar with four other guys.

Maria turned to him, a bright smile on her face. "You're just in time."

"For what?" He watched the others, especially Lobo, looking for any sign they were on to him.

"We just got the call." She paused.

He'd been in this game too long to get jumpy over a vague statement like that.

Lobo filled in the silence. "Scratch and his wife just had a baby boy."

Viper smacked his hand down on Lobo's shoulder.

"That's awesome. Mom and baby are good?" He loved that the members of the MC were so close and celebrated everything together.

He just wished the rest of the time some of them weren't out killing people for money.

"Everyone is great." Maria touched his arm. "In fact, we're taking baby presents to them in just a little while. I can't wait to hold the little guy in my arms. Will you help me get the bags from the back?"

He'd chipped in to the baby-shower fund a couple weeks ago. "Sure." He left Lobo and the other four guys celebrating at the bar and followed Maria through the door that led to a hallway and the storeroom, a kitchenette, and the office.

Lobo kept the office locked, but Maria had a key and walked right in. She closed the door behind him and stood with her back to it. "How did it go?"

He didn't like being backed into the room alone with her. Especially when he wasn't sure if she just called the shots or liked to get her hands dirty. "You already know." He pulled out the fifty grand he had in his jacket pocket.

Delight sparkled in her greedy eyes.

Instead of taking the eight she owed him, he kept ten. He needed her to see him as a dominant force she couldn't push around. Not like the others.

She pouted. "Hey. That's not what we agreed on."

"Travel expenses," he said and waited to see if she balked at it.

"It's a good thing I like you." Her sweeping, sultry gaze down his body did nothing for him. Not when he belonged so wholly to Lyric.

Maria snatched the rest of the money from him and dumped it into a large purse, then pulled out a small notebook, opened it to a certain page, and used a pen to make a note. "Another one bites the dust."

So cold. So callous.

It made him appreciate Lyric's generous heart even more.

It reminded him that he'd been playing this game so long he'd become accustomed to treacherous, selfish cutthroats and he acted like them more often than not in order to play the game. And over the last many years, it felt like he was becoming as heartless as them in his pursuit of justice.

Maria clicked the pen closed and tossed it and the notebook into her bag again.

He made it seem like he wasn't paying attention and was more interested in the stack of baby clothes and infant toys in the bags on the chair by the desk. "Do you need to wrap this stuff, or what?"

She pulled an extra-large gift bag out and started arranging the items she'd bought inside it. "Why were you at the police station this morning?"

He went perfectly still. "Who says I was?"

She stopped what she was doing and stared at him, a hard look in her eyes. "I know you were there. And so was she."

He caught the jealous look. "Seems someone tried to run over Lyric." He left it at that and let Maria fill in the blanks.

The dismissive shrug rubbed him the wrong way. "It wasn't you?"

"No. I was somewhere else, doing something else, for someone else."

She knew that, so of course she knew he hadn't tried to hurt Lyric. Which meant this was more fishing for information about him and Lyric. His gut tightened with dread. He'd been so careful not to let his feelings for her show.

Maria continued to arrange the package, but her focus remained on him. "So why do they suspect you?"

"She's got people looking out for her, who don't like the fact that maybe a time or two I looked her way. They think I'm bad news."

"Bad can be a good thing." A wicked grin. "So what did you tell the cops when they asked where you were last night?"

"I was at home. Alone."

She tsked. "Not much of an alibi."

Exactly, but he wanted her to believe he spent his nights home alone. "They're going to need more than suspicion to nail me for attempted murder."

Another mistrustful look. "What motive would you have for trying to hurt her in the first place?"

"Her brother seems to think I took offense to her noninterest in me."

"Did you?"

"I told you already, she's roses and rings and carpools. She's a picket-fence life, and I'm a lone wolf."

She grinned at that. "My lone wolf." The possessive tone irked him.

"Not yours. I told you, I'm not looking to be with anyone right now."

She fiddled with the tissue paper. "Oh, but you are mine because we share a secret." She thought she had him under her thumb.

"A mutually destructive secret," he reminded her. "So don't go thinking you've got something on me."

She stood tall and faced him head on. "Just so long as you understand I run things."

He raised a brow and challenged that assertion. "You? Not Lobo?"

She waved that off like it was nothing. "He's a fucking idiot who's all about the pack and loyalty and ride or die." She rolled her eyes. "He believes in the brotherhood and working together for all of you." The dismissive tone told him she really believed that all to be meaningless. It meant a lot to the guys who belonged to the MC.

He studied her. "You don't think that's a good thing?"

"In the last five years, the legit side of this MC has brought in very little money. Enough to sustain the club, buy the booze, pay the rent, and help out a few guys who found themselves in a jam."

Sounded right to him. "Isn't that the point of paying the dues and taking on a few legit jobs here and there to benefit *all* the members?"

"And yet I've pulled a few of the guys out of debt and provided the means for them to better their lives. I'm giving you a way out of all that manual labor, scraping by on jobs with low margins just so you can win the bid and get the work." Smart thinking.

He didn't underestimate anyone on the job. People may look and talk a certain way, but you never knew who they really were, or what they were hiding, until you dug down deep and allowed them to show you the truth.

For months, she hadn't even been on his radar.

Now he knew the fun, flirty woman hid a cold-blooded side.

"Construction is honest work."

She cocked her head. "Don't you want more?"

"I took the job, didn't I?"

She studied him more closely. "And it didn't seem to impact you the way it did the others. Scratch, Cueball, Bleaker, Spike . . . they all came back from their first job amped but also in a kind of shock, like they couldn't believe they'd done it, even though they had past experience with such deadly things."

Viper appreciated her giving him a list of the players. He'd already put the four on his short list of possible suspects because of their backgrounds. It didn't get past him that she'd done her homework, too, and only approached those in the club who already had the capacity to commit murder. None of them, except for Spike, had ever taken a life prior to working for her, but they all had violence in their past.

"If you're concerned about my mental health, don't be. Last night . . . not my first rodeo." And that was the sad truth. Though he hadn't killed that asshole's wife last night, he'd killed before. It weighed on him, but it didn't stop him from doing the job and meting out more justice.

He wasn't a cold-blooded killer.

He did what he had to do to protect the innocent or defend himself and his fellow agents.

Maria issued death orders like handing out homework assignments. She expected the work to be done on time and with A-plus precision.

She smiled. Disturbingly, it was warm and affectionate. "You're exactly what I need. I think we're off to a very beneficial partnership."

"Not if you don't make me an equal partner on the jobs. And I want confirmation on the contract. I want to see exactly how much it's worth. You fuck me over, you won't see me coming."

She stared at him so long he wasn't sure she'd go

for it. Then, she went to the laptop on the desk, typed in a few things, then spun the computer toward him. He saw a simple order form.

Now he had the web URL and the log-in and password she'd used: he had a knack for being able to watch a person type and decipher what they wrote without seeing the screen. He had what he needed now to take her and the rest of them down.

"The buyer can only find this order link once they've made contact through the message board. They simply fill in their name, a phone number for contact, the meeting date, and the date of execution."

He didn't find it funny at all that she used it in the literal way to kill someone. "Then you call using a burner phone that can't be traced, set up the meeting place, keeping that somewhere open to avoid witnesses and so you can see the cops coming. You only let the contact know where with enough time for them to get to the meet. The deal is struck and the money paid in person, right there on the spot. The *execution* of it completed soon after that."

She nodded, a look of pride in her eyes that he'd gotten it all so easily. "Simple. Clean. Only a few people know about it beforehand."

"How do you know you're not talking to a cop during the chat?"

"I do my research on the person, ask a lot of personal questions, and make sure it all adds up. If there's something even a little off about it, I back out."

"I can't believe it's this easy to hire a killer."

She gave a one-shoulder shrug. "I'm more surprised by the reason people do it. It's usually petty. Money, mostly. Divorce seems to bring out the worst in people."

"You coming, or what?" Lobo yelled down the hallway.

Maria rolled her eyes. "I guess we better hurry up." She cleared the computer screen and shut it down, then stuffed the gift bag with some cute tissue paper that had ducks and bunnies on it.

He went to turn for the door and accidentally knocked the gift off the chair. "Oh damn. Sorry."

"It's okay, klutz." She bent to pick it up and fix what spilled out.

While she was distracted, he snatched the notebook out of her purse. "I'll take that." He held his hand out for the present. "You grab your stuff."

She did, and he followed her out to the main part of the club. The other guys were already headed for the door.

His phone rang, since he'd texted a code to his brother to call him. "Hey, let me grab this and I'll meet you outside." He accepted the call. "Hey, man, can you believe it? Scratch and his wife had the baby. Lobo, Maria, Cueball, and a couple others are headed down to see them now. You should join."

Nick knew exactly what he was saying. "On our way."

Viper gave his brother all the players and where they were headed.

Before he walked out the door, he heard something out the window.

"I told you not to come here," Maria's sharp voice drew him over.

"What the fuck were you thinking, doing that to her?" Rick stood right up in Maria's face.

Her, who? Viper wondered.

She quickly looked behind her at her brother and

the others getting into two cars. "I can't talk now. I'll meet you later."

"I thought you were helping me. All you did was make her hate me. Now the cops are after me, too."

Because of the hit-and-run?

Viper seethed.

"Let's go," Lobo called out.

Maria shoved Rick away. "I said later. Now, go." She turned and walked away.

Viper wanted to go after Rick, but right now he had bigger fish to fry. Instead he called his brother back and said succinctly in a deadly tone, "Call locals. Rick just left the clubhouse. Tell them to find him and put him in a fucking cage."

He put on his mask of indifference and walked out of the clubhouse for what he hoped was the last time. He was so done with this job.

Maria, of course, wanted him in the car with her and Cueball. Lobo and the other three rode in another car in the lead. A block from the hospital entrance, they were cut off by black SUVs front and back, two more in the lane beside them. Agents jumped out, guns drawn, Nick ordering them, "Out of the vehicles. Hands up."

Lobo and his crew complied immediately, though cautiously.

Maria pulled a gun out from under her seat.

Viper knocked it out of her hand to the floor.

"What the fuck?" She glared at him.

Luckily, the feds knew he was in the car and waited. "Those are fucking trained agents. What do you think you're going to do? Start a shoot-out with six heavily armed men?"

Cueball bounced in the back seat, glancing out every window. "Man, we're fucked."

"Get out. Keep your mouth shut," Maria ordered both of them. "They don't know shit." She put her hand on the door handle and got out slowly, raising her hands.

He and Cueball exited the other side.

Viper immediately went down on the ground, hands out in front of him on the pavement. As expected, Cueball followed his lead.

Nick cuffed Viper.

Another agent took Cueball into custody.

When Nick sat him up on his knees, Viper spotted Scratch in the back of one of the SUVs. Poor bastard just had a kid, and now he was headed to jail with his wife left to raise their child on her own.

Viper felt bad for the little guy who, because his father had made bad choices, would never really know him.

He wanted to be everything to the ones he loved.

Maybe now he'd get the chance.

Nick bent down close to his ear. "Is this everyone?"

"We'll question the guys with Lobo, then let them go if they have no outstanding warrants. Any word on Rick?"

"He disappeared. Cops couldn't find him."

"Fuck." How did that weasel keep getting away? He focused on what he could do right now. "Left back pocket."

Nick took the notebook out and thumbed through it.

"You fucking asshole," Maria shouted.

He turned and found her pinned, belly to the car hood, a fellow FBI agent searching her.

She glared hard at Viper, then at the book in his brother's hand. "You fucked with the wrong woman. Payback's a bitch."

Viper took the threat seriously and would take steps to neutralize her. But first, his brother hauled him to the SUV with Lobo in it and left the two of them together while they cleared the scene.

"What the fuck is this all about?" Lobo asked.

"You tell me," he shot back, giving Lobo a chance to confess to what he really knew.

"Fucking Maria. She's into something, but I haven't figured out what. The girl is always scheming and whispering with some of the guys." Lobo shook his head. "Whatever she's done, she took a father from his child today." The disgusted scorn on his face only made him look angrier.

"You seriously don't know?" Viper didn't trust Maria's word that she'd done this all behind Lobo's back.

"My guys are loyal. Like you. They love the club and the brotherhood. But when there's a woman . . . they fucking go brain-dead. I've seen her sniffing around you. She's fucked just about everyone else, so it doesn't surprise me. You know why I was so angry about her keeping that baby a while back?"

"Why?"

"She wanted to ransom her back to her family. She said the club would make a lot of money if we used our brawn. What she wanted to cultivate was a deadly reputation. I don't mind when behind that is a *You fuck with us, we'll fuck with you*. But to actively harm people just to earn a buck?" Lobo shook his head. "I know MCs have a reputation, and maybe there's some shady shit we do, but we aren't monsters. We don't keep babies from their families."

"What do you think she's been doing with some of the guys?"

"I'm guessing some sort of enforcement kind of

thing. Someone owes money to someone, and one of the guys makes sure he gets what's owed."

Viper knew Lobo and the guys did that kind of work sometimes.

He spilled the hard truth. "It's more that she eliminates a problem in someone's life."

Lobo's eyes went wide, and then he turned and stared at Viper, looking for a lie and seeing only the truth. "No."

"Yes. I did a job for her."

"What? No." He shook his head. "I'm not going down for murder."

"I have a feeling she's going to try to pin it all on you."

Viper's prediction came true an hour later when he was standing in a room next to the interview room where Maria said for the third time, "Lobo ran the club. Those guys will do anything he says. It wasn't me. I'm just his sister, one of the women."

Viper had to give her credit for using the hierarchy in the club against the members. Women weren't given any power. In fact, they were subservient to the dominant men. But Maria had used sex and money to lure the men into doing her bidding.

Nick sat across from Maria and held up the notebook Viper had stolen from her. "This is an interesting list of names and figures. All in your handwriting."

"I kept the records for Lobo."

Viper wasn't surprised she'd sell out her own brother. She didn't feel things like others did. She was only out to save her own ass.

Nick flipped open the laptop on the table, the one the tech guys had no trouble getting into since Lobo himself had given them permission to search it. Viper had supplied the URL, username, and password. That got them into the site where Maria took the orders, but there were also other files on the computer, hidden files, that the tech guys also found that gave them the chat logs for all the customers who hired Maria.

She was blackmailing them after the fact, too. They paid for the kill, then she made them keep on paying.

"We have everything. Including the bank-account information where you've stashed all the money."

Maria gasped. "How is this possible? How did you even know?"

Viper wondered how she'd known he was at the police station this morning. He'd snuck in the back and only two people had seen him. Officer Bowers and the lieutenant. He also wondered how Maria made sure the people who hired her were legit. Google? Yeah. You could find a lot on an internet search, but she seemed so sure about who she agreed to work for.

The answer to his questions walked into the office.

Viper met him right outside the door where Maria sat dumbfounded by her arrest. "Lieutenant. What brings you here?"

The lieutenant didn't miss a beat. "I heard about the arrests and came to get some information about what's been going on in my town."

Viper knocked on the interview-room door.

Nick opened it, leaving the door wide enough for Maria to see her visitor.

"Rob! Tell them I didn't do this. Get me out of here."

Viper held the lieutenant's gaze. "Rob? Sounds like you two have a *close* relationship." Especially since Maria believed he'd get her out of murder charges.

The man's cheeks went ruddy. "It's a small town. I know nearly everyone in some capacity."

"I wondered how she knew so soon after Spike had been arrested. I wrote it off that she figured it out when Spike didn't check in. Now I'm wondering if she got a call or was with someone who'd receive that kind of information as part of his job. Because the second I saw Maria today, she said she knew I'd been at the police station." Viper stared the man down, daring him to lie to him.

He gave in with a frustrated huff. "I told her you'd been there. But that's all I told her."

"But you hoped she'd figure out the rest."

Nick closed the door on Maria and waved his hand out for the lieutenant to go into another room where Maria didn't hear the rest. "Talk. Because right now, I have men in your office checking your computer, looking for any information you might have looked up and investigated on the people we've tied to Maria's murder-for-hire business."

The lieutenant tried to pull off surprised, but Viper didn't buy it. He was sure Nick didn't either.

"I didn't know why she asked for the information. She just wanted some basic facts on the names she gave me."

"Like were they law enforcement? Did they have a record that might come back to bite her in the ass? I mean, they might not want to be tied to the crime they asked her to commit. She also didn't want them to silence the one who set it up and knew about it, too. Because blackmail is a dangerous game to play with someone who might have it in them to do something about it." Viper saw the second the cop figured out how serious this was and that he was going down as an accessory.

"I swear, I didn't know what she was doing."

"Bullshit," Viper snapped. "You looked up the man in Willow Fork who wanted to kill his wife. It's only one town away. You'd have seen the news reports as well as been told about it from the WFPD. You knew what you'd done to help Maria fulfill her contract. You're here to make sure she doesn't rat you out. All it's going to take is her lawyer telling her she can get a deal for her cooperation. But let's face it, you didn't hide your tracks. The only thing you did that does help you is not tell her that I'm FBI."

"I knew you'd figure out it came from me," he admitted. "So yeah, I hoped she'd figure it out by telling her you were at the station when there was no reason for you to be there."

Which meant he'd hoped Maria would take Viper out before the lieutenant got caught. The fucking bastard thought getting him killed would solve his problem.

"Except Maria thinks my reputation put me there. Big, bad biker guy who has a thing for the chef at Dark Horse Dive Bar gets called in for an alibi when someone tries to kill Lyric."

The lieutenant swore. His face paled.

"Yeah. You didn't really think that through, did you? You'd have probably gotten away with this if you hadn't told her about me at all. You weren't on my radar. She probably wouldn't have thought to give you up."

The lieutenant swore again.

Viper got in the man's face. "Who was behind the wheel of the car that hit Lyric?"

The lieutenant eyed him. "We're working under the

assumption it was Rick Rowe. My officers tried to find him earlier today when Agent Gunn notified us he'd been spotted at the Wild Wolves MC. Why? Is that not your working theory anymore?"

He didn't know if the cop was lying or not. "I just find it interesting that Rick and Maria know each other."

The lieutenant didn't waver. "I don't know anything about that."

Nick stepped forward with a pair of cuffs. "Then, we're done talking. You're under arrest for accessory to murder."

Viper disarmed the cop, while Nick cuffed him and read him his rights.

Another agent came forward and took the lieutenant to be booked.

Nick smacked Viper on the back. "Outstanding work, Mason."

Yeah, he didn't have to be Viper anymore. And a dark-haired angel with blue eyes needed to know exactly who he was. "We got them." It felt damn good to *finally* close the case.

"*You* got them. Including a corrupt cop."

"Maria had her claws in a lot of men." He caught his brother's stare. "What?"

"There's something still bothering you about seeing Rick and Maria together."

"What if we have it all wrong, and Rick isn't the one who tried to kill Lyric? He's obsessed with her. Why kill her when he wants her so badly?"

Nick's gaze turned grave. "Because if he can't have her, no one will."

Mason wasn't buying it. "But that's a crime of

passion. He'd try again to change her mind, then kill her if she refused. It would be in the moment. Violent. Hands-on. He'd want to see her face when she realized her mistake in not accepting him."

Nick mock-shivered. "Dude, that's dark."

"But true. The car thing, it was spur-of-the-moment. It was happenstance that Lyric was in the parking lot at all. So what if Maria was the one who went to the bar that night looking for a chance to get rid of Lyric?"

"Why?" Nick asked.

"Because she knew I was interested in Lyric. I wanted her, not Maria. I shot Maria down every time she flirted with me or asked me to be with her. I told her I wasn't interested in Lyric, that Lyric wasn't interested in a guy like me."

"She didn't believe you."

"As hard as I tried to make it sound real, I guess I fucked up." He'd never forgive himself for putting Lyric in harm's way.

"It is not your fault Lyric got hurt." Nick had a knack for reading his mind like that.

He hung his head. "Isn't it?"

"You don't even know if that's true."

"You work on Maria. I'm going after Rick." He took a step away.

Nick grabbed him by the arm and halted him. "That's not your job. The cops will find him. Go find Lyric. Be with her. Protect her from Rick. And if it was Maria who tried to kill her, well, she's in custody and won't ever be able to do it again."

He met his brother's earnest gaze. "I need to know, Nick. I have to know if it was Maria or Rick."

"We'll get the answer." Nick put both hands on Mason's shoulders and squeezed. "And it still won't be your fault."

Mason knew that it was and didn't want to see Lyric walk away from him because his job had put her in jeopardy.

Chapter Twenty-Eight

Mason walked into the packed bar. The after-work crowd filled the tables, dance floor, and bar-stools. Gabby Barrett's "Pick Me Up" blared through the speakers. He wouldn't mind taking Lyric down some back road, her by his side, them kissing under a full moon.

Lyric was probably working, even though she should be resting. Yes, he'd used the tracker he gave her to find her here, though he'd hoped she'd be tucked away safe and sound at her family ranch.

He wanted to go after Rick but wasn't sure where to start.

And he'd neglected Lyric long enough. For the job. But that wasn't an excuse he wanted to keep using.

He didn't see her through the pass-through into the kitchen and headed to the bar where Aria was serving drinks.

She spotted him immediately. "Hey, stranger. She's upstairs and pissed off." She filled six shots, passed them out to the cowboys in front of her, then waved him to follow her.

He walked along the bar and followed her into the kitchen. "Why is she mad?"

"Because we won't let her in here tonight. She needs to relax, but she's not good at doing nothing." Aria started making two plates of food. Sliders and mac and cheese. "She hasn't eaten. You look like you could use some food and time with her."

He sighed out his agreement. "It's been a hell of a day."

"I heard about you and the other MC guys getting arrested. Since you're out, I assume my suspicions are right and you're one of the good guys." She raised a brow, waiting for his response.

"I am," he confirmed, able to finally talk about it now that it was over.

"Well, I'll assume you want to tell her all about it first, so head on up. I hope we don't see you two for a couple of days." She gave him a suggestive look he read all too well.

"I'll take care of her," he promised.

She grinned, the same blue eyes as Lyric's, sparkling with mischief. "Oh, I know you'll put the smile right back on her face."

He shook his head. "I didn't mean it like that."

"I know. But I also know she needs you right now."

"I need her, too." The confession was real and easy to admit.

Aria put her hand on his back and pushed him toward the door. "She's got beer and wine and food upstairs, but she'll appreciate you bringing her dinner." Aria smiled, turned, and left.

The rest of the kitchen staff looked at him with interest, knowing why he was there and who he'd come to see.

He left out the back door and headed up the stairs to the small landing. He noted the brand-new lock on the door. The frame had been repaired. He breathed a sigh of relief that she was relatively safe.

With the plates in his hands, he couldn't knock, so he lightly kicked the door and waited. A few seconds later, she pulled the curtain aside. A huge grin spread across her face. She unlocked and opened the door in record time.

"M. You're here." She looked him up and down, the tears gathered in her eyes. "Are you okay? I heard you were arrested."

Small town. News traveled fast.

He wanted to hug her, but his hands were full. "That was just for show," he assured her. "Can I come in? Food's getting cold."

She seemed to catch herself. "Jeez. Yes. Come in." She backed out of his way and closed the door behind him.

He noted the changes in the apartment since he'd last been here. "I don't like what that asshole did to the place."

"You make it look a hell of a lot better."

That right there soothed him in a way only she could do to him. With one sentence she'd reassured him she remained interested in him and that she was happy he was there with her.

She waved him toward the new dark brown leather sofa. The blue chairs that used to be in front of the fireplace were shoved into a corner, their fabric torn like a gaping wound spilling out stuffing. "I plan on getting them reupholstered."

He went to the sofa and set the plates on the new coffee table. A fire crackled and burned in the hearth, keeping the room warm and cozy. He glanced at the bed behind the sofa and noted the new bedding.

"Looks like you were able to get a few things in short order."

"You like?" She'd gone with pale green sheets and a thick blue comforter.

"I could crawl in and sleep for a week." He was so tired. But more than anything, he wanted to spend time with her. He found her pretty blue eyes still on him. "We need to talk."

"That can wait. Sit. Eat. Beer or wine?"

Yes, they'd share a meal, then clear the air. "Do you have some of that red?"

"I do." She went into the kitchen.

He took a seat on the couch and waited, staring at the fire, letting his mind and body catch up to the fact that the job was done: he could relax and just be with her.

She turned off the kitchen light, leaving the room dark with only the strung lights over her bed on the damaged birch-tree branch and the glow of the fire in front of them. The room was quiet, except for the sound of the firewood cracking and popping every so often.

She handed him his glass and sat beside him. "To a job well done."

He eyed her. "You know."

She put her hand on his knee and squeezed. "You told me you weren't a criminal. I know you're a good guy. So what was it? Drugs?"

"No. Murder-for-hire, actually."

She gasped. "Okay. Wow. So you're not DEA?" Such a smart woman.

He grinned. "Good guess, but I'm FBI."

"Wow." She looked him up and down. "Nice cover. You look like a thug."

"Thanks?" He wasn't sure if that was a compliment or not.

She brushed her fingertips along his jaw. "You're sexy as hell, and I want you desperately."

He leaned in and kissed her, wanting her just as much.

She leaned back and broke the kiss. "I have a million questions. How long have you been undercover?"

"This time, less than a year. Before this, I was undercover in a militia group. Took them down along with the leader of a commune of farmers after he turned against the community because he wanted power and money."

"Damn. Okay. So you do all the really dangerous stuff."

He shrugged that off, even though it was true. "It's the job."

"So what happened with the Wild Wolves MC?"

"I'll answer all your questions, I swear, but first, I need some food."

She caught herself. "I'm sorry. The rest can wait. You look exhausted."

"This case . . . being away from you . . . it's taken everything out of me. Now that it's over . . . God . . ." He scrubbed his hand over his face. "I just want to be with you." He hoped the desperation in his voice didn't turn her off.

"I'm right here." She handed him his plate. "We don't have to rush. Stay as long as you like."

Forever? "Do you mean that?"

"Every word," she assured him. "Plus, my family won't let me lift a finger downstairs, so I'm all yours."

He loved the sound of that.

Hunger gnawing at his gut, he downed two sliders

in four bites, then took a breath to sip the excellent wine.

Lyric ate more slowly beside him, just watching him.

"What?" he asked around a bite of the third slider.

"I just . . . It feels like some of the pieces fell into place and others I'm still trying to figure out. Most of all, I'm just happy you're here. I could just stare at you for hours."

He chuckled. "The view will be better after I have a shower, a shave, and a haircut."

She slid her arm over his shoulders and leaned into him. "I like you all dark and dangerous."

He rubbed his hand down her thigh.

She hissed in pain.

He immediately released her. "I'm sorry, Angel. I didn't mean—"

She kissed him to shut him up. "I know. I'm fine. The other side of me isn't bruised."

"I'll keep that in mind." He'd take care of her and kiss all the hurts better.

"So was everyone in the MC arrested?"

He shook his head and forked up the last of his mac and cheese. "No. Lobo has probably been released already. He didn't know what Maria was running out of the club with four of the members." He took the bite and set his empty plate aside and turned to her. "I killed Bleaker in December when he tried to kill Kenna."

Her eyes went wide. "Wait. You were at Max's ranch when they were attacked?"

"I was in the truck with the guy who wanted to eliminate Kenna before she IDed him to the cops."

"But that means you knew he killed Kenna's friend and was after her. Why didn't you stop him before he tried to kill her?"

He raked his fingers through his hair. "Because he'd been hired to get something from her. And the FBI was trying to get to her brother and another man. Bleaker wasn't supposed to kill her friend. Things went sideways. When he went after her, I let her protective detail know he was coming. I had backup on the way. Like today, I expected my brother and his team would arrest us at the scene, Kenna would ID Bleaker as the killer, then I'd be free to go back to the MC and finish my case."

She narrowed her gaze, a furrow appearing between her dark brows. "But it didn't go as planned, and Kenna got shot."

He regretted that more than he could say. "And I took out Bleaker."

Understanding dawned in her eyes. "To save Max and the FBI agents."

"Yes." He scrubbed both hands over his face. "I'm sorry she got hurt. You have no idea how relieved I was that she survived." He laid his head back on the couch and stared at the fire.

Lyric turned next to him, one leg bent at the knee on the couch. "Max had to have seen you. He knew you and I had something going. He never said anything."

He rolled his head and stared at her. "Because the FBI agents with him told him they had an undercover agent with the suspect, and my cover had to be protected."

"Or you'd lose your chance to finish your case."

Or my life. But he couldn't say that to her. "People were dying."

She brushed her fingers through his hair. "Max is the one who encouraged me to be with you."

That surprised him. "He did?"

"I told him I didn't think you were what everyone thought you were. He told me to trust my gut. The way he said it, he sounded so sure that I was right."

He needed to thank Max for keeping his secret and nudging Lyric his way. "You were right. Now I get a chance to prove it to you."

"You already have."

He sighed, knowing he needed to get it all out in the open. "There's more I need to tell you."

She shook her head. "You're wiped out. Go take a shower, then come to bed."

Oh, how he wanted to wrap her up against him and love her. "Angel, this is important."

"It can wait. You've worked really hard these last many months. I can see the toll it's taken on you. So give yourself a break, and let me take care of you."

That sounded amazing. So he took the reprieve, vowing silently to tell her everything in the morning. "Are you sure?"

"That I want to make you feel good? Yeah." The sexy smile made his gut tighten and his dick swell.

"I won't be long."

"Take your time. Let the hot water help you relax. I'll do the rest." That suggestive smile tied him in knots and undid him all at the same time.

He wanted her so damn bad it hurt.

He kissed her, letting her feel his desperation and desire, then broke the kiss, grabbed his wine, and headed for the shower, because the least he could do was wash away this day and spend the night showing her how much he appreciated having her in his life.

The second he closed the bathroom door, he downed the last of the wine and stripped. His cut shoulder protested every movement, but he ignored the stinging pain, turned on the shower, and stood under the spray, letting the hot water work on his tense muscles.

He used the bar of soap instead of the body wash she always smelled like. He shampooed his hair and scrubbed the stubble that was more a beard now. He wished he had a razor, but that would have to wait.

Rinsed and feeling better, anticipation riding him hard to be back in Lyric's arms, he debated pulling on his jeans or just sticking with the towel around his waist. He went with the easier-to-remove option, opened the bathroom door, and stopped dead in his tracks and just stared at the beautiful woman sitting in bed across from him, her legs bare, hair down. She wore nothing but a simple white T-shirt, the V-neck showing off a lot of cleavage.

His mouth watered.

She stared at him over the laptop she'd been using. Her gaze hot and intent on him. "Drop the towel."

Chapter Twenty-Nine

Lyric picked up the laptop, set it on the nightstand, and rose to her knees on the bed all without taking her eyes off the gorgeous man in front of her.

His eyes blazed with heat as he swept that hot gaze from her head down to her bare legs. "Lyric, baby, I really thought I could take this slow and easy tonight."

She appreciated the sentiment, but . . . "Who says I want slow or easy?"

His thick erection stood proud behind the towel, letting her know just how ready M was to be inside her. Right where she wanted him.

To show him she didn't need him to leash his passion, not with her, she pulled the shirt up and over her head and let it sail across the room as she tossed it away. "What I want is you, naked, on your back, in my bed. Right now."

"Angel, I'm holding on by a thread, and just looking at you is about to send me over the edge."

"Then, stop making me wait to get my hands on you."

He did exactly what she'd demanded, dropped the towel, and slid onto the bed, landing on his back next to her.

She rewarded him by turning and straddling his thighs, her hands sliding down his chest and back up. "How's the shoulder?" She leaned over and kissed it right above the worst part of the cut, then rose back up.

"Hurts. Make me forget."

She grinned down at him. "I'll give it my best shot." She leaned over him again, planting her hands on either side of his shoulders, and kissed him like she'd never get to do it again. She poured out all her love and appreciation for this man, who'd worked so hard to finish his business so he could get back to her.

She left his mouth and ran a trail of open-mouthed kisses down his neck.

He sighed, his hands brushing up her back and down to her hips. He somehow navigated her body without hitting any of her bruises from the hit-and-run.

She kissed him all along the line of stitches across his shoulder and over his bicep. Then she raked her nails softly over his pecs and nipples.

He groaned.

She glanced up at him. "Oh, I like that sound." She repeated the caress, got the same response and another deep growl when she pressed her lips to his heated skin and started making her way down his rock-hard abs.

"Angel."

She grinned at the plea in his voice. "I think you've earned a bit of the devil tonight." She scooted back, dipped her head, and licked the head of his dick with her flat tongue.

He swore and growled at the same time.

She did it again, then took him deep into her mouth. His fingers splayed through her hair as he held her to him, his hips rocking to the slow up-and-down nod of her head as she sucked on him, all the while rubbing her hands along his thighs. Feeling the urgent need building inside him, she clamped her hand around the thick base and slid her mouth up and down him again.

"Enough." He hooked his hands under her arms and dragged her up his body.

"Your shoulder," she protested, landing on her hands, so she didn't hit the stitches. Hers were nothing compared to his and didn't hurt at all anymore.

"I want to be inside you when I come." He took her mouth in an urgent kiss as his hand slid down her belly, over her mound, one long finger sliding along her folds and deep inside her. "You're so fucking wet for me."

She moved against his hand.

He slipped a second finger inside her as she kissed him long and deep.

She broke the kiss, cupped his cheek in one hand, and nipped at his bottom lip. "Give me what I want."

His finger slid out of her, brushing against her clit, making her moan, her inner muscles clenching. Desperate to be filled, she pressed down, slid along his hard length until the head met her entrance. She'd barely taken an inch when he thrust in deep. One arm hooked around her waist holding her down to him so they both could enjoy the feeling of being locked together, pleasure so deep and all-encompassing if they didn't take a breath it would all be over. His other hand took her by the back of the neck and brought her down for another searing kiss.

And then she rolled her hips against him, letting the sweet friction and glide of their two bodies take them both into the dance.

"God, you feel so good. Don't stop," he begged.

She kept the pace as she kissed his neck and savored the feel of his hands rubbing her back, over her ass, along her sides, and cupping her breasts, his fingers squeezing her tight nipples. She increased the pace, bringing him up to the edge, then she slowed things down again, drawing it out, enjoying the closeness, the feel of him, the way he held her close, the way he looked as she lavished him with her love.

And then one of those traveling hands found its way between them, a nimble thumb swept circles over and over against her clit as she rose and sank on his hard length, the feeling exquisite, then blindingly fantastic as the pleasure climaxed and he pumped into her again and again, spilling himself, and prolonging the rolling orgasm.

She tried not to fall too heavily on top of him but found she'd lost the strength to hold herself up. She did manage to land on the side opposite his stitches, her face buried in his neck, her lips pressed to the pounding pulse beneath his heated skin.

Neither of them said anything for some time. It took a while to catch their breath.

The popping, crackling fire cut the silence, but it was his steady heartbeat that held her enthralled along with the man himself. "I'm so glad you're here. I know it hasn't been that long, but I can't seem to feel whole when you're not with me."

He held her tighter. "I'm not going undercover anymore," he confessed. "I can't. I don't want to be without you either. I want to be me again. I want a life that's mine. I want you. I want us."

"I'm yours. And you're mine."

"Mason."

She grinned knowing he'd feel it against his skin. "Mason Gunn."

He cupped her face and made her rise and look at him. "How did you know my last name?"

"Well, there aren't many guys named Hawk who own a distillery in Montana."

He grinned, shook his head, then kissed her. "You cheated and went digging?"

"Can you blame me? You can't give me clues and not expect me to fall prey to my curiosity. All I did was find Hawk Gunn and Gunn Brothers Distillery, which gave me your last name since you're cousins, related by your dads. Which you told me, I'll remind you. But I didn't follow the family tree, because I wanted *you* to give me your name."

"You have no idea how much I want to."

It took her a second to comprehend what he was saying. She couldn't stop the smile that took over her whole face and filled her heart with love and warmth. "You do?"

"More than anything. I've waited a long time to find you. I don't know how long I can wait to have it all."

"Why waste time when it's what we both want?"

"I'm going to do it right, Angel, because you deserve all the best of everything I can give you."

"Bring it on. I'm ready. I'm with you."

He pulled her in for a soft, sweet kiss, then hugged her close as she settled at his side, hooked her leg over his, and pulled the covers over them.

"Mason?"

"Mmm, I love the way you say my name." His voice was soft as he began to drift off. "What is it, Angel?"

"Are you going to be okay?" She hadn't missed the desperate need she sensed in him that he wanted that life with her because of all the bad he'd seen on the job. He'd killed someone just a month ago. That had to weigh on his heart. Because he had a good one, and it had to be a heavy burden for him to carry.

"If someone asked me that before I met you, my answer would have been *I don't know*. And inside, I'd have known that I was in deep trouble." The quiet that came over him told her he was thinking about those dark thoughts.

"And now?"

"I have a lot of really good things to look forward to, including your smile when I wake up in the morning." He kissed her on the head, his arm tightening around her.

She snuggled in, letting him know she appreciated the sentiment, she'd always be there for him, and she loved him.

Chapter Thirty

Mason woke up happy for the first time in so long that he couldn't quite remember when he'd last felt this way. But today, he had the woman he loved in his arms, his body wrapped around hers, her sweet ass snuggled into his aching erection, her hair draped over his neck, and her head resting on his arm. He kissed the back of her head and rubbed his hand down over her hip and thigh.

"Mmm." She put her hand over his and squeezed but remained content against him. "Do you have to go to work?" The words were slurred with sleep and mumbled. The grip she kept on his hand said she wanted him to stay.

"I'm on paid leave for the next month, so I can decompress and finish the counseling sessions I started back in December." He hugged her close. He was never anxious to share his feelings about the bad shit that went down on the job. He didn't want to rehash the details over and over again, and in the past he'd said and done what he needed to do to get back to work.

But he'd realized something in those weeks he'd been away from Lyric over the holidays. The nightmares in his life had piled up. He didn't sleep well. He had a short fuse. And he couldn't enjoy being with his family the way he used to.

He didn't know how to be happy and carefree anymore.

But when he was with Lyric, he could breathe and let everything else go because she made it so easy for him to focus on one thing. Her.

And while he loved their time together and found himself easily opening up to her because he wanted everything between them to be honest, he'd still been lying. He didn't want her to see the broken parts of him. He'd tried to hide them.

And what he really needed to do was heal them.

He needed to change his life so he could be in hers.

She shifted in his arms and turned to face him. Her beautiful blue eyes were filled with understanding and sympathy. "I can't imagine what it's like being undercover and away from your family and friends, lying day in and day out, with a threat hanging over your head every second."

"You imagine it very well, Angel."

"Those are just words. You lived like that. I can't fathom the disappointment you felt when you missed a family event, or your friends invited you out, but you couldn't go."

It sucked. Each and every time. And every time it happened, it felt worse. "I lost most of my friends. When you never show up, they stop calling and asking you to come. Most of the people in my life now are fellow agents who get the job. But then it's just us blowing off steam and rehashing cases."

She traced his lips with her fingertip. "Because they get it, and they know you get it."

"Not exactly good times," he admitted.

Her fingers swept over his brow, and she looked deep into his eyes. "You must have felt very alone."

"Most of the time I am while on a case. I have Nick and other agents I check in with as I funnel information to them, but . . ."

"It's not like having someone there with you experiencing it, supporting you through it."

He didn't know what to say because it was true. It was his ass on the line. He had backup, but that only came when he called. He could be dead before anyone knew his cover had been blown. He was good at his job, but even he'd come close a couple times to being outed as a cop. The people and groups he infiltrated had little trust or mercy for traitors.

Lyric's soft fingertips traced along his hard jaw. "I respect what you do. It's incredibly brave and necessary. And if you want to keep doing it, I will support you, because I know it's something you believe in doing." Such faith, such trust, and so much generosity to allow him to do what he loved if that's what he wanted, even if it meant it took him away from her.

He slid his fingers into her silky hair and held her softly. "I'm done. I've already told Nick I can't do it anymore. My heart's not in it. My head . . . I can't take anymore. Bad people, doing bad shit with glimpses of good few and far between. It's sucking the life out of me. Now, it seems, I see a couple and I envy them. I see a dad with his wife and kids and wonder if I'll ever have that. And I know if I keep doing what I'm doing, the only thing I'll have is an impressive arrest record and an early grave. That's not a life, Angel. I've been mired in the darkest parts of humanity. I want the good stuff back in my life." He kissed her softly. "I want to spend real time with my family. I want to get to know all of them again. Most of all, I want to be with you. I want to love you and be loved by you. You want to buy a house, let's do it. You want to have some kids, I can't wait. You want to travel, you tell me where and we'll go. Whatever you want, anything you want, I'm in."

"Montana."

"What?"

"After I introduce you to my parents, I'd like to meet yours. I'd love to see your place up there. You must want to go home. And I'd love to properly meet your brother."

He pulled her to him, his forehead to hers, eyes locked. "Right now, I'm really happy right here with you." But yeah, he wanted to go home. So badly. Soon.

But first, he needed to eliminate the threat against her. "There's something I need to tell you."

"Me first."

He brushed his fingers through her hair again. "What is it?"

"I want you to know, you can share anything and everything with me. You don't have to hold anything back."

"I know. You proved that last night when you didn't kick me out because of what happened with Max and Kenna. They're your family. And I put them in danger."

"You did your job. You saved them."

"I can't help thinking that if Kenna had died because I didn't stop that asshole before he got to her, I wouldn't be in your bed, let alone your life."

She shifted onto her elbow and stared down at him. "That's not true. I would still feel like you did everything you could to protect them."

Mason raked his fingers through his hair, groaning because he'd used his sore arm.

"Be still." She kissed his chest. "Let that arm rest."

"You don't understand." His frustration felt like a living thing inside him.

"I know if you keep moving it, it's going to hurt more."

"It's not about my damn arm." He held her gaze and gave her the truth. "I think Maria was the one who tried to kill you because she was jealous about me coming to the bar all the time to see you."

The silence that followed was deafening.

The blank look in Lyric's eyes turned his gut and tightened his chest with worry.

"Did you and her . . ."

He slid his hands into her silky hair on both sides of her head and held her close. "No! Never. In all the months I was with the Wild Wolves MC, we barely interacted."

"Wait." She shook her head. "My mind is still trying to catch up. You're FBI, not a contractor at all."

He grinned and kissed her softly, liking that all those pieces she had were falling into place for her and creating a truer picture of him. "No. My dad is good with his hands and taught us how to fix things around the house. Construction comes easy to me. I like fixing and building stuff. Whatever I couldn't do, I had the other guys in the MC who knew what they were doing, so I'd take on the easier stuff while they did the work that required permits and inspections."

"Smart."

He chuckled. "I'm a good liar, remember?"

"It's your confidence and attitude. People don't question you because of it."

"Fake it till you make it."

She shook her head. "It's more than that. Not everyone could pull it off the way you do."

He kissed her softly. "You saw what everyone else didn't."

"They were looking at you to confirm you were who you appeared to be. That's what you showed them. You lived that persona, so that's all they saw. I knew there had to be something more behind the intelligent eyes, because I caught glimpses of the wanting in them."

"I was so desperate for you, I couldn't hide it all the time. And now I don't have to anymore."

"So why do you think it was Maria who tried to kill me and not Rick? I had rejected him quite publicly and definitively."

"Right before we made the arrests yesterday, we were leaving the MC. I hung back to call Nick to let him know the op was a go. I overheard Maria outside the club talking to Rick."

Her brows went up. "What was he doing there?"

"That's exactly what I wondered when I saw him through the window. I'd never seen him there before, but it was obvious he and Maria had some sort of acquaintance or relationship."

"Maybe she's how he found me at the ranch when he came to town?"

"She works at the hair salon next to the diner—" He abruptly cut off his sentence.

"What?" she asked.

He squeezed her arm. "The car that hit you . . . Someone took the keys out of the owner's purse while she was paying her bill at the diner counter."

"You think it was Maria?"

"She works right next door. She'd be in and out of the diner all the time. That's why no one thought twice about her being there. If it had been Rick—"

"Someone would remember a stranger."

"Still, it's not proof. I need to find Rick. If he can point the finger at Maria, then that's another charge to her long list of crimes. If it was him, I don't want him thinking he can come back and finish the job."

"I finally get to claim you as my badass boyfriend." Her grin made him smile back.

He brushed his fingers through her hair. "You own me, Angel. My heart, my soul, all of me."

"Well, whatever am I going to do with you?" The sexy look in her eyes said she had some ideas.

He palmed her ass and pulled her body snug against his. "Whatever you want, sweetheart."

"On your back, baby."

He grinned and complied, loving the feel of her rising and straddling his hips. "You like being on top."

She took his wrists and moved his hands to her breasts. "I like your hands on me."

"So do I." He molded the soft mounds to his hands, her hard nipples pressed to his palms.

She sighed and rubbed herself against his thick erection as she leaned forward, her beautiful hair spilling around him in a curtain, her lips taking his in a searing kiss. Their tongues tangled and glided over each other's until they were both desperate to breathe and lost in the building passion. He broke the kiss and pulled her up over him so he could take one pink-tipped breast into his mouth. With her up on her knees, he slid his hand down to her wet center and stroked his fingers through her soft folds, teasing, tempting, and making her moan. He gave her other breast some attention and slid one finger, then two into her tight core. He kept the push-and-pull rhythm slow and easy, but she had other ideas and rode his hand, her breath coming in pants. He circled her clit with this thumb and sent her over the edge. He enjoyed bringing her back to herself with featherlight strokes of his fingers and a kiss that melted her into him.

And then she sank back on him, taking his hard length into her in a slow glide that made him want to plunge fast and deep, but he let her take him in her way, in her time, until she was seated on him all the way to the hilt. She rocked once, and he clamped his hands on her hips as she rose up and rocked again, her head falling back, her long dark hair brushing his thighs.

He looked up at his angel and saw the ecstasy, felt the connection between them, and let pleasure reign as he thrust deep and moved with her.

She fell forward, her hands on either side of his head. The kiss she gave him scrambled his brain and amped up the desire riding him hard. She took him up to the very edge, held him there until he wanted to beg, and then her body tightened around his cock. He followed her into pure bliss. And when she collapsed on his chest, he held her close, kissed her on the head, and said what he needed her to know more than anything. "I love you."

He'd said it before. She knew he meant it. He just really needed to say it. She deserved to hear him say it to her every day.

She pressed up on one hand, the other went over his heart. "I love you, too, Mason. So much. Never doubt it."

"I don't. I won't. Because I see it every time you look at me."

•

"Well, I like looking at you." She smiled. What a gift. She had no idea how much he loved this peaceful, normal, impossibly important and poignant moment in his life. He'd wanted this for so long, and now he had it.

And nothing and no one was going to take this from them. Ever.

Chapter Thirty-One

An hour later, Mason and Lyric finally made it out of bed. Mostly because they'd worked up a big appetite. He was sitting at the table finishing another pancake and his second cup of coffee while Lyric showered, when someone knocked at the door.

This time, he didn't have to worry about who saw him here. Though he did pull on a T-shirt to go with his jeans before he opened the door barefoot and still rumpled from his tumble in bed with his angel.

He didn't expect to see his brother this morning, but it put a smile on his face.

Nick stared.

"What?" Mason asked, confused by his brother's silence.

"You look . . . happy."

Mason felt it for the first time in a long time. "I'm where I want to be, not where I need to be."

Nick got it immediately. "And where is she? I owe her a huge thank-you for making you feel that way."

"Oh, I thanked her. Multiple times." He was in such a good mood, he caught himself teasing.

Nick caught it, too. "You know, until this moment, I didn't realize just how different you'd become on the job. You used to joke and laugh all the time. For the past few years, until today, I can't remember you being lighthearted at all."

"What was there to joke about when I was surrounded by thieves, murderers, anarchists, traffickers, and all the other bad elements that come with the job?"

Nick nodded, letting him know he got it without having to say anything. He bent and picked up the two large duffel bags at his feet and carried them in. "We cleaned out your place this morning, got all the surveillance stuff." Nick dropped the bags by the sofa. "Are you going to stay here for a while, or head home?"

"I'm staying here until we find Rick."

Nick's gaze filled with approval. "And you want to spend time with her."

"She wants to introduce me to her parents." He ignored Nick's wide-eyed surprise. "I want to take her home to meet the family. I want Mom and Dad to see me happy for a change."

The bathroom door opened behind him. "M, who are you talking to?" She stopped dead in her tracks when he turned to her.

Hair damp, wearing a simple Dark Horse Dive Bar T-shirt and jeans, she was gorgeous. And his.

"Come officially meet my brother, Nick." He held his hand out to her.

She took it and immediately leaned into his body, then held out her other hand. "Hi. I'm Lyric. It's so good to meet you."

Nick took her hand but didn't shake, he held it in both of his. "Thank you for bringing Mason back."

Lyric glanced up at him, then back at his brother. "He doesn't have to hide to survive anymore."

Nick's gaze locked with his. "She's perfect."

Mason knew exactly what Nick meant. Lyric understood him in a way few others did. Not unless they did the job he did. Nick got him, but even he hadn't dug deep enough to the core of Mason and what had slowly chipped away at him all these years. Because Nick didn't want to see the damage done to his brother at Nick's command as his boss.

Nick tugged Lyric's hand, bringing her right into his chest. He hugged her close. "Welcome to the family."

Lyric stepped back into Mason's embrace. "Oh, well, we haven't quite gotten that far."

Nick held Mason's gaze. "Oh, I know my brother. It's a done deal. He's never going to let you go."

"That's good," Lyric replied, "because I decided to keep him a while ago. So yeah, he's stuck with me."

Nick grinned. "It's good it worked out this way, then."

Mason wrapped his arms around Lyric, keeping her back to his chest, close. Exactly how he liked her. "Any updates on the case?"

"You're on leave. So let me handle it."

"Okay." Mason's answer surprised Nick again. Mason never let anything go. He had to see every detail of the case done. But this time, he had other priorities.

"Who's in charge of finding Rick now that the lieutenant has been arrested?"

"What?" Lyric gasped. "Why?"

Nick filled her in. "Because he nearly outed Mason to the Wild Wolves."

Mason appreciated Nick's fury at the officer. "He

didn't blow my cover," he explained to Lyric, "but he was helping Maria check out the people who hired her to kill someone for them."

"What did he get out of that?" she asked.

Nick frowned. "Maria. He put his whole career on the line for some hot-and-sweaty nights with her. She used their affair to make him keep doing the background checks for her or she'd tell his wife he was cheating. He couldn't afford the divorce or for his kids to find out he's an asshole. Cheaters are the worst."

"My sister Aria agrees with you."

Interest lit in Nick's eyes. "Mason told me about her putting her ex in his place."

"She booted him right out the door," Lyric confirmed.

Nick got back to the question Mason had asked. "Officer Bowers said he knows Lyric and was here when her place got broken into, and he's not resting until he finds Rick." Nick looked back at her. "I think he has a crush on you."

She squeezed the arm Mason had across her chest. "I'm taken."

Mason nuzzled his nose into her hair right behind her ear. "Don't forget it."

"You won't ever let me." Such confidence and pleasure in those words.

"I'll leave you two to your time together. Keep in touch, Mason. Let me know how you're doing."

"You don't have to beat around the bush. I told her I'd be going to therapy to work out my shit. We have no secrets."

"Then, she knows everything about Maria."

"That she may have tried to kill me? Yeah," Lyric confirmed. "Is it me? Am I the one who makes people violently possessive?"

"Some people are just bad," Nick said. "Mason adores you. He'd never hurt you because he's good. Rick and Maria, there's something twisted in them. It's not your fault. And we will make them pay for what they've done."

Mason reluctantly released Lyric to go to his brother and wrap him in a bear hug. "Thanks, man. It means a lot that you always saw me."

"We're brothers. I know you. You know me." Nick smacked him on the back, hugged him hard, then let him go. To Lyric he said, "I'll see you soon."

Lyric closed and locked the door behind his brother. "I like him."

"The feeling is definitely mutual between you two." He pulled her back into his arms and stared down at her. "What's your plan for the day?"

She rolled her eyes. "Aria texted that we got a big catering order this morning, but I'm not allowed to help with it. So I'm all yours." She needed to rest and let her own many bumps and bruises heal.

"Nice. You're all mine."

Her sweet grin made him want to kiss her. "If you're staying here with me, we need to get some groceries. Maybe we could head into town, see a movie, have lunch, shop, then head back here for a quiet night."

It sounded like a normal, everyday thing, but it made him so damn happy because he got to do it with her. Because this was the start of his life with her. "Yeah. Let's do all that. I'll just jump in the shower, and then we can go."

"While you do that, I'll go downstairs and make sure Aria and Melody have everything in hand for the catering order and kitchen rush tonight."

He kissed her and waited for her to leave before he grabbed what he needed out of his bag and went into the bathroom to shower and complete his transformation from Viper to Mason.

Chapter Thirty-Two

Mason loved the shocked and surprised look on Lyric's face when he walked into the bar after his shower.

"Holy hotness," she blurted out, her gaze fixed on his shorter hair and clean-shaven face.

"What?"

She shook her head like she needed to rattle herself back into reality. "M. Seriously. That's too much gorgeous goodness for one woman to take."

He walked right up to her, cupped her beautifully shocked face, and kissed her like he hadn't seen her in forever. Like he could do it any time he wanted, anywhere he wanted. Like now. Right here in front of her stunned sister, Aria. "I thought you might like to see me looking less disreputable and more me. I know I did. Bonus that I blew your mind."

She fisted her hand in his shirt and tugged him down until they were face-to-face, her lips a tempting inch from his. "It's not about how you look. It's who you are that I love." She kissed him back like he'd kissed her a moment ago. "But I love that you're stepping out of the role you had to play so you can be you with me."

"So obviously something has changed." Aria stared at him from behind the counter. "Care to share?"

It was Lyric who turned to her sister and answered. "Aria, meet FBI Special Agent Mason Gunn. The man I'm going to marry."

Aria's eyes went wide, and so did his. He never expected that. Not now. Not when things were so new, even if they'd talked about it.

Aria nodded like it was a done deal. "Lyric doesn't hold back when it comes to what she wants." The smile said Aria approved of Lyric's choice. "I knew there was something about you, I just didn't know what. Now I guess it makes sense, all the cryptic things you said to her, and how you tried to keep her at arm's length."

"To protect her." He wanted that clear, because he'd always wanted her.

Lyric put her hand on his chest. "To keep you safe."

Aria held his gaze. "So what now? Are you staying in town, or is your job done and you're headed home? Wherever that is."

He looked down at Lyric. "I am home."

She grinned, then met her sister's sentimental gaze. "We're making plans."

"Are you leaving with him?" Aria asked, a touch of worry in her voice. She obviously didn't want her sister to go.

He answered for her. "Lyric's life is rooted here with her family, this bar, her music. I won't ask her to leave everything she loves. My life has been all over the place for years. While I have a place up in Montana with my family, I want to be with Lyric, and that means I'm staying here."

Aria and Lyric shared a look that conveyed a conversation he didn't even try to decipher, but he knew Aria was happy for her sister. And maybe Lyric was letting her sister know how sad she was that things hadn't worked out for Aria and her cheating boyfriend but that maybe someone who deserved her would come along soon.

"I'm really happy for you guys." Aria squeezed Lyric's hand and looked at him. "I know you'll take care of her. But if you don't, they won't find your body."

"Threatening a federal agent?" he queried, mostly joking with her.

"It's a promise, tough guy. Plus, Lyric would have your balls if you arrested me."

Mason frowned and looked down at Lyric's serene face. "Are your parents going to be this hard on me?"

"They're going to love you because you love me."

About to kiss her, he stopped a mere second before their lips touched, stood back, and took out the phone he'd used on the case. He saw the caller ID and frowned.

"What is it?" Concern. Lyric read him so well.

"It's Lobo from the MC."

"Don't answer it. You're done with them."

Yeah, but he still had to live in this town with those guys, so he needed to know if there was a threat to him. And Lyric because of him.

"Hello?"

"We need to talk. Come to the clubhouse. Now. It's not a request. Don't make me come for you." Lobo hung up.

His mind sharpened as he thought through all the angles. Lobo knew he was a federal agent. Mason was the reason five people close to Lobo were in jail, including his sister. Calling up, ordering him to come to him . . . It didn't make sense. If he wanted to harm or kill Mason, why ask him to come?

It had to be something else.

"I'm sorry, Angel, we'll have to delay our plans for today. I need to take care of this." He turned to head back up to her place to get his badge and gun. A stark reminder of who and what he was, even if he was supposedly on leave.

She followed him out through the kitchen, up the stairs to her place, and into the apartment. "Tell me what's going on."

"I'm not sure. Lobo wants to meet."

"So you're just going."

He pulled his gun and badge out of his bag and attached both to his belt, letting her see him as an agent for the first time.

Her eyes went wide at the sight of him armed. "Seriously, you can't just go there alone."

He cupped her face and stared directly into her eyes. "I'm a trained federal agent. He's no match for me. Plus, I'll call in backup and have the local cops cover my ass."

Her blue eyes filled with worry. "I don't like this."

He didn't either, but . . . "I understand, Angel. But this is my job."

"You're on leave. Send Nick."

He should, but Nick probably wouldn't get anything but silence. "Lobo wants to talk to me."

"What if it's a setup and he wants to kill you?"

"Then, he's very stupid for asking me to come when he knows I'm an agent. I think this is something else."

She held her hands out and let them drop. "Then, what's the point? You've locked up everyone associated with the case. Anything he has to say he can say over the phone."

He put his forehead to hers and looked her deep in the eyes. "I need you to trust me."

"With my life. Always. But if you're not back in a reasonable amount of time, I'm coming for you."

He kissed her like his life depended on it, showing her how much her words meant to him. Because he didn't doubt that she'd storm into the Wild Wolves MC and raise hell to get him back. "My angel's got vengeance in her."

She held him by the shoulders, her nails digging into him. "I can't lose you now."

"You won't. I promise. I'll be back soon." He kissed her softly, taking his time, letting her feel how much he meant every word he said and that being with her was all he wanted. "Rick is still out there. Do not leave the bar. Do you have your tracker on you?"

She cupped her breast. "Want to see if you can find it?"

He growled. "Yes. Definitely. But later." He kissed her quick again, then headed for the door.

"Text me the second you're on the way back," she called out.

"Lock the door," he ordered her. He didn't like leaving her alone, but Aria and several people were in the kitchen downstairs, so she'd probably be fine. Trouble was, *probably* didn't ease his concern or protective instincts.

He'd get this done, then be back with her.

He climbed into his truck and headed for the MC, calling Officer Bowers on the way.

"Bowers," the cop answered.

"This is Special Agent Mason Gunn. You know me as Viper."

The long pause didn't surprise Mason. "What can I do for you, Agent Gunn?"

"Meet me at the Wild Wolves MC. Lobo's asked for a meeting, and I could use some backup after I arrested his sister and four members of the club."

"Why me and not another agent?"

"You're closer. You know these guys, too. This is your town."

"All right. I'm like, four minutes away. What's the plan?"

Mason laid out the simple plan and thanked the officer for the backup. He didn't really think he needed it. He was used to working alone and walking into danger. But because of Lyric and how badly he wanted a life with her, he wasn't putting himself in undue jeopardy.

Plus, he believed her when she said she'd come for him if he didn't return to her in a timely manner. For all he knew that meant in the next half hour, so he better make this quick before she did something reckless.

He pulled into the clubhouse parking lot right behind the cop.

Bowers parked with his cruiser angled to the club door, several yards back so he could see the front and side of the building where he could cover the two doors into the building. Smart.

Mason approved of the cop's tactic and climbed out of his truck, his gun in easy reach, his senses heightened for any danger around him. He walked to the club door, turned to Bowers, gave him a nod, and held up five fingers, letting the cop know the time started now.

The door opened then with one of the club members waving him inside, a look of surprise in his eyes at Mason's new look. The door closed at his back. Mason shifted so the guy behind him and the other two in front of him couldn't pull any moves without him seeing it.

"Relax," Lobo said from the table near the bar. He sat with cool casualness. "I just want to talk."

"You have less than five minutes. If I'm not out that door by then, the cop calls in backup and things get sketchy."

"Not only do you sound like a cop now, you look it." Lobo shook his head and dove right in. "How long did you know about Maria?"

"I didn't know who was running the murder-for-hire business until a week ago."

Lobo remained cautious but relaxed. "You thought it was me."

"I never assume anything, but yes, you were a suspect."

Lobo leaned forward in his seat, hands on the table in front of him. He obviously didn't want Mason to get any ideas that he was a threat or had a weapon. "Why wasn't I arrested for anything?"

"While you run the club, your boys have their side hustles. Some of the money funnels into the club. They pay their dues. I wasn't here for misdemeanors. That's for the local cops to investigate, though my report is focused on Maria and her guys. They've racked up a lot of charges. I'm satisfied the people who needed to be arrested and charged have been, and so is the FBI. So why am I here?"

Lobo gave him a firm nod. "You did your job."

"Yes." Without regret or guilt. He took down the bad guys.

Lobo pressed for more information. "Are we on some watch list now?"

"Should you be?"

Lobo frowned. "Just give it to me straight."

He did. "Local cops will be watching you. They have been for some time. But the feds have the guilty in custody. The case is closed. I will be staying in town for personal reasons."

"Lyric." Lobo narrowed his gaze.

He was at the table in seconds, his fists planted, his face in Lobo's. "I'd be very careful about saying her name and looking at me like that. I might take it as a threat. And anyone who threatens her had better watch their back."

Lobo fell back in his chair, all at ease and looking disgruntled that Mason had gotten in his face. "I like her. She's kind. She helps the people of this town. She's helped people I care about. That thing with Mindy and her kids . . . Mindy was my high-school girlfriend. I hate what's happened to her. I don't like what that asshole did to her, or the way he attacked Lyric."

Mason read in Lobo's eyes that he wanted to make sure it never happened again. The man obviously respected Lyric and the help she provided to others.

"Violence against women is the worst kind of thing a man can do, especially to someone they supposedly love. So before my five minutes is up, I'll tell you why I asked you here."

Mason backed off and stood, holding Lobo's steady gaze. "What is it?"

"Maria was spending time with that new guy in town. She wanted him to keep Lyric away from you."

Mason went on alert. "I know." And he hated that he'd put Lyric in danger.

Lobo didn't break eye contact. "My sister ruined this place. She seduced men into doing things they'd have never done if not for her promises. She helped that ass-hole get close to a good woman. I don't know what he did to Lyric, but I don't want him to do anything else, because then who will look out for the lost and broken in this town? He's squatting in an abandoned property out on Sycamore Road, number 327. You can't miss it. White house, boarded-up windows, trees all along the back side."

"Did your sister try to kill Lyric with that hit-and-run at the bar?"

Lobo's eyes filled with weariness. "Until the FBI arrested her and the others, I didn't think her capable of something so deadly, but look how wrong and blind I've been."

"Did she do it?" He needed to know.

"I don't know." The sadness and uncertainty in his eyes said he wasn't lying.

"Thank you for the information. Am I going to have a problem with you or anyone else from the club if I stay in town?"

Lobo shook his head. "No. And if you do, you let me know. I'll put a stop to it. We are not a gang. And I'm going to make sure the remaining members re-member that."

Mason held his hand out and shook with Lobo. "Then, I'll leave you to it with my thanks for helping Lyric with her problem." Because he knew Lobo had done this for her, not him.

Mason left the clubhouse with no time to spare.

Officer Bowers rolled down his window. "Every-thing cool?"

"Yes."

"Good. I've got a domestic disturbance call to get

to." With that the officer tore out of the parking lot, leaving Mason to find Rick on his own.

He climbed into his truck, pulled up a map of the area on his phone, found the place was located on a large parcel of land, the nearest neighbor quite a ways away. The perfect spot for someone to hide.

He sent the location information to Nick.

MASON: Possible Rick Rowe hideout. Checking it out. I'll text you if I find anything.

NICK: Send me updates every 10

Mason drove out of the lot and headed for the property. He didn't see a car out front when he drove past the house. Nothing to indicate anyone was there, but with the boarded windows, it was hard to tell if anyone was inside.

Why hadn't Rick simply left the state and gone home?

His obsession for Lyric wouldn't allow it.

Mason parked in the trees on a barely-there dirt track and climbed out of the truck. He avoided the wide-open field and took the long route through the trees to the back of the house. Nearing the second ten-minute mark to check in with his brother, he hid behind a tree watching the back of the house, noting the rental car hidden from the road back there. He pulled out his phone and texted Nick.

MASON: At the house. Surveilling now. Suspect car hidden out back.

He didn't wait for Nick's reply, set his phone to

Silent, checked the upstairs windows, saw no sign of anyone inside, and snuck up to the back porch where all the windows were also covered. He put his ear to the door and listened, not hearing anything.

Then something cracked him in the back of the head, and the lights went out.

Chapter Thirty-Three

Lyric was sitting in the middle of her rumpled bed, her guitar on her lap, the final sounds of the song she'd written fading to quiet. She grinned at the lyrics written on the pages next to her. Proud and excited, she couldn't wait to sing this song to M. He'd know the words and feelings were inspired by him.

She checked the time on her phone and noted he still hadn't texted her. Worried he was taking too long and something might have happened, she was about to call him when his number popped up on her phone.

She swiped to accept his call. "I was just about to come after you," she teased.

"Good." Rick's voice chilled her to the bone. "It's a seventeen-minute drive from the bar to 327 Sycamore Road. If you're not here in the next twenty minutes, he dies." Rick hung up on her.

For a second nothing seemed real. Her mind went blank with shock.

Then the fury hit. "I don't think so, asshole." She set aside her guitar, searched for the phone number online, and sent the call through. As the phone rang, she leaped off the bed, stuffed her feet into her boots, grabbed her purse and keys, and ran out of her place. When she was halfway down the stairs, someone answered the call.

"Gunn Brothers, how can I help you?" The cheery voice grated right now when her world seemed so dark with M in danger.

"I need to speak to Hawk."

"Regarding?"

"It's a family emergency."

"And you are?"

"Look, I don't have time for this. Just put him on the phone." She jumped down the last few steps, hit the pavement, and ran for her car.

"Mr. Gunn is in a meeting. If this is about business, I'm happy to take a message."

"This is personal."

"Then, you'd have his cell number if he wanted you to contact him."

She climbed behind the wheel and started the engine, her patience gone. "This is life-and-death. Now, put him on the fucking phone."

The line went silent.

"I swear to God, if she hung up—"

"Who is this?" the deep, annoyed voice didn't faze her.

"Hawk, this is Lyric Wilde. Mason's in trouble. I need you to call Nick, give him my number, and tell him time is running out."

"On it." He hung up.

She placed another call, speeding through town and one red light, her gut in a knot, her heart in her throat, and all her hopes and dreams of a life with Mason hanging in the balance. "I need your help." She detailed exactly what she needed as quickly as possible. "Please hurry," she pleaded. "I can't lose him." She choked back a sob, concentrated on the road, then disconnected her call for help to accept the incoming call from Nick. "I'm on my way to him right now," she explained to Nick before he could say anything. "I have seven minutes left or he claims he'll kill Mason. I'll make it. I won't let anything happen to him. 327 Syc—"

Nick cut her off. "Mason already gave me the address. I'm headed there now, since he missed his check in. Don't go in there. Let the FBI handle it."

"No. He wouldn't wait if it was me. I promised him if it was him in danger, I'd come, just like he'd come for me." Her voice cracked. "I won't break that promise." She hung up and pushed down on the gas pedal when she turned onto the long straightaway of Sycamore Road. "I'm coming, baby. You hold on."

Chapter Thirty-Four

Mason came awake, first listening to his surroundings, then slowly raising his head to take in the silent room. He glared at the man, who appeared to be in his midtwenties, standing in front of him holding Mason's phone and gun. "You won't get away with this." He pulled at the electrical wire binding his wrists to a ladder-back wood chair in the middle of a living room. Light seeped in from the two windows on his right through a two-inch gap at the top that the boards didn't cover.

Rick looked both determined and scared. "You don't understand."

Mason took a breath to clear his head and met the guy's nervous gaze. "Explain it to me, because you're right. I don't understand why you'd want to hurt someone as sweet and kind as Lyric."

"She's the one who's a tease."

"No, she's not," Mason defended her. "She's just not interested in you."

"That's what you think. She promised me we'd work together. Man, it was amazing. She just got me. It was like she read my ideas and looked into my soul and just knew what I was trying to say, what I wanted her to see."

Mason understood exactly how Rick felt. To be seen by someone, it was everything.

But Rick had taken Lyric's innate ability to read people and used her amazing talent to write a song that meant something to Rick.

"We laughed and connected, and she put her hand on my arm and flirted with that amazing smile of hers." Rick's euphoria at the memory showed on his face.

Mason understood it all too well because she made him happy, too.

But Rick misinterpreted Lyric's kindness for something more.

"Maybe I tried to take things too fast. But she didn't have to push me away like that and tell me to go home. I don't have any fucking place to go. Stupid roommates kicked me out."

"Why?"

Rick seemed to remember he was talking to Mason, not rehashing his gripes in his head. "What?"

"Why did they kick you out?"

"Because of a girl." He rolled his eyes. "She was seeing my roommate, but she was all eyes for me. We had these moments when she'd stay over. He got pissed, said she wanted to be left alone. I knew better. But he didn't want to believe that she was into me, not him." He caught himself. "This isn't about her or my fucking asshole roommate."

Mason tried reason. "It sounds to me like what happened with Lyric is what happened with this other woman. They were nice to you, and you took it to mean they wanted something more. But they didn't."

"You don't know. You weren't there. You just don't

want to face up to the fact Lyric was all over me behind your back."

"Lyric would never do something like that. She'd never hurt someone like that. And why the fuck would you want a woman who would do that to a guy?"

"It's them. They just like to mess with our heads."

Mason had enough of this twisting of the truth. "Did it ever occur to you that maybe it's not them, it's you?" Mason probably shouldn't antagonize the guy, but he seemed to be in a chatty mood, and he needed to stall for time so Nick could get there and save the day.

Mason didn't even care about the ribbing he'd take from his brother for getting taken by surprise by this prick when worse men hadn't been able to touch him. But as long as he got back to Lyric, he didn't care.

Rick rolled his eyes. "They say one thing, then they change their minds."

"Lyric tried to be nice at first, but then she told you she wasn't interested. You didn't want to hear it. I get it, man. She's a beautiful woman. Smart. Talented. Kind. Caring. She takes care of people. I get why you're drawn to her."

"Maria told me you had a thing for her. You think you're so smart. I saw you with her at the hospital. Her sister drove you two to your place."

So that's why Maria had showed up the next morning, asking about Lyric.

"You've been trying to take her from me."

That sounded a lot like something Maria might drill into his head to get him to do what she wanted and keep Lyric away from him.

"Lyric and I were something before you ever met her in Nashville. It's not her fault she wanted to be with me and not you. She feels the way she feels. And you need to respect that."

Rick turned his back on Mason. "You have no idea how she feels about me."

"I know how she feels about *me*. And I won't let you hurt her."

The front door flew open, and Lyric stood in the opening, her breath coming in quick pants like she'd run from the car and up the porch steps to get to him.

"Angel, get out of here. Run!" He tried to break the bindings but remained trapped in the chair.

She met his gaze and breathed a sigh of relief. "I promised I'd come for you."

His heart overflowed for this woman, even as a feral need to protect her came over him. "Damn it, Lyric, leave me and go."

She dismissed him with a disgruntled sneer and focused on Rick and the gun in his hand.

Luckily, it remained at his side.

Lyric moved.

Rick did, too, keeping Lyric from getting to Mason, but also blocking him from seeing her. And then someone put a hand on the nape of his neck. Too small to be Nick's. He couldn't have gotten here this fast. But Lyric hadn't come alone.

He went still. A knife blade cut through the plastic and wire on his right hand. Blood rushed into his fingers.

"What do you want, Rick? Another song? More of my time? What?" Lyric sounded ready to give him anything while keeping Rick distracted. "Tell me, and it's yours. Just leave him alone."

Rick raised the gun and pointed it at her. "I just want you to listen to me."

"Okay. I'm listening." She'd gentled her voice, spoken slowly and with interest, keeping Rick focused on her.

"I didn't try to kill you. It wasn't me. It was her."

"Maria?" Lyric asked.

"Yes. You have to believe me. I wouldn't do that to you. *She* wanted *him*. You were in the way. She was supposed to help me get you. Instead, she went behind my back and tried to take you away from me."

"Okay. I understand." She sounded so calm, but Mason knew she had to be frantic to get to him. "You didn't want to hurt me."

"I want you to be with me. But now everything is messed up. I saw you go with him that night after I came to the hospital to take care of you."

Lyric didn't say anything for a moment. "You trashed my apartment."

Rick's body went rigid. "You deserved it, after what you did!"

"What did I do, except be honest with you from the beginning that I didn't want that kind of relationship with you? You keep trying to force it, but all that does is show me that I don't matter to you at all."

Rick took a step toward her. "You do. I love you."

Mason's left hand was free. He didn't bother to look behind him to identify who helped him. He slowly stood behind Rick.

"Then, if you really do love me, let me go, knowing you did it to make me happy."

He shook the gun at her. "Why can't we be together? Why can't you just try?" Anger laced with frustration, sadness, and defeat filled those words.

"Because my heart belongs to him. It has for a long time."

"He can't love you the way I love you."

"He loves me with his trust and understanding and care. He doesn't take anything I don't want to give. He accepts me for who I am and allows me to live the life I want to live."

"I can be better. You can show me how to be better."

"That's not my job, Rick." Her soft voice kept Rick calm. "I can't fix you. You need help before you really do hurt someone."

"What's the point?" He put the gun to his head. "Every time I try, it turns to shit."

"Don't. You don't want to do that!" Lyric reached for Rick.

Mason grabbed the gun and yanked it away from Rick. "You don't get to do that and put that nightmare in her head." He holstered the gun and pulled Rick's arms behind his back. "Cuffs, Nick?"

Nick came out from hiding just outside the front door and tossed the cuffs to Mason. "You're supposed to be on leave."

"Yeah, well, it's a small town, and the cops were busy with something else." Mason shoved Rick into Nick's waiting grip, then he pulled Lyric into his arms and hugged her close. "Are you okay?"

"I'm fine. Thank you for saving him."

"The idiot never took the safety off the gun." He dropped that nugget of luck, then held Lyric by the arms away from him. "Why the hell did you walk into this house? You could have been killed. Do you have any idea what that would have done to me?"

She cupped his face and kissed him hard. "I love you. There was no way I wasn't coming for you. Get used to it."

He dragged her back into his arms, buried his face

in her neck, and held her close until his heart stopped trying to pound its way out of his chest.

It took a minute, but he finally let her loose, though he kept her close with a hand at her waist. He turned toward the back of the house and shook his head at the couple standing there. His gaze settled on the woman Lyric resembled more than a little bit. "Thank you for cutting me loose, Mrs. Wilde. That was a huge risk."

"Anything for Lyric."

"I feel the same way," he told her, earning a firm nod of approval from Lyric's father, who stood next to his wife with a rifle in hand.

Lyric turned into him and put her hand on his chest. "Mom. Dad. This is Special Agent Mason Gunn and his brother Nick. They're FBI. And this one is mine."

He looked down into her possessive and love-filled gaze, then turned to her parents, not missing the subtle rise of the rifle, Mr. Wilde sending a message to Mason about treating his daughter right. Mason dismissed it because he'd never hurt Lyric. "Mr. and Mrs. Wilde, I'm so happy to meet you. I just wish it was under better circumstances."

"It's nice to finally meet you." Mrs. Wilde grinned at him, then gave Lyric an eye-twinkling glance of approval. "And it's Robin and Wade."

He had to ask. "What are you doing here?"

Lyric answered for them. "As the crow flies, Wilde Wind Ranch is a little over a mile behind this property. By road, it's about a fifteen-minute drive around the way."

"But by horse, it's a quick ride," Wade answered.

Lyric pressed her cheek to Mason's chest. "I needed backup, so I called them to help right after I called Hawk to get to Nick. I didn't have his number or know how to reach him. Going through the FBI seemed like it would take forever, so I looked up Gunn Brothers Distillery and called Hawk."

Nick held Rick against the wall by the front door. "Hawk is probably going nuts waiting to hear back." Nick notched his chin toward Mason. "You're bleeding."

Mason felt the blood on his neck. "Asshole clocked me with a log."

"That's twice in a matter of weeks." Nick shook his head. "You're losing your stealth skills."

Mason pointed to Rick's bare feet. "He planned to sneak up on me."

Rick struggled against Nick's hold but didn't get anywhere. "I needed her to listen to me."

"A phone call would have done it," Lyric snapped. "I've given you every opportunity to do the right thing, and every time you've mucked it up because you only care about what you want."

Rick hung his head. "Well, I'm fucked now. I hope you're happy."

She would be. Mason would make sure of that.

But his sweet Lyric went to Rick and showed her heart yet again to someone who didn't deserve it. "It will make me very happy if you use this experience to see that what you're doing isn't working and you need to learn a better way to interact with people, especially women. Otherwise, you'll never have the kind of relationship you seem to want. You can't make people do what you want them to do. You can't make them feel something they don't. You have to allow them to be who they are."

"I've lost everything."

"You have a chance to be better and have better."

She stepped back from him. "I'm starting a new chapter in my life with someone I love. You need to start your own. Don't come back here."

Nick walked him out the door. "You're going to need a lawyer. Kidnapping and assaulting a federal agent . . . Not good, man."

Mason hoped that was the last he'd see of Rick. Maybe not, if the case went to court.

Lyric stepped behind him and gently brushed her fingers over his hair, checking out the scrapes and goose-egg knot on his skull. "You need to get checked out at the hospital."

"I'm fine."

"Listen to her, son," Wade admonished. "You were unconscious for a few minutes."

Mason stared down into Lyric's worried gaze. "I hate that we spend so much of our time together at the hospital."

She chuckled. "As long as you're okay, where we are doesn't matter."

He could think of one place he'd rather be with her. In bed. Because right now, he was so damn happy she didn't get hurt or killed he wanted to spend the next hour or more holding her, touching her, loving her.

"Later," she whispered, reading his mind.

Nick came back in. "Rick is secure. I'll get him booked. I'll need all of you to write up your official statements about what happened here today. Email them to me." Nick handed Robin his card, then gave one to Lyric. "Anytime, anywhere, anything you need, I'm there. No matter what. My cell number is on the back. Use it." Nick bear-hugged Mason. "I love her, man. She came through for you in a big way today. Keep her, or I'm taking her."

"I thought you had a thing for Aria?"

Nick released him and glanced at Lyric. "I wouldn't mind you putting in a good word for me with her."

Lyric grinned. "I think she's already noticed my hot boyfriend has a hot brother."

Nick kissed her on the cheek. "I really like you." And then he left.

Mason shook his head. "I need to call Hawk, let him know I'm okay."

"We'll leave you to it," Wade said. "Call us later and let us know what the doctor says about that head injury."

Mason took the hint that he wasn't getting out of another hospital visit. Lyric probably wouldn't let him sweet-talk her out of it, anyway. She cared too much, loved him too much to take a chance on his well-being.

Robin came to him and gave him a hug. "Take care, Mason. We'll see you for dinner at our place on Sunday." She made the statement without it sounding like the order it was, reminding him of his own mom.

Mason waited for the Wildes to depart before he pulled out his phone.

"What the fuck, man. Are you all right?" Hawk, normally calm, cool, and collected, sounded on the ragged edge of desperation.

"I'm fine. My angel, she took care of business."

Hawk's sigh of relief echoed through Mason. "Thank God. Okay. So I take it the asshole's in custody."

"Nick's got him. I'm headed to the hospital to get a head wound checked out, but otherwise I'm fine."

"You're sure?"

"All good." Mason hugged Lyric to his chest. "Lyric's just looking after me."

"You deserve it."

"So do you," Mason reminded his troubled cousin.

Lyric snatched the phone from him. "Hey. I have a question."

"Anything you want, sweetheart, it's yours."

With Lyric pressed to him, Mason could overhear everything.

"How many women call you at work desperate to talk to you and get a date?"

Hawk took a long time answering. "Yeah. Sorry about that."

"That is not an answer," Lyric pointed out, a wicked grin on her face.

"I don't know," Hawk grumbled.

"The quiet ones always seem like a challenge."

"I'm not playing anyone's game." Hawk was a loner. Had been for a long time now. Maybe too long.

Maybe like Mason, he was hoping to find someone worth taking a chance on.

"Thank you for helping me today." Lyric seemed to understand that, like Mason, Hawk was hiding who he truly was under a mask of what he showed to the world.

"You're family now."

Tears gathered in Lyric's eyes as she stared up at Mason but spoke to his cousin. "Next time I call, make sure the person answering knows who I am."

"Why would you be calling me again?"

Lyric grinned, not caring one little bit about his cousin's grumbled tone. "Because we're friends now."

"We are?" Hawk sounded oddly curious about Lyric's assertion.

"We are. And when Mason brings me up to see his family, I'm going to hug you so hard."

"Why would you do that?" Hawk sounded disgruntled and maybe scared.

"Because you need it. I'll talk to you soon, Hawk." She hung up on him.

Mason stared down at her. "Why all of that?" He acknowledged the touch of jealousy but knew she wasn't interested in his cousin that way. But he didn't get why she was pushing for a friendship Hawk would probably resist. And then it hit him. "You hear me in him."

"Loners don't actually want to be alone."

Mason had felt alone for a long time, even though he'd been surrounded by people. His job meant no one really knew him.

Hawk had his family, most especially his brothers, but he kept them all at a distance, not wanting his pain to become their burden. Though it did, because they loved him. And seeing him unhappy and isolating himself weighed on them. Just like it did on Hawk.

Lyric rubbed her hands up and down his chest. "You said he's been through a lot. I'm not his family."

"You heard him. You are."

"I'm a connection because of you, yes, but I'm also new to him. I don't know his past. I can meet him where he is now and be a friend who accepts him as he is."

"You make my life a million times better. Hawk could use your kind of light in his life."

"He got me to Nick today so he could help you."

Mason didn't tell her Nick would have come when Mason didn't check in, but maybe if things had gone a different way today, Nick getting the heads-up from Lyric and arriving sooner could have made all the difference.

"What do you think of this place?" Lyric glanced around the room they were standing in.

"It looks like someone started a remodel." The wiring had obviously been replaced. There were still some supplies, including the wire used to tie him up, in the corner of the room.

"It's four bedrooms and two and a half baths. There's a formal dining room through those doors that could be your office. The kitchen needs to be gutted and redone."

He eyed her. "How do you know all this?"

"This is the property I thought about buying a while ago. It's between my parents' place and the bar. But it was too much house for just me. But for us . . ."

Yeah. For them, it could be perfect. "I like Shaker cabinets in the kitchen. Clean lines. Simple. What kind of countertops do you want?"

Her smile brightened. "White quartz, the ones that sparkle a little. And a big farmhouse sink." She nipped at his chin. "But first, I'm taking you to the hospital."

Chapter Thirty-Five

Lyric wanted to give Mason more of the normal days he'd longed for while undercover. So two days after the doctor checked him out at the hospital and declared him fit and fine—and yes, he was—and they'd rested and decompressed at her place, they did all the date things he'd wanted to do with her since they met months ago. They went out to eat, saw two movies, went shopping downtown to replace some of the things that had been smashed in her apartment, and even went horseback riding at the ranch.

The pure joy on Mason's face to be up on a horse and in the saddle, out on the land, lost in the quiet beauty of it all . . . It did her heart good to see him finally relax like that and find peace in the moment.

And on that ride, she'd let everything go, too. Rick was out of her life. He'd lawyered up and would probably make a deal with the prosecutor, but that was no longer her concern. Maria was facing serious charges. More than likely, Lyric and Mason would have to testify, but then Maria would be in prison for a long time, maybe forever. And Lyric planned to live her life. With Mason.

She never knew it could be this easy, this right, to be with someone.

Mason was a piece of her heart she didn't even know had been missing.

Tomorrow she was back to work at the bar.

Mason started his therapy in the morning and wanted to plan a trip home. She sensed how desperate he was to reconnect with his mom and dad.

But tonight, she wanted to give him something special. Something that was theirs. Something to make him smile. A gift he'd inspired.

She left the bathroom where she'd been getting dolled up and found him sitting on the sofa with his laptop, writing his final report on the case. "Hey, M, come down to the bar with me. I've got something I want to give you."

He closed his laptop and looked up over his shoulder at her. "Wow. You look amazing." The blaze in his eyes told her she looked sexy as hell and he wanted her.

She grinned. "Thank you. I thought I might make you want to see what I have on under this dress later."

"I like the dress. I love what's under even more." He placed his laptop on the couch, stood, and came around to her, his loving gaze moving over her, leaving behind hot ripples of desire coursing through her. "We could just stay up here." The sexy suggestion tempted her, especially when he dropped his voice like that and looked at her like he was stripping her bare in his mind.

"Date night first, then me and you dancing in the sheets."

His eyes went wide with understanding. "Okay, Angel. Let's go have some fun." He held his hand out to her.

She took it and followed him to the door, down the

stairs, and to the bar's kitchen door. The second he opened it, the music spilled out, along with the smell of pulled pork sliders and French fries.

Nervous butterflies fluttered in her belly. She didn't know why. She'd sung on stage hundreds of times. Even in front of Mason. But this time, it was her song for him, and she really wanted him to like it.

She said hello to everyone in the kitchen as they walked through and out to the bar where Aria was ringing up an order.

"You ready?" Aria gave her an encouraging smile.

"Pour him a glass of my red."

Aria knew the wine she loved and had become one of Mason's favorites, too.

He squeezed her hand. "Are you going to clue me in to what's going on?"

Aria handed him his drink.

Lyric pulled him behind her toward the stage and pointed to the chair beside where Melody stood ready to record her performance, so she could post it to their YouTube channel. Lyric had snuck down to the bar earlier this morning, while Mason showered, to record the song and put it up for sale. She had a feeling the song could be something people related to and liked enough to download.

She took the stage to a round of cheers as the playlist song ended and everyone waited for her to sing. She grabbed her guitar and sat on the stool, then started the way she always started. "Hello, Dark Horse Dive Bar."

"Hello," the crowd answered back.

"Who wants to hear a brand-new song?"

"We do," the crowd roared.

She met Mason's intense gaze. "Ever since we met,

all the songs I write now are songs about you. This one is yours."

The start to the song resonated with how they began, slow and steady, the chords and rhythm rising like the spark of love had in her heart all those months ago, and now grew stronger with every beat.

And then she sang to him, seeing the spark of surprise and love and pride and joy as she spoke to him in a way that he understood came from her soul through her music.

> *You walk into my bar*
> *Sparks fly like a shooting star*
> *Looking good in black denim*
> *You take a seat and I'm silently beggin'*
>
> *What's your name?*

A surprised smile lit up his whole face.

> *Is it luck I'm havin'*
> *A moment worth saving.*
> *A lifetime I've been waiting.*
> *What's your name?*
>
> *I see you*
> *You see me*
> *Can't take my eyes off you*
> *When you're looking at me*
>
> *You're still and quiet*
> *My heart's in a riot*
> *We lock eyes*
> *And the world goes by*

What's your name?
Is it luck I'm havin'
A moment worth saving.
A lifetime I've been waiting.
What's your name?

Lost in this moment
My heart's all in it
I'm holding my breath
Hoping you'll claim it.

What's your name?
Doesn't matter.
One look from you and
My thoughts scatter.
Everything on the line
I secretly call you mine.

What's your name?
Is it luck I'm havin'
A moment worth saving.
A lifetime I've been waiting.
We meet, we touch, we kiss
A love so deep keeps growing

And then you look at me and love me that way
And all I want is . . . your last name.

The crowd went wild, but the applause was just white noise, because the second she sang that last line, everything about Mason went still, his gaze sharp and penetrating. And then he grinned, stood, and prowled to her as she set her guitar aside. Whitney Houston's version of "I Will Always Love You" played over the loudspeakers and couples gathered on the dance floor. Mason took her into his arms and for the first time, right in front of everyone, he claimed her with a searing kiss, picking her right up off her feet and holding her close.

And although the song was about letting someone go, she broke the kiss and sang out loud and clear the words to him as an unbreakable promise that she would always love him.

He pulled her back into the kiss, turning up the heat, though she didn't know how that was possible without her going up in flames.

The crowd cheered again. Her sisters made whooping sounds.

But Lyric was lost in her lover's embrace and didn't notice until the cold air hit her as they left the bar that he was taking her back upstairs to bed, where he showed her just how much he loved her.

Chapter Thirty-Six

A lot can change in an instant. Mason had learned that quickly on the job. But he never thought he'd settle into a relationship so completely and so effortlessly the way he did with Lyric. Two weeks and it felt like they'd always lived together in the apartment above the bar. Their lives so intertwined now, he missed her when she was working, so he ended up down in the bar with her, watching, talking, just being together.

Maybe it was because he didn't have the distraction of work.

Mostly it was how much he enjoyed her company.

"Um . . ." She didn't say anything more for a moment from the seat beside him as he pulled into the driveway of his parents' Montana ranch. Nick was meeting them here, along with his aunt, uncle, and cousins. They were having a big family dinner. Mason couldn't wait to introduce everyone to Lyric.

"Um, what?" He slowed the car, seeing that she needed a second to pull her thoughts out of her head and spill them off her tongue.

She was never unsure about anything, least of all speaking her mind.

He stopped the car and turned to her. "What is it,

Angel? Are you nervous about meeting everyone? Because you shouldn't be. They're excited to meet you." She'd already met his parents through their video chats.

She shook her head. "No, it's not that. I did something, and I'm not sure how you're going to feel about it." She scrunched her lips, then bit the bottom one before confessing, "I bought the house." She held up her phone. "It closed today. It's mine." Her gaze dropped to her lap. "Ours."

They'd talked about doing it together. "Why didn't you tell me?"

"I'd spoken to the realtor a while back. Before we got together. She knew I was interested in the property but not quite sure about pulling the trigger."

He held on to his patience, trying to understand why she'd do this without him when everything else these last weeks felt like they were true partners. "Then, why did you buy it without asking me to go in on it with you like we talked about?"

"She called to give me a heads-up that someone was interested in buying it, but because I'd shown interest, she wanted to see if I wanted to put in an offer while the other party was still looking at other properties in the area."

Okay, that made sense. There'd been a clock on it, and she didn't want to miss the opportunity. But . . . "You said you weren't sure you wanted it after what Rick did to us in that house. You didn't want those memories every time you walked in the door."

Her pleading eyes held his, begging for him to understand. "But it's also the perfect place for us. We talked about that, too. And I just couldn't let it go, because I know that we'll make that place our own. The apartment is too small for both of us. I know you don't mind it, but you shouldn't have to step outside in the cold to take a work call or ask me to leave so you can have your privacy to do your video therapy."

A sense of worry came over him. "Do you feel like I'm hiding things from you?"

"No. Not at all. I know the work stuff is sensitive and maybe not what I really want to hear about anyway. And your therapy . . . that's a safe place for you to talk about anything you want and know that it's private. I don't need to know everything, because you always come to me when you need me."

He ran his hand over her soft hair. "I always need you." He sifted his fingers through the silky strands and held her at the back of the head. "We've been open and honest with each other from the start."

"I know. That's why I feel so bad that I kept the purchase from you. I just didn't want to put any pressure on you or push you to take a step you're not ready to take yet."

He pulled her close, pressed his forehead to hers, and looked deep into her eyes. "Angel, baby, for the first time in my life I feel like I know exactly what I'm meant to do and where I'm meant to be. And the answer to those two things is loving you and being with you. You bought the house." He couldn't believe it.

"With the money I made off your song," she blurted out. "It went viral. People loved it. It's still selling like gangbusters. I've had offers from other artists to cover it. But it's yours and mine, and I thought why not use that money to build our future together? So I bought the house."

He didn't know what to say. He had no idea the song had done so well. Except that he'd shared in her excitement about how it shot up in the rankings and that it was her highest-ranking song to date. Apparently he'd not translated that to sales and income.

"I'm so proud of you, sweetheart. I know what it means to you that others connect with your songs. I think it's great that you used the money for us. But in the spirit of us doing things together, I'll pay for the remodel. Then, it really will be ours. Deal?"

She sighed out her relief. "Deal."

"And Angel?"

"Yeah."

"Always know, home is you, not the place. Though, I love the place," he assured her. He saw in it exactly what she saw in it. A place close to her family's ranch. A place where they could raise their kids. A place that gave them space to grow and make memories.

She pressed her palm to his cheek. "So long as I have you, I'll be happy anywhere." Then she looked down the road in front of them at the house he'd grown up in. "If this is where you need to be—"

"I need you." He appreciated that she'd even entertain the thought of moving to Montana with him, but he couldn't ask her to do that, and he liked Blackrock Falls. "Yes, this place is a part of me. My family is important. I'm not losing this or them. I'm just doing what I've wanted to do for a long time, living the life I want. And that's with you."

"Then, you're not mad?"

His heart melted for this beautiful woman. "That you bought a house because you want to make a life with me in it? No, Angel. I'm happy. And I can honestly say, it feels damn good after all the shit I've been through. But if that's what it took to find you . . . Worth it. Every second. All the pain. I'd do it all again just to have you." He fisted his hands in her beautiful hair and pulled her into a deep, demanding kiss, knowing she'd feel the connection that kept getting stronger, the love that grew each and every day.

They lost themselves in each other, like they always did when they kissed.

The blast of a car horn popped their intimate bubble.

Mason glanced past Lyric's beautiful face and kiss-swollen lips to stare at his three cousins in the black Range Rover pulled up beside them.

Hawk drove with his big brother, Lincoln, in the front passenger seat and baby brother, Damon, in the back.

Hawk shook his head and shouted, "Get a room."

Mason grinned. "Jealous."

Hawk growled and drove off.

Mason settled back in his seat and drove the rest of the way to the house.

The guys were all out of their car waiting.

"Who is who?" Lyric asked.

He pointed out each of his cousins by name. And even though he knew she was going to do it, it still shocked him to see Lyric jump out on her side, walk right up to Hawk, throw her arms around his neck, and hug him.

Mason was close enough to hear her say, "Thank you for bringing him to me when I needed him."

Lyric didn't let Hawk go after the polite amount of time you'd hug a stranger. But Lyric had decided Hawk was her friend, and that was that for her.

Mason knew how it felt to be hers, so it didn't surprise him that Hawk remained unsure about what to do with her, but he also didn't back away.

Hawk stood there, hands at his sides, face a mask of

no emotion. But Mason knew deep down, he couldn't resist Lyric's love, that bright light that drew Mason and everyone else.

Lyric waited Hawk out. So did Mason. Even Lincoln and Damon stood, staring and waiting and probably hoping to see something come alive in Hawk.

Mason understood and could sense something deep inside of Hawk needed this to break through to the part of Hawk that didn't want to feel anything anymore.

Lincoln and Damon held their breath, hope filling their gazes that Hawk would finally let someone in.

Ever so slowly, Hawk wrapped Lyric in a hug and whispered something in her ear that made her laugh. He held her for another moment, then looked to Mason. "If you don't make her stop, I might decide to keep her."

Lincoln and Damon both let out relieved laughs.

Mason didn't have to do a thing.

Lyric stepped back, sliding her hands along Hawk's jaw and saying, "We're best friends now, but I will always and forever be his."

Mason gave Hawk and the others a cocky grin. "Don't forget it," he warned his cousin.

Still, Lyric hooked her arms through Hawk's and Mason's, and they walked together up the porch steps, Lincoln and Damon bringing up the rear.

Lyric glanced up at Hawk. "How did the meeting with Charlie pan out?"

Hawk gave a disgruntled sigh. "Thank you for the contact. We got into the spirits competition. Damon will represent the brand in June. I don't know how you did it."

"I sang at Charlie's wedding two years ago. He owed me a favor."

"And you used it on me, instead of asking for a gig at his Nashville bar?" Hawk seemed taken aback by that.

Mason had to agree, since Charlie owned one of the best bars in Nashville where singers would kill to perform. He was also tied to several country-music festivals so it was no small thing for Lyric to use the favor for Hawk.

"We're more than friends. We're family." She smiled brightly up at Hawk and the front door opened.

Aunt Donna gasped when Hawk leaned over and kissed Lyric on the forehead, then smiled at her. His aunt stepped closer to Lyric. "I don't know how you did it, but thank you. I haven't seen that smile in so long, I thought he forgot how to do it." Aunt Donna hugged Lyric so hard she squealed. "Can you work on Lincoln next? He's far too serious."

"What about me?" Damon asked, looking like he'd love some of Lyric's attention.

His mother grinned at him but spoke to Lyric. "That one is full of mischief."

"My younger sister, as well."

His aunt hugged Mason next. "Look at you. Happy. Your mom's in the kitchen desperate to see you. Go."

Nick and his dad were in the house on the sofa watching a football game. Mason smacked a hand on both their shoulders. "Good to see nothing has changed."

Nick set his beer down on the coffee table. "Where's my favorite girl?" He turned to Lyric.

She didn't miss a beat and teased his brother. "Aria's at the bar, probably wondering when you're coming back."

Nick's eyes lit with interest. "Did she say that?"

"My lips are sealed." Lyric did hug Nick, though, then turned to his dad. "It's so nice to finally see you in person, Noah."

Mason had done a couple of video calls with his parents so they could meet Lyric and he could catch them up on his life and plans for the future. His parents seemed to love Lyric from the moment they met. Mostly, they liked that he was happy.

Mason shook hands with his uncle Mac, then went to his grandfather, reclining in the chair next to the sofa, and bent and hugged him. His granddad held him for an extra few seconds and whispered in his ear, "Glad you're back. Missed you, boy."

Lyric took his grandfather's outstretched hand. "It's so nice to meet you."

His granddad pulled her hand to his lips and kissed the back of it. "Pretty, pretty girl." He winked at her, flirting, the old buzzard.

Lyric blushed.

Mason pulled her back to his side. "Don't get any ideas, old man."

His grandfather chuckled, then yelled at the TV, "That's holding."

"Where is she?" His mom, Adeline, burst into the room, arms out, ready to take Lyric in for a hug.

"No love for your favorite son," Mason grumbled.

She gave him a mock glare. "I'll get to you." She turned back to Lyric. "I'm sorry I didn't come out to greet you, sweetheart. I am so over the moon you're here."

"What about me?" Mason complained again, understanding his mom was overjoyed that he had finally brought home someone he planned to make a part of this family. She wanted Lyric to know not only was she welcome, she was appreciated.

His mom rolled her eyes at Lyric. "Men. They think the world revolves around them."

He knew his mom was teasing and pulled her into his arms. "Don't I get any love for bringing her home?"

His mom held him close. "Your happiness means everything to me."

"Hey," Nick grumbled from the couch.

"I love you both." Adeline stepped back, then gathered her nephews one at a time into her arms for hugs and kisses on the cheeks. Lincoln, Hawk, and Damon all took their turns, then headed into the kitchen to grab a beer.

And just like that, Mason was surrounded by all the people he loved most. He got into the game with his dad, uncle, grandfather, brother, and cousins. Lyric found herself pulled into the kitchen with his mom and aunt. He found her there laughing and chatting like they were all dear friends when he went to grab more beers for the guys. She held her glass of wine up to him and smiled, her eyes bright with delight. So he skipped the fridge and went to her, kissing her right there in the kitchen where his mom had spoiled him.

His mom and aunt both ran their hands over his head, like they'd done so many times when he was a kid.

He only had eyes for the woman in his arms. "I love you."

"That's perfect, because I love you, too."

"Do you want to come watch the end of the game?"

"No, baby, you go have fun with your dad and the guys, while I get to know your mom and aunt."

He knew she wanted him to reconnect with all the men who'd shaped him. Before he grabbed the beers, he turned to his mom. "Did you have time to stock the cabin?"

His aunt gave him a look. "Actually, your cousins volunteered to get it ready for your return." Aunt Donna looked at Lyric. "I'm thinking Hawk wanted to do something for you."

Lyric looked shocked. "I'm surprised. He's been so resistant to my calls."

Mason had expected Lyric to get the cold shoulder from Hawk. And mostly, she did. The handful of calls they'd shared over the last two weeks were short, nothing but Lyric asking about his work, his day, any plans he might have for going out. Which he never did. Lyric talked about what she was up to with a song, at the bar, with Mason, all without being asked just to fill the silence coming from the other end of the line.

And then the last call had been subtly different. Hawk asked her about the song she'd been working on, then asked her to play it for him. Then he'd asked her if she'd send him a couple easy recipes that he could whip up at home on a late night when he needed something fast. And just like that, Lyric breached the walls around Hawk's heart.

Mason knew his cousins and asked, "Am I going to have to kill them for whatever prank they've pulled?"

Aunt Donna gave him a soft frown and a shrug. "Not sure. But they might surprise you this time. You've been gone a long time. They've missed you." The look in her eyes, and his mother's, said he'd been missed by everyone.

"I miss all of you." He took Lyric's hand. "We'll be spending more time here, even though we'll be working on our new house."

His mom gasped. "You bought a place in Blackrock Falls?"

"Lyric did. This beautiful old house I'm going to fix up for us."

"Does that mean you'll sell the cabin here?" his aunt asked.

"Absolutely not," Lyric interjected. "That's home when we're here." She hadn't even seen the place, and yet, she knew it meant something to him to keep his place here near his family.

"You heard her," he said to his mom, to reassure her that she'd be seeing a lot more of them.

He couldn't wait. Because dinner with his family was lively and filled with stories about him, because everyone wanted to be sure Lyric knew what she was in for with him. He didn't mind. She laughed along with his family about the antics he used to get into with *the boys*, as his parents and aunt and uncle referred to them most of the time. It reminded him so much of how things used to be before he'd taken the undercover assignments and had missed more than just dinners like these.

Now he was home, and Lyric was the center of his world, not work, the job that had been his life while everyone else's went on without him.

It was his grandfather who held up his glass at the end of the meal and said, "We're so proud of the work you've done, Mason, but we're happy to finally have you home. And with such a beautiful woman at your side. I hope she turns you inside out and steals your heart and maybe someday gives us a much-needed sweet little girl to add to our table, though I'd never turn down another little rascal like you."

Mason couldn't help himself: he wiped away a tear.

Lyric squeezed the hand she held resting on his thigh. "You definitely stole my heart."

He stared into her blue eyes and knew without a doubt he'd love her forever and beyond.

Chapter Thirty-Seven

Lyric loved spending time with Mason's family. They were so kind and close, just like hers. But after being around all those men and trying her best to connect with his mom and aunt, all she wanted to do was be alone with Mason.

They pulled up to the A-frame cabin with the tall windows and cute cherry-red door. Surrounded by trees and lost down a long driveway, it felt like they were in the middle of nowhere, even though they were only ten minutes from his parents' place.

"I love it," she said, smiling at him.

"You haven't even been inside."

"It feels like a secret place, just for us."

He grinned. "It is now." He caught her gaze. "This used to be the place I'd come to hide away from everyone and everything. Now it feels like a romantic getaway with the woman I love."

Lyric leaned over and kissed him. "That's very sweet."

"Don't tell anyone. It'll ruin my badass reputation."

"Your secret is safe with me." She loved that he could let his guard down with her.

Mason got out and grabbed their bags from the back seat. She met him at the front of the car, and they walked up to the small porch and front door together. He set their bags down and pulled the keys from his pocket and unlocked the door.

When he didn't open it and walk in but turned to her, she stared at him confused.

He held out the key, dangling from a song-note key chain. "This is yours."

She'd given him the spare key to her apartment the morning Nick arrived and dropped off his stuff. It had been more a convenience for him to come and go as he pleased when she was working because he didn't have his apartment anymore.

But this felt like a step toward their future. "I love the key chain."

"I got it just for you." He kissed her quickly, then his grin fell. "God knows what my cousins did this time."

That raised a brow. "What'd they do last time?"

"TPed the whole place and tossed confetti everywhere. It took days to vacuum it all up and handpick pieces out of the carpet and furniture."

She laughed. "They love you a lot."

"Uh-huh." He opened the door and flipped on the light.

Lyric stood and stared at the huge room and caught her breath. "Oh, Mason, it's beautiful. You didn't have to—"

"I didn't. They did." His voice was filled with wonder and thickened with emotion.

A fire had been laid in the hearth, ready to be set ablaze. The bed looked like a white cloud with the thick coverlet and plump pillows, red rose petals strewn across the top and all over the floor. White spider mums burst out of cobalt blue vases on both sides of the bed. A large bouquet of red dahlias sat on the kitchen table. Pink roses and white snapdragons filled a crystal vase on the kitchen counter.

The place was clean and smelled like flowers and citrus.

Mason found his words. "I can't believe they did this for you."

"He won't admit it, but Hawk likes me." She kissed his cheek. "They're happy you're happy."

He still looked stunned. "I owe them."

"No, you don't. It's family."

He met her gaze. "Hawk said that to me."

"Then, you understand what you mean to him."

Mason nodded but said, "I think he definitely likes you more." He picked up their bags, carried them in, dropped them by the sofa in front of the fireplace, then went to the dining table where a box of chocolates and a basket of bath products sat. He read aloud the note the boys had left behind.

Mason and Lyric sitting in a tree, k-i-s-s-i-n-g
You know the rest and we hope you have it all. The love we see. Can't wait to be there for your wedding. And no doubt you'll keep her in bed until there are little Gunns playing cops and robbers in the yard again. You deserve it all.
We've missed you.
Spend more time here with us.
There's wine and food in the fridge.

Hawk, Lincoln, Damon

They'd all signed it.

"I'm going to hug that man again," Lyric declared,

tears in her eyes, knowing as he did that Hawk had been the instigator in this.

"Me first." Then he took her in his arms and held her close, staring down at her. "This is all because of you."

"All I did was love you."

"And that's everything."

* * *

HAWK OPENED HIS front door at the god-awful hour just past dawn and fell back three steps when he was practically tackle-hugged by Lyric and Mason. Their arms tightened around him and held him up before he fell on his ass.

"What the fuck!"

He knew they were heading back to Blackrock Falls this morning. He didn't expect them to say good-bye in person.

Mason held him with a hand around his head and kissed his cheek. That startling gesture woke him up even more. "Thank you."

Lyric was snuggled into his shoulder, her head resting on his chest, one of her arms around his back, the other around his cousin. "The flowers were beautiful. All my favorites."

Yeah, he'd had the most bizarre conversation with her about flowers after he'd been assigned the task of ordering them for June at work for her five-year anniversary with the company. Lyric had helped him out, telling him what she liked.

So he remembered. Not a big deal.

But by the way she held him, and them showing up like this, it was to them.

Lyric squeezed him again, not seeming to care that he was practically naked. "I've got them packed in the car. I'm taking them home."

He didn't expect her to go through all the trouble. They were just a bunch of dead flowers. Or would be soon. So why bother? Except the grin on her face when she looked up at him told him how much she loved them, and his cold heart might have melted a little.

Mason released him first.

Lyric stepped back when Mason gave her room. Her eyes roamed over him. "Damn, Hawk, I seriously do not understand why there isn't a horde of women camped outside your door."

Mason covered her eyes with his big hand and pulled her back. "That's it. We're never coming back here. That's the last time you hug him."

Lyric chuckled and gave a mock frown.

Hawk didn't want to admit that the thought of Mason reining in her freedom to spread her affection with abandon, which seemed to give her so much joy when she foisted it on him, irritated him. "Leave her be. She's perfect."

"I know. That's why I'm trying to keep her away from you." The grumbled words held a world of fondness, because Mason knew Hawk would never tread on his relationship.

"Hawk?"

"Lyric?"

"Whoever gets your heart will be a very lucky woman."

Because Mason still held his hand over her gaze, she couldn't see Hawk glare at her. His heart was a solid chunk of ice wrapped in barbed wire with a toxic symbol sign hung up as a warning that he didn't have the capacity to feel anymore and would more than likely hurt anyone who dared to come close. He couldn't even shut out the nightmares anymore.

And although he pretended well enough to be a normal human being, the fact was he was a messed-up pile of broken bits and pieces inside. Someone dug too deep they'd cut themselves to shreds on the shrapnel.

"You're the only one brave enough to confront such a feral beast." He felt that way most of the time, like he was one step away from losing it.

She gently removed Mason's hand from her face and stared at him. "You are good and kind and worth it. I couldn't have picked a better friend."

And that was the thing. She had picked him, forced it on him, even. Like she knew that was the only way past his defenses, so she could stake a claim.

It awoke something in him. It made him think that maybe there was something left inside him that cared.

She came back to him, went up on tiptoe, and kissed his cheek. "I'll call you." She fell back to her feet. "Or, you know, you could call me sometime. Because you like me. Right?" She was teasing.

Of course he liked her. You couldn't not like her.

He grumbled, "Get out."

She only smiled brighter.

So did Mason. "Catch you later."

"Pick a later time," he groused, sounding like a disgruntled old man.

"See, baby, he's inviting us back." Lyric gave him a wicked grin over her shoulder as she walked out the door.

Mason waited until she was a little ways away before he stood in the doorway and said, "I know what it's like to be lonely like you've been for a long time. She changed everything for me, because I let her in. Let someone in, Hawk, because it doesn't have to be like this. You can be happy despite all the shit you've done in the name of duty and honor and for the greater good." Mason knew what he was talking about there because of the nature of his job. He got Hawk on a level most people didn't. "Think about it, then do something about it, because I can tell you for certain, it's worth facing that pain, learning to let go, and finally living *your* life."

Hawk didn't say anything. He didn't know what to say.

"Thanks for making my angel smile." Mason's eyes narrowed. "Now, knock it off. That's my job." Mason closed the door without letting him reply.

Hawk decided poking at his cousin by flirting with his girlfriend was too fun to stop now.

And if it crossed his mind that he hadn't played like this and taken joy in it like this in forever, well, he ignored it and his instinctive need to squash the fun took over.

He liked riling his cousin and making Lyric smile.

It was better than the brooding hell he usually suffered through every day.

He wanted to go back to sleep but headed for his kitchen and the coffee maker, knowing the only thing he'd be doing was thinking about Mason's words and whether or not a man like him could ever be the kind of man a woman needed and deserved him to be.

If Mason could do it, maybe he could, too.

Chapter Thirty-Eight

Mason missed Lyric with every breath he took, every beat of his heart. She'd skipped her February trip to Nashville to write with her partner Faith so they could finalize the renovation plans for their house and start construction. So she'd moved the trip to the end of March. The house was coming along. Only a few more weeks until it was done.

"How long has she been gone?" his therapist asked.

Mason stared at the computer on his desk in the unfinished office in their house. "Six days. She'll be back later tonight." He couldn't wait.

"And how are things between you two?"

His problems had never been their relationship. That part of his life was easy. "She worries about me when I wake up in a cold sweat from a nightmare."

"You said those are getting better."

"They are." It seemed when he'd decided to change the nature of his job, his brain had finally had a chance to start processing all the trauma and bad shit he'd done and seen on the job. Like taking a vacation, only to relax and end up sick. "Lyric and I are great. I couldn't ask for a better partner."

That's exactly what she was to him.

When he'd expressed to his therapist and her that

he felt like he was using her to try to get over his mental damage, she'd put him in his place.

"If you hold me and comfort me when I wake up from a nightmare about the hit-and-run or Tim trying to beat the shit out of me, am I using you? Would you tell me to suck it up and get over it?" His disgruntled angel had socked him in the belly, then kissed him stupid. "I love you. I'm here for you, the way you are for me. So get over yourself, and let me ease the hurt and hold you through the pain, and tell me all the things you hold inside you so you can get them out. I will still be by your side no matter what."

Her words and devotion and absolute conviction humbled him.

"Lyric loves with everything she is," he told his therapist. "I'm so damn lucky, I sometimes can't believe she's mine."

"Do you feel worthy of that kind of love?"

He grinned, thinking of the way Hawk tried to deny her friendship and love, though it was a different kind than the one they shared. "You can't feel unworthy of what she gives because of the way she gives it. It's so open and honest and pure. It's so real, you can't help but know she sees you, all of you, and still feels that way. So some part of you, even a small part has to be worthy of that. And if it is even just a small part of you, then it must be enough. I'm enough to deserve that love."

"Maybe all my patients need someone like her."

Mason agreed.

A gleeful shout came from the kitchen, and Mason smiled so big his cheeks hurt.

His therapist smiled, too. "I take it she's home."

"Early." He was so damn happy, it felt like he might burst. "And she found her surprise."

"I think we'll leave things with you knowing you're enough. Enjoy the rest of your day." The therapist signed off.

Mason left the office on the hunt for his beautiful angel, though he knew exactly where to find her.

The second he stepped into the kitchen, she tapped her phone and the chorus to Tina Turner's "The Best" rang out, along with his angel's powerful voice, letting him know she thought he was *the best* by pointing her finger at him. Then she hugged the brand-new professional six-burner gas range. She stood and continued singing, dancing, and pulling the simple white T-shirt she wore over her head, revealing the pale pink bra hugging her breasts. She danced to the double ovens, put her back to them, closed her eyes like she was in ecstasy, shimmied down, then back up them, and undid the button and fly on her jeans.

He simply grinned and kept his eyes glued to her, loving her voice in his ears, her spirit filling the room, her body calling to his.

She hit the chorus again as she ran her hands down the two ovens and bent at the waist, her ass out toward him. Then she hooked her fingers in the waistband and pulled those jeans and her panties all the way down to her ankles in a sexy striptease that had him hard and aching.

He groaned.

She kept singing and somehow kicked her shoes and the clothes away, leaving her gloriously naked, except for a bandage on her wrist.

He wondered what had happened but forgot that thought the second she put her back to his chest and shimmied down him to the beat of the music. She glided back up, her body rubbing against his, making him throb with need. It had been way too long since he'd been inside her, and his cock wanted to take the reins and put a stop to this amusing and wonderful moment. But he enjoyed watching her too much to take her now and found the strength and will to hold out.

Lucky him, because she kept running her hands all over him and singing how he was the best, and it reminded him of the conversation with his therapist moments ago about him being enough. His angel thought he was so much more to her.

And all of this dancing and singing because he'd upgraded the kitchen appliances from the ones she'd settled for because of the cost to the ones he knew she really wanted. She was worth the expense, and he would benefit from her amazing cooking skills.

Her hands swept down his back and over his hips, her hands grabbing his ass. He reached back and gripped her swaying hips, holding her close. She slid her hands under his thermal and pushed up, taking the material with it.

He took the hint and pulled it off over his head.

Her hands came around him and undid the button and fly on his jeans. Then her hand was locked around his hard cock, and he swore as she hit the part of the song about being torn apart. And he thought she could bring him to his knees in an instant.

He pulled her close in front of him, picked her up by the back of her thighs, set her lush ass on the brand-new countertop on the island in front of him, and took her mouth with his, cutting off the final verse of the song, letting Tina's voice ring out with what they both believed about the other. Because the best was having the person you loved more than anything in your arms.

He lost himself in the kiss and wanted to thrust his aching cock inside her, but he managed some finesse and stroked his fingers along her sensitive inner thigh to her soft, damp folds, one finger, then two sliding into her heat. "You're so wet for me."

"I missed you," she said against his lips.

"I'm pretty sure you're more excited about the appliances."

She chuckled, grabbed him by the hair, and made him look at her instead of kissing her again. "Nothing is better than you."

The words made his heart overflow with love for this smart, kind, beautiful woman.

Then he lost all thought when she grabbed his hard length, freed it from his boxer briefs, and rubbed the head of it against her soft folds. "Love me."

He didn't need to be told twice and thrust into her, burying himself deep.

She sighed out her satisfaction, planted a hand just behind her on the counter, and started to move with him. The loving was urgent and intense, both of them needing to be close, but also desperate for release. He wanted to make it last, make it good for her. She locked her legs around his waist and pulled him in again and again.

He held her with one arm and slid his other hand down to where they were joined and brushed his thumb over her sensitive clit. She fractured in his arms, her legs pulling him deep into her core as his orgasm rolled through him, setting off aftershocks in her.

He leaned into her, cradling her head against his chest, his fingers buried in her long hair as they both caught their breath and settled back into their sated bodies.

"I love the kitchen," she said, so much joy in her voice.

"Yeah? I wasn't sure." He teased. "I love the way you express yourself." There wasn't a day that went by that she didn't show and tell him in some way that she loved him. He loved the songs she either sang to him or sent him to listen to when she was busy but still wanted him to know she was thinking about him.

"Don't expect me to dance naked in the kitchen all the time."

"Not even if I ask real nice and love you like this again?"

She leaned back and looked up at him. "You'll have to ask me *real* nice."

He nuzzled his nose into the sensitive and soft skin behind her ear, taking in her sweet and floral scent, reacquainting himself with the feel of her against him, the softness of her hair, the way she breathed with him.

"The house is nearly done. When can we move in?" she asked.

"Painters will finish the rooms upstairs day after tomorrow before they do down here. After that, it's just some small stuff to finish. Weather's getting warmer. We'll need to decide what we want to do with the yard."

"I want flowers."

"Whatever you want, Angel, it's yours."

"I want you. Always you."

He turned his left hand toward her to show off the tattoo he'd gotten while she was away.

She took his hand and stared at the compass tattoo he'd had since he was twenty, but now showed his true north, his way home, pointed to her name now inked in his skin.

She was already inside every cell of his being, the most precious part of his heart.

Her gaze went teary. "M." Just that soft, sweet sigh of the name she called him.

She pressed a kiss to his hand over her name, then gently pulled the bandage off her arm, held it up, and showed him her new and only tattoo. "Great minds," she teased.

A heart enclosed an *M*, the letter made out of musical notes to form the lines. One of the bars leading to the round bottom of the music note wasn't a line at all, but his name. *Mason* spelled out in stacked letters. She brushed a kiss on his lips. "You're mine. The song in my heart."

He kissed her, knowing she'd done this for him. He marked his skin with things that were important to him. They told a story about what he believed in and cared about, and who he was. This was her way of showing him that he was as permanent in her life as he was on her skin.

He didn't know what to do with the enormous love he had for her inside of him, so he poured it out in the kiss they shared and spun out until they were both panting. "You didn't have to do that."

She took his left hand and pressed it to her heart. "You're all over me, inside of me. I wanted it to show. The way you show things."

"But you didn't know I was getting your name tattooed on my hand."

"You show me in so many ways that I am the center of your world."

"You're home to me, Angel."

"Just like you are to me." She kissed him again. "God, I missed you."

He smiled down at her, feeling exactly the same way. "Any other places you want to christen in the house?"

She raised a brow. "Do we have hot water? I could use a shower after my flight."

He scooped her up, her legs still wrapped around his waist, his hands clamped on her lush ass and carried her upstairs to their completely updated master bath.

They didn't have any furniture, let alone towels. But if she wanted a shower, he'd make sure she didn't care about anything but the way he loved her.

Because he planned to do that until the day he died.

The tattoo wasn't the only surprise he had planned for her.

Chapter Thirty-Nine

It wasn't often they opened the bar late on a Saturday, but this was a special occasion. April tenth. Mason's birthday. One he got to spend with everyone he loved, instead of on a case that kept him away from family and friends.

Lyric had invited everyone. His whole family arrived in Blackrock Falls early to check out their finished house. Then they all made their way here for an early dinner. Between his family, friends from the FBI, and her family, they had quite the crowd gathered in the bar. Far too many to have at their place all at once. Mason told her when they planned the event.

It had been a great party. She saw the appreciation he had for the people in his life. Most especially her. She wanted this to last a little longer, to keep the joy on his face and in his heart as long as possible. He'd take the memories with him. Ones he'd wanted to make for a long time when he'd been deep undercover, protecting those he loved by staying away and doing an important job.

She stood by his side as everyone sang him "Happy Birthday," his arm around her back, hand on her hip. He'd kept her close all day, wanting her to be a part of everything with him.

"Make a wish," she said before he blew out the candles.

"Sing me *my* song again."

She couldn't deny him the request. "Of course I will."

He blew out the candles, took her hand, and led her to the stage, where her guitar had already been set up.

She eyed him, sensing that strange nervous energy about him that she'd felt several times today. To please him, she took the guitar, stood at the mic, and sang him his song.

Her fingers strummed the strings, the chords filling the room, along with her voice as she stared into his eyes and sang, "What's your name?" The song and words flowed out of her. His gaze locked on her, intense and filled with love.

Everyone else in the room disappeared from her awareness. It felt like it was just her and him and the love they shared.

And then she got to the end of the song and sang, "And all I want is . . . your last name." Before the final chord whispered out, he dropped to one knee and held up a beautiful, oval diamond ring.

"All I want is you."

She pressed her fingers to her lips and tried so hard not to cry, but the tears gathered in her eyes and slipped down her cheeks.

"You want to know my wish?" he asked. "That the smart, strong, loving, brilliant songwriter, the kindest person I've ever known, would be my wife. You have my heart, my soul, everything I am. You can have my last name, too. Will you marry me?"

She'd nodded all through those words.

She barely noticed when someone released the

guitar strap and took the instrument away, because she was too busy saying *Yes*.

She reached for Mason as he stood and came into her arms, kissing her like she'd granted every wish he'd ever had.

"I love you," he said against her lips, then deepened it again, holding her close, making her feel loved and protected and cherished like only he'd ever made her feel.

It took her a second to realize the noise surrounding them was their family and friends clapping and cheering.

Mason brushed his lips to hers once, twice, then stared down at her. "Were you really surprised?"

"Yes." She'd had no idea. "It's your birthday. I didn't think you'd propose today."

"You're the only gift I really want." He pulled up her hand and kissed her tattooed wrist, then slid the diamond ring on her finger. "Do you like it?"

She placed her hand on his chest and stared at the glittering stone. "It's beautiful, but no comparison to the way you love me."

He swept his hand up under her hair, tilted her face up to his, and kissed her again.

Before they knew it, they were showered with congratulations. She got a lot of hugs. Mason received a bunch of hearty smacks on the back. But it did Lyric's heart good to see Hawk kiss Mason on the head, then try to come to do the same with her. Mason stopped him, but Nick snuck in and kissed her on the forehead instead.

It had become a game for Nick and Mason's three cousins to get past Mason to kiss her like that. Not that Mason actually minded them showing her affection. It was just a way for all of them to show Mason he was back in the fold and a part of their fun and games.

Apparently the proposal was no surprise to her parents, who hugged her and Mason, all smiles and happy for one of their kids to be in love and starting a life with someone.

She stood with Mason on her right side, her parents on her left and smiled as her three siblings held up their drinks from across the room in a toast to her and Mason.

"Who do you think will be next?" she asked her parents.

"Aria, if Mason's brother, Nick, has anything to say about it," her dad grumbled, though without any real reservations behind it.

Mason squeezed her side. "They're still circling each other. Maybe Melody. There's a guy who comes in more and more. I think he's got his eye on her."

She bumped her shoulder to his. "Sounds like someone I know."

"Angel, you had me so tied up in knots, it's a wonder I could do anything but love you."

Her mom sighed. "Mason, honey, I hope whoever Aria and Melody fall for is as good to them as you are to my little girl."

Mason didn't seem to know what to do with those words.

Her mom still stared at her kids. "I hope it will be Jax. He's been keeping things casual far too long. But it will take a special kind of someone to steal and hold his heart."

Mason glanced at her mom. "I hope whoever she is, she has a heart as beautiful as Lyric's."

Her mom's soft gaze met theirs. "You two are

perfect for each other. I hope you have a long and happy life together."

Mason turned Lyric into his body and held her close, looking down into her eyes. "Forever won't be long enough. But we will be happy."